MASTERCRIME

JAMES BURKE

A Present for Santa

J.M. Dent & Sons Ltd
London Melbourne

First published by J.M. Dent & Sons Ltd 1988
This paperback edition published by J.M. Dent & Sons Ltd 1989
© James Burke 1986

Printed and bound in Great Britain by
The Guernsey Press Co. Ltd., Guernsey, C.I.
for J.M. Dent & Sons Ltd
91 Clapham High Street, London SW4 7TA

British Library Cataloguing in Publication Data

Burke, Jim, *1921-*
  A Present for Santa.
  I. Title
  813'.54 [F]

ISBN 0-460-12589-3

This book is dedicated to Mary,
who knows why

A Present For Santa

Prologue

It was raining hard, but the brunt of the rush hour traffic was off the streets, so the dark coupe was making good time up the Drive. The blond man, driving alone, was handling the car mechanically, his mind far from Chicago's glistening streets.

He turned left off the Drive and headed west, then north again. He stopped in front of an apartment building entrance and touched his horn. A woman who'd been waiting just inside the heavy glass doors came out and dashed across the sidewalk to his car. She climbed in quickly with a splattering of water, shaking more from her plastic head cover as she took it off and laid it on the floor next to her wet bag. She reached over and kissed the man's cheek, but he didn't seem to notice as he pulled the car back into traffic. He turned right at the second intersection, drove a couple of blocks east, and began looking for a parking place. He found one and skillfully maneuvered the car into it, then got out, opening his umbrella as he did, and moved around to the other side to let the woman out. They walked quickly to a nearby building, she clutching his arm.

Inside the lobby the woman shed her raincoat and dabbed at her tanned cheeks with a kerchief as they waited for the elevator. On the fourth floor, they stopped in front of an apartment door while the man used two keys to open a pair of formidable-looking locks. Then he pushed the door open and stepped back politely to let her precede him. As she crossed the threshold there was a blinding flash of light and then a deafening roar as the walls seemed to disintegrate and the floor erupted and bucked. Time seemed suspended for one lucid fraction of a second as the man saw the woman literally fly apart in every direction—blood, bone, flesh, gore, and cloth, just seeming to hang in midair. Then a million needles tore at his face, his eyes, his body; a giant fist slammed into his middle, hurling him backward and crumpling him against the steel of the elevator doors. There was an instant of consciousness in which he heard the clattering madness of a thousand trains and felt the reverberations of their wheels passing over his head. Then at last there was the silence of oblivion.

The young nurse was sick with compassion. How could the poor man be alive? But he was—and conscious. He was battered beyond belief: blind, legless, one arm amputated above the elbow, the other a mangled mess, head and internal injuries they couldn't even count or locate, much less diagnose; still he hung on. She had been standing by his bed, just watching, when his hand had moved. And then he had struggled to form words, trying until he did it with such force and distinction that she had understood and obeyed. She'd brought the paper and pencil, and he'd used that mutilated hand to write his request. When he had finished he'd dropped the pencil and his bandaged fingers had grasped her wrist, holding it tightly until the gauze began to turn pink and she told him gently that she understood. He had relaxed his grip and she'd left, taking the paper to the chief resident. The chief had looked at it, listened to her explanation, and then reached for the phone. He dialed a number, waited, then asked to speak to the U.S. district attorney.

1

As Morley rounded the curve in the path he could see the old man sitting quietly on the bench, looking across the lake toward the mainland. He was a handsome old guy. Dapper as hell. Always looked like he was dressed for lunch at some ritzy hotel. Dapper Dan. That's how Morley had thought of him since the first time. The old man smiled as Morley approached, moving toward the end of the bench and patting in invitation the space he'd vacated.

Morley sat down. "Morning, Dan."

"Morning. You're early today."

"Nothin' better to do, so I decided to take a little extra walk. How 'bout you? You're pretty early too."

"Too nice a day. Couldn't stand it inside any longer. Besides, I've got to go back North tomorrow, and from the latest weather reports I'll need all the Florida sun I can store up."

"Hope you don't have to stay long."

"I don't think so. Maybe a week at the outside. I'm too old for all that snow and ice."

"Hell, Dan, *I'm* too old for it."

They both laughed at that, as the disparity in their ages was great and obvious. Morley was still on the sunny side of forty, and Dan, well preserved and tailored as he was, had seen sixty quite a few years ago. The older man got serious. "I've got a pickup and delivery for Saturday. Could you handle it for me?"

"Don' know why not. Same deal as usual?"

"No, not quite." Dan looked away, hesitated a moment, then turned back to the younger man and went on. "No, it's really very different this time. I've never lied to you before and I won't start now." He smiled. "Of course, I've not always told you all the truth—but you've known that."

Morley raised an eyebrow, nodded in assent, but said nothing.

"Okay. I'll tell you what I think you need to know about this one, and you decide if you're in or not. No hard feelings if it's no, but I'd sure appreciate it if you'd take it."

Again Morley said nothing, so again the old man went on.

"This one is different, but in degree. We'll use the same procedures—although the timing will be tighter and we'll have to hold to it—but the package is more important, more secret, more valuable than before."

Morley nodded; Dan continued. "I do not believe there will be any danger for you, and it's certainly not illegal for you. There could be danger before it gets to you, and even after you send it on its way but I repeat, not for you."

"May I ask why the big distinction?"

"Yes, that's an acceptable question." The old man laughed. "Because the knowledge of all the procedures in this operation, and of your part in it, is held by only one person—me. The other two parties don't know each other's roles, nor does either of them know who you are."

"Hmm. I think I like it that way. May I ask why this particular package is dangerous?"

"Yes, as long as we don't get into specifics. This is a very negotiable package. Whenever you've got something like this, there's always a chance somebody or something will go sour, somebody whose greed exceeds his discretion." The old man smiled again. "You know, Pat, there are people—some of whom we deal with—who firmly believe that 'fair shares' start after they get theirs."

"I won't ask what people."

"Good. That is *not* an acceptable question."

"And you still say my piece of this action is legit?"

"I assure you so although I'll admit that the overall deal might not be considered kosher in some circles."

"I've known that, Dan." Morley smiled widely. "The work's too easy and the pay's too good. There has to be a wrinkle somewhere."

"How did you get so cynical at such an early age?"

"Just lucky, I guess."

"Any other questions?"

"Yeah, but I know better than to ask."

"Are you in?"

"I'm in."

"Good. Pickup will be at Miami International, Saturday, one P.M., Eastern information desk. Use your Carradine papers. You won't need anything else. Envelope for Carradine will be there no later than twelve-forty-five. Your pickup no later than one P.M. Okay?"

"Okay. That *is* a tight schedule."

"That's what I meant, but it's not too tight, is it?"

"Not for me, Dan. Just so your other boy makes it."

"He will. I assure you."

"And how about delivery?"

"West Palm Airport, five P.M. same day—Saturday. United desk. Use key, or check if no keys available. You can even use the bus station if necessary. This man *will* have leeway. He's not booked out 'til seven-thirty on United to New York, but you should observe the five P.M. deadline."

Morley nodded and Dan continued. "The envelope with this ticket"—he handed Morley a one-way ticket from West Palm Beach to La Guardia—"and your key or check should be left for Mr. Merle Sandstone. Any questions?"

"Have I ever seen Sandstone?"

"Not to my knowledge."

"Has he ever seen me?"

"I can't imagine how. No. I'm sure. No."

"And you think we should try to keep it that way?"

"I think we *have* to."

"Hmm. You've never felt that strongly before."

"I told you. This time it's different. Believe me."

"I do. I've got it. I can't make sure Merle Sandstone doesn't see me, but I can make sure he doesn't see the real me."

"Good. Exactly what I meant. I'm not trying to scare you, but the less other parties know, the better I like it."

"Agreed."

"Ernie Pro will arrange for your stipend in the usual way, as soon as the transfer is confirmed."

"That I don't worry about, although I've gotta admit I live better'n I used to." Morley smiled at this. It was true.

The old man shook his head, waving an index finger at him playfully. "Just see you don't live so well you get those tax bastards snooping around."

"C'mon, Dan, it's not that much. Unless you gave me a raise."

The old man laughed again, then quickly got serious. "There will be a little something extra this time. After all, you're getting some seniority in your profession."

"That's great. Now if I only knew what my profession *was*."

The old man smiled but said nothing. He stood up, brushed off the seat of his trousers, and started to walk away. He stopped after a couple steps, turned, and lifted his hand in a half salute. "See you next week, Pat. Usual signals." As he started away he turned back again. "Be careful."

Morley returned the wave and just as seriously said, "You too." He stayed there on the bench, watching as the old man carefully crossed the highway and disappeared into a nearby oceanfront high rise. Morley felt sad. He couldn't have explained why; he just did. After a couple of minutes he got up and headed south along the shore, hands in pockets, a worried look on his face.

Friday was a bright, gorgeous day, with just a few puffy clouds, none of them big enough or high enough to deaden the warmth of the January sun. Morley had been fishing at Lake Okeechobee all day Thursday and then out late with fishermen companions that night. Still he was up early and out on the street long before the "snowbirds" had begun their daily pilgrimage to the beach. Hot or cold, rain or shine, each morning Morley walked over the huge arched causeway to the mainland to pick up his paper. His paper was the *Chicago Tribune*, and the newsstand held it for him each day. He'd had to make a special order and pay weekly in advance to get the regular city edition, as the various out-of-state editions did not carry the want ads and personals.

This paper business had begun early in his relationship with Dan Casper—in fact, right after his first pickup and delivery and his first stipend. Dan had suggested to Morley that they use the want ads and personals of the *Tribune* to "assist and protect their communication." What he'd meant was that he would use them to send Morley pickup and delivery instructions when he, Dan, was out of Florida, which at that time was quite often. At the time, Morley had been more amused than impressed, but it had worked well.

At that same time, Dan had given him a code name, "Santa," which was a source of amusement to both of them. He'd also given him a rather extensive open code of letters and words, which were used in the *Tribune* and in all other communications to disguise their messages.

Back in his apartment, Morley settled into his lounger to study the pertinent parts of the *Tribune*. It was possible that Dan might change some aspect of Saturday's job. It had happened before. But there were no messages, so Morley began to read the rest of the paper. He turned the front page, looked down, and gasped.

Lead column, page three, a two-column write-up with pictures—SUSPECTED SYNDICATE FINANCE CHIEF AND SECRETARY GUNNED DOWN IN WASHINGTON D.C. STREET. The pictures showed a smiling Dan Casper and a serious Ernie Pro, both looking very much alive. Dante Cappacino (evidently his real name) and Dorothy E. Prohaska (obviously hers) had just left a fashionable downtown restaurant and were strolling east near Lafayette Park, only a block from the White House, when the killers opened fire from a car that had pulled up at the curb beside them. The victims had fallen in the traditional hail of bullets; the gunmen had raced off in the traditional tire-squealing getaway car; the police were following the traditional myriad leads with alacrity. Cappacino had been pronounced dead at the scene; Miss Prohaska was in critical condition in a Washington hospital.

Morley came out of shock slowly but completely. He had heard something about a gangland shooting in Washington on the radio yesterday over at the lake, but he'd missed the names and details, so it hadn't meant anything to him. But this changed everything. He forced himself to be calm, to think, to try and turn this unexpected occurrence to his own advantage.

He thought back to the first time he'd met Dan, and later, Ernie Pro. Could it have been only nine months ago? Time has a way of playing tricks on an idle mind—and idle he'd been ever since Monnie's death. A few months of going through the motions of work, knowing that neither his head nor his heart was in it. And then coming down here to Florida, supposedly on a sabbatical aimed at getting his head screwed back on, a sabbatical that had stretched on and on, with no end in sight. Fortunately, or perhaps unfortunately, money had been no problem. His uncle's estate and the proceeds from holdings that Monnie had had in her own name meant that he hadn't *had* to work at all for a few years, so it had been easy to exist, just blowing the days, weeks, and months in idle pursuits. But he was too young, too healthy, and too energetic to be forever content with self-enforced idleness; maybe that was why he'd been so receptive to the Dan Casper overture. Maybe. He knew he didn't want to go back to the military job from which he'd resigned. It was too hooked in to all the "Monnie memories," especially the final one: tangled, smoking fabric and metal, and blanket-covered bodies in a torn-up grain field. But then, he wasn't sure he wanted to get involved in something new, either; he had finally admitted to himself that he just didn't know what he wanted to do with the rest of his life. He had consoled himself with the assurance that one day he'd find a direction, and then he'd know.

In those empty days nine months ago Morley had often walked along the bike path that followed the eastern shore of Lake Worth. It was a pleasant three miles, quiet, relaxing, and most of all, conducive to thinking. That particular day he'd found Dan sitting on a bench across from the northernmost group of high rises, and, in the local fashion, had wished him a good morning. This had happened a number of times before the older man invited him to share the bench and chat. They'd begun to talk, feeling each other out like strangers do, sometimes walking the path, but more often sitting on a bench—the old man made it known that he wasn't much of a walker. They were pleasant talks, learning a bit about each other, the kinds of things you're willing to tell strangers. Gradually, their conversation had become more broad-based and general, and Morley had been impressed by the man's knowledge, especially on a number of Morley's favorite subjects. But most of all he liked the old man's whimsical sense of humor, his ability to mock gravity with absurdity, and his willingness to laugh at himself.

Morley began to notice that his new friend Dan was skillfully edging many of their conversations onto the subject of background, personal experience, jobs, family, and so forth. Although he volunteered some information and seemed to answer quickly and frankly any of Morley's questions about his own background, the old man seemed much more intent on encouraging Morley to talk about himself.

It was a hot, humid day in early May when their relationship had gone from the fraternal to the fiduciary. Morley still didn't know whether the incident was contrived or real. As he became exposed to more of Dan's maneuverings in the ensuing months, his better judgment told him that the affair had been a well-staged fake. Now that the only two who knew for sure were dead or dying, he would never be sure. But on that day it had seemed very real.

They had walked a few blocks down the path and then returned to the bench. Although the weather had cut the walk to a short and leisurely stroll, Dan had appeared a little woozy and breathless. When he mentioned he was experiencing some discomfort in his chest, Morley had accepted it as he was supposed to. Then, at Dan's request, he had gone to the old man's apartment and brought back his nitroglycerin pills. Ernie Pro was out at the time. The pills seemed to ease Dan's pain, but Morley had insisted on accompanying him back to the apartment to make sure he was okay. The old man was adamant about not wanting a doctor.

It was on this second visit that Morley had begun to notice things. First, that Dan's apartment was luxuriously furnished. This he had expected, but the degree was impressive. He figured it had cost upwards of forty thou to put in the basics. Then his trained eye noted all the security features—doors, windows, locks, wiring, even an electric eye. It went way beyond the means or desires of the usual condominium owner. And Dan's office compounded his suspicions: complicated phone system comprised of several phone lines. One phone had no numbers, no dials, no identification at all. There was also a taping system, with remote, auto, or manual; an answering machine; recorders; and on and on. A cabinet was filled with phone books from all over the world and airline schedules of all kinds and from all countries, both master books and smaller seasonal schedules. It had been immediately apparent that Dan was neither retired nor vacationing when he wintered in Florida.

Dan, of course, had been fully aware of Morley's surprise, but he pretended he wasn't. Sitting back in a lounge chair and still looking a bit groggy, he had asked Morley to do him a favor—to pick up a "package of business papers" from a "friend in Palm Beach." Dan had explained convincingly that because of certain problems (not further defined) surrounding a very large and touchy land deal (not further described), his friend (not further identified) would simply leave the package at the check room of a certain hotel. For all the same reasons, Morley would have to use another name when picking it up, and then instead of bringing it to Dan, would check it in turn at the West Palm bus station and bring the key to Dan later that night. Morley had agreed to do it.

It proved to be a piece of cake, and of course the next time Dan went out of town he had a similar "favor" to ask. It had grown more frequent and usually more complicated, and finally he got his coded instructions from the *Chicago Tribune* when Dan wasn't there. Each time he performed this favor—even after the first one—Dan had insisted on his receiving a "stipend." Morley took it, and it was useful, though not sufficiently generous to change his lifestyle or make him beholden to Dan. The buildup was gradual but relentless; Morley, who'd used the same techniques successfully himself, recognized the pattern clearly and soon. He realized Dan was leading him down the garden path, but it was kind of exciting and definitely interesting. And despite Dan's repeated assurances to the contrary, probably illegal. To Morley, who'd been bored and languishing, the combination was irresistible. Like an old fire horse smelling the smoke, he couldn't hold himself back.

Morley found it fascinating to watch the system at work. Dan was a very efficient and professional man. The pickups and deliveries were often tightly scheduled and always fairly complicated, and Dan had furnished him with several sets of documentation and corresponding disguises to protect his identity. Morley never saw any of the other parties, never talked to them, and never got mail from anybody in the system. He never got phone calls from anybody except Dan and Ernie Pro, and he knew they always called him from a pay phone.

He only questioned Dan when there was something in the "form" of the pickup or delivery that he didn't understand; he never inquired about the "substance." Once he did ask Dan if the "hijack checks" at the airports caused him any problem. Dan had given him a funny look, and Morley thought he wasn't going to answer. Then Dan had laughed and said, no, they hadn't bothered him very much. Surprisingly, he had gone on to say that "people with legitimate reasons for carrying things" never have to worry about the "contents of their bags." Morley was impressed. What the old man seemed to be telling him was that his couriers had documentation and "arrangements" that eliminated problems if airport checks required them to open their bags. Morley was smart enough, and by now experienced enough, to realize that Dan had told him about an important aspect of his system. He interpreted this as meaning that the old man trusted him.

By the time Dan had settled in for the winter, arriving "permanently" with Ernie Pro and announcing that *this* year he would *not* make so many trips North, Morley's relationship with him had evolved into a routine. Jobs were spaced erratically, but they averaged about two each month, and by then Morley was handling them all. (He had no idea who had handled them before.) The old man had begun to rely on him more and more, even discussing possible modifications in the procedures with him or asking his advice on certain problems that arose. They became good friends, but conversely they began to see less of each other; the lakeside meetings were rare, held only when something had to be discussed face to face. Morley came to like the old man a great deal. It was funny. Whenever he thought about that it had made him sad. He guessed that

12 . . .

now he could at last figure out why: it had been one of those strange premonitions.

And then there was Ernie Pro. It had been obvious to Morley that she was a hell of a lot more than a secretary. Companion? Friend? Mistress? Yes, and more. She was Dan's alter ego, his social conscience, his solicitous mate, and his doting mother. Morley had learned a good bit about her one morning when they'd had a long breakfast and driven to Miami. Dorothy Ernestine Prohaska. Chicago's West Side, small parochial girls' high school, secretarial school, marriage to a well-meaning, charming drunk who gave her a beautiful daughter and then took it all away one night on a rain-slick road ten miles from home. The daughter lingered for three weeks before dying, mercifully, of massive brain damage. Ernie had gone back into the job market, rusty, cynical, hard, and smart. She met middle-aged businessman Dan Casper and climbed the ladder with him, never to be separated again. Love and marriage? Yes, and no. Yes, she undoubtedly loved him, but Dan was a religious enigma: like Ernie Pro he had been raised a Catholic, and though he hadn't been to church since he was fourteen (and even then under protest), he would not divorce his wife, even though she'd been in a private mental institution for more than two decades. So he and Ernie Pro made the best of their situation, more like husband and wife than many husbands and wives—except when they were in Chicago. Ernie's old-country, peasant-poor, strait-laced parents had watched their daughter's progress through life sadly at first, later with understanding, and finally with pride. They stayed warm in their split-level in a northwest suburb, never knowing or wanting to know where Ernestine got all that money, or what, if anything, her good friend and boss, Mr. Cappacino, had to do with it; nevertheless, they would never have accepted a union unblessed by religious trappings. So in Chicago Ernie Pro and Dan maintained separate households. In their Florida home it was quite different. There was no subterfuge, and they were

. . . 13

content to let the neighbors—with whom they sought no contact—assume that they were man and wife. Dan first introduced Ernie Pro to Morley as his "secretary" and never deigned to correct or elaborate on this description. Morley realized early on that this was a true, if understated, depiction. Ernie Pro indeed ran Dan's "office."

Morley's fevered mind went back to Dan's "business," clicking off the facts as he knew them. From the start he had made two assumptions: Dan was running some kind of illicit courier system, and at least one of the parties involved was the syndicate. The packages he handled had to be money, stocks, bonds, documents—paper of some kind; the weight, size, and obvious value dictated as much. The paper had to be illicit or they'd have sent it by normal means. And who played those kinds of games with that kind of paper? Only the syndicate.

Later, he figured out some of the refinements. There had to be two basic clients, one domestic (the syndicate) and one foreign (a similar, or maybe related but independent outfit). Dan had to be running a service operation, and running it from his hip pocket. It was a truly private deal he wasn't sharing with anybody, and one that was making him a very handsome income. This was where Morley came into the picture. He figured his role was that of clean, anonymous middleman, or "cutout," who kept the two clients from ever meeting each other and who was clean as far as the law was concerned, and therefore able to handle the critical in-country transfers with a high degree of safety. Morley thought Dan was probably technically truthful when he said that Morley's role in the procedures was not illegal, since he always had a good cover story and never personally traveled between countries or even between states. Nevertheless, he'd have hated to try and convince some mean-eyed district attorney that he was just an innocent victim being used by those "dirty, unscrupulous wolves."

Putting all this together, it made sense to Morley that Dan would have gone to considerable lengths to hide Morley's identity from all parties concerned. Morley would have done the same to protect his own system from theft or takeover. On the other hand, assuming that the parties who had killed Dan had done so with the objective of taking over his courier system, it made little sense to kill the old man before they had all his secrets. But then, maybe that wasn't the reason for the hit. Was it just coincidence that Dan had been killed in Washington, the home of all those investigating committees, not to mention the FBI, the IRS, the DEA, the ATU, and assorted other alphabetically configured tentacles of the federal bureaucracy? Maybe, but maybe not.

Back to the current problem. Could he assume that Dan had died without divulging the secret of his system? Probably not, although the timing and method of the hit spoke more of frustration than tidying up. Could he assume Dan had died without divulging the identity of his bagman? Then he remembered, and his fear subsided somewhat. Just three days ago Dan had told him that only three people knew all the procedures for the latest pickup, and that the "other two"—who had to be the foreign courier and his principal—did not know who he, Morley, was. He had to assume that Dan's domestic clients—the syndicate—had had him killed, and he felt he could conclude that they hadn't known him or the pickup details three days ago. From what he knew about Dan's habits and style, he doubted that they had learned in the interim.

So logic said his secret was safe, and now he could consider how to go after that package. But wait—Ernie Pro was alive, and she knew his name. Yeah, but she didn't know the pickup details. Besides, she had to be under guard in the hospital, so that even if she were conscious she'd be unavailable to syndicate hoods. That seemed to make sense.

There were two other positive angles. Even if the syndicate had his name and description, he'd be in disguise, and he would take all kinds of evasive actions on the way to Miami. More importantly, even if they caught him making the pickup he would only be doing his bagman job. How could they object to that, or see anything sinister in it?

But if he made the pickup clean and nobody hassled him, picked him up, or tailed him, what then? Hell, he'd be home free. Why not? What if they were waiting for him at home? Unlikely. It damn well better be, because once he made the pickup and then didn't show for the delivery, the syndicate would be like a horde of locusts over South Florida.

Damn it. He decided to give it a try. So it might be suicide for him to drive within five miles of Miami Airport tomorrow! But what the hell, nothing ventured . . . The odds were acceptable. The foreign courier, undoubtedly on his way already, would probably just continue on and do what he was supposed to do. "Merle Sandstone," whoever he was, would just have to sit at West Palm and wonder.

Once he'd made up his mind, Morley began to move and think at a pace and with an intensity he hadn't achieved for too many years. He was surprised how good it felt to be stimulated and challenged again, to have his future, maybe even his life, hanging on his ability to outthink and outmaneuver a tough and talented adversary. Damn good.

2

Morley guessed that once he made the pickup and failed to show for the delivery he'd have four days of grace, maybe five at the most, before the vultures moved into the area in earnest. Best to get started. He went to a nearby motel phone booth and called a Miami number. A soft, sexy voice informed him that he had reached the offices of Rourke Associates. He told the voice who he was and asked to speak to Mr. Rourke. A couple of clicks and a pause later, a deep, non-sexy bass came on. "Patrick, my boy, good to hear from you. And how's everything up there on the Gold Coast?"

"Not bad, Terry, not bad at all."

"So? Then to what do I owe this honor?"

"C'mon, Terry. I don't call you only when I have problems—it just seems that way. Besides, you and Barbara owe me a visit. When the hell are you coming up for that fishing weekend?"

Rourke laughed heartily. "Same old Morley—best defense is a good offense. All right, you win. We'll have to do it soon. I promise. Meanwhile, what the hell *is* the problem?"

Morley's voice got serious. "Terry, I need a bit of professional help, and at the moment I can't give you all the background. You'll have to take me on trust."

"So what else is new? You sound just like the rest of my

clients, though you I'm inclined to trust more than most. What's up?"

"First off, it's not illegal. Honest. But it is important."

"Okay. I gotcha. Give me the bad news."

"Right. I need some disguise materials—first-class stuff, two sets—ID and pocket litter to go with them."

"That's all? I thought you had a *big* problem."

"Well, I may need some other stuff, like passports, later, but the disguises, those I need yesterday."

"I won't ask why, will I?"

"No, you won't, old pal."

"All right. Give me the names and tell me what you want to look like and I'll have the kits ready by, say, noon tomorrow. Okay?"

"I'm sorry, Ter, but I need 'em before that. Tonight? Or before nine tomorrow morning?"

"With friends like you, Patrick . . . Okay, we can do it. My man will bring the package tonight. Before ten, your place. What's your number again?"

"Fourteen C."

"Got it. He'll be there. Anything else? How about some complicated investigations in Alaska or maybe Rangoon—reports to be in by sundown?"

Morley laughed, and Rourke joined him. "Okay, Patrick, you win. I won't give it another thought."

"Thanks, Terry. I knew I could count on you. Incidentally, I just might need some investigations run in the next few weeks; could you handle 'em for me?"

"Why not? It's how I put the bread in the kids' mouths, not to mention in Barbara's purse. Sure. Sure. Just give me some lead time. It's not like disguise kits, you know."

"Yeah, I understand. Speaking of Barbara and those kids, it has been too long. My God! I'll bet Fred is bigger than you are. And Dolly? Dates and boys?"

Rourke made no effort to conceal the pride and pleasure in his voice. "Fred is six-one, one eighty-five, and lettered in both football and basketball. You'd like him, Patrick. He's our kinda kid. Dolly—whoa, I mean Dolores, no more of that undignified, childish 'Dolly' stuff—she's prettier than her mother and almost as smart. You'll have to see 'em, Patrick. It has been too damn long."

"I know, Terry, I know. Where the hell does the time go? I promise, we *will* get together soon. It's not as if we lived a long way apart."

"Yeah, let's do it. Meanwhile, I'd better get on with this crazy job of yours. Now tell me exactly what you want; spare no details, my boy."

Morley began to itemize his request. Rourke listened carefully, injecting an occasional question, until they were both satisfied they understood each other. They rang off with reiterated promises to get together soon.

Morley left the booth, got his car, and drove toward Palm Beach. Good old Terry. It was a real break having him and his facilities available—but then, Morley wouldn't have considered trying to pull this deal off without "a little help from his friends," even though it meant spreading the knowledge of his intentions around more than he'd have liked. Terello Michael Rourke had what he himself termed a first-class investigative service. It was too big and too successful to be called a private eye outfit. About six years ago he had become bored with his reasonably lucrative but routine legal practice and decided to take a fling at P.I. work. He was a native Floridian, and since his mother was Cuban he'd been raised bilingual; when he hung out his shingle, he had gotten his start with the local Latin business. Then he had begun working the Caribbean and on down into South America. Finally, established as a fast-rising enterprise, he had nailed down a good piece of stateside business through an affiliation with a nationwide outfit.

Terry was a big, dark, good-looking man, combining his father's heavy Hibernian frame with his mother's olive complexion and Latin features. He and Morley had met in the army when they shared a barracks room, and they had been good friends ever since. They'd kept in touch, mostly through Christmas cards over recent years, and Morley had spent a weekend at the Rourke's beautiful Coral Gables home a couple of years ago when he first arrived in Florida. Terry had always told Morley to holler when he needed something, but this was the first time he'd needed to do so. He was pleased with the response, and certain there'd be a few more hollers before he finished this job.

Morley crossed the bridge onto the island of Palm Beach and turned into a tony shopping center, parked, and walked toward a tony looking office sporting the legend HURST GLOBAL TRAVEL. Friend number two. Roger Hurst was Morley's age and had been a college classmate, but the resemblance ended there. He was a born extrovert, as ebullient as he was efficient in the business world and he carried the same qualities into his personal life. Roger's clothes, hairstyle, and other accoutrements were those of a generation half his age; he liked flashy cars and flashier women and was in almost every way the opposite of the kind of person one would expect to find as Morley's friend. But friends they were and had been since that first week of freshman year up in Evanston. Despite career paths as different as their personalities and a meager ration of contacts, they had maintained a flourishing friendship.

Like Terry, Roger was Florida-born and couldn't understand why anybody would want to live anywhere else. He had parlayed his family name, a small piece of family dough, and some good airline and hotel contacts into a thriving travel service. Roger had been delighted when Morley arrived, more or less permanently, in the area, and he had continually tried to entice Morley into working for him. In accord with the plan he was now forming, Morley believed that the time had come to take Roger up on his offer.

Roger was at the door saying good-bye to one of his dowager clients when Morley arrived. Roger patted her shoulder as he walked her onto the sidewalk, and then turned to

Morley with a deep, affected bow. "And you, Señor, can we be of assistance to you?"

Morley played along, amused as always with Roger's histrionics—Roger seldom talked in his own voice or acted in his own character. "I am only a humble laborer seeking employment, sir."

Suddenly Roger became Roger. "Patrick, you're serious! Aren't you?"

"Very much, my friend. Any openings?"

Smiling widely, arm around Morley's shoulder, Roger led him toward his private office. Once inside, door shut, he turned to Morley seriously. "Okay, what's the gag?"

"No gag. I just decided I'd like to take a look at the travel business, and since you'd mentioned it once or twice, I thought I'd see if you'd really give me a job."

"Patrick, if *you're* serious, of *course* I'm serious. Can you start soon? Next week maybe?"

"Why not? Sure, next week's great. Tuesday be okay? What time do you open?"

"Nine-thirty, but it's okay if you're not on the dot. We don't really start to function 'til after ten. Oh, shit, what am I saying? Come in when you want to, buddy. Afternoon if you want. No problem."

"I'll be here at nine-thirty Tuesday morning."

"As you wish, my boy, as you wish. Any ideas as to what kind of work you'd like to do?"

"Yeah, I think so. You mentioned before that you thought I'd be a natural in the European tour line; how about that?"

Roger beamed. "Super. I still use some of those contacts you introduced me to; I'm sure they'll put out even better for you. I've got some great ideas for the summer season I'd like to float for you. Then let's talk about some specific tours." Roger was getting excited. "But we can talk about that on Tuesday, can't we?"

"Sure thing, Rog. Sounds terrific. Just what I think I'd like, and the sooner the better. Let's iron out the details Tuesday as you said, but I'd like to get started in the European market as soon as possible."

"You name it, pal."

They shook hands, both obviously pleased with their agreement, and Morley left.

Roger stood thoughtfully, watching Morley through the window as he drove away. What the hell brought that on? he wondered. Not that he wasn't tickled; Pat Morley would undoubtedly be worth five times whatever salary they would agree on. It was the surprise. After needling Pat for two years, knowing that the best possible therapy for his friend was to get involved and busy in *some* line of work, Roger had almost given up. Then, suddenly, here he was, asking for the very thing he'd tried so hard to force on him. He'd worried about Pat when he'd first showed up down here, still dazed over Monnie's death, with some sort of crazy complex that it was his fault she'd died. Roger had partially succeeded in arguing and laughing Morley out of the depths of his despondence, but only partially. Then, today, in comes Pat, laughing like the old Pat, ready and willing to work. Roger shook his head. Not to question fate, he thought, just count your blessings. He felt so good about the way the day was going he decided he'd take that rich, round-heeled widow to lunch. He reached for the phone, smiling.

While Roger was making the arrangements for his afternoon's dalliance, Morley was busy with more mundane tasks. He drove to his West Palm Beach bank and removed a number of large manila envelopes from his safety deposit box, putting them in a briefcase. Retracing his route to Palm Beach, he parked in the lot of a second bank, waited for a quiet moment, and then slipped on his old salt-and-pepper wig and attached the matching mustache. Inside the bank he presented a key and signed the entry record card for the perfunctory inspection of the young female attendant. As she was comparing the card with her master signature file, Morley palmed her date stamp, substituting a duplicate he had ready in his other hand. She turned back, stamped the entry card without looking at the date, and placed it in the file drawer. As the woman turned to lead the way to his deposit box Morley reversed the procedure, leaving behind the original stamp showing the day's date.

He opened the box in a private cubicle, removing from it some envelopes identical in number and size to those he'd brought in his briefcase. He put the latter in the box, the former in his briefcase, and buzzed for the attendant to replace the box.

Then Morley drove to a third bank a few blocks away, this time switching to a black wig and pencil-thin mustache in the parking lot. Using his false identity papers, he rented a safety deposit box and paid the deposit and rental fee in cash. Again in a private booth he removed the envelopes from the briefcase and locked them in the new box.

In a fourth bank back on the mainland in West Palm Beach, he repeated the procedure he'd just used and rented another new box, telling the attendant he'd be back early the next week to deposit his valuables.

Morley was pleased with the way things had gone. He smiled as he drove north toward the Singer Island bridge. He was thinking about the syndicate boys getting into Cappacino's safety deposit box. He had no illusions about their ability to do so, and when they did—well, it might shake them just a little bit. When they had their experts examine the contents, they'd realize the books were phonies, and they'd undoubtedly conclude—since the last recorded entry was by Cappaccino himself four days ago, just before he left on his last trip—that the old man had "had" them. That would be nice, and it might give Morley some time, but he knew he couldn't count on this theory holding up for very long. He had to assume that later, when they'd thought it out, they just might conclude that the missing bagman had worked the switch. Then they'd know it was a planned caper and they'd come after him with their first team. At least the disguises should cloud the issue a bit, until he made his move.

Morley smiled again as he remembered the first time he'd seen the contents of those envelopes—the real ones that now reposed in his own box. Morley had only been in the Casper apartment four times, including the two visits the day of Dan's angina attack, but it had been enough. He'd noted that Dan did not like to keep things in his pockets, and his first move on entering his apartment was to empty them—keys, wallet, change, everything—into a small velvet-lined box on the dresser in his bedroom. Morley had also noted that one of the keys on Dan's ring had the distinctive size and shape of a safe deposit box key. Instinctively he had known this was important. From then on Morley had carried a small box of modeling clay to every meeting, and it was not long before he got the opportunity to use it. Dan had asked him up, and during the course of their visit he had excused himself to go to the bathroom.

That had been the easy part; once Morley had located the right bank (it was not the one in which Dan maintained his checking account), it had been a matter of timing and luck. He'd chosen the most crowded time of the day and had helped his luck along by hours of practice forging Dan's signature. When he presented the key and signed in, the busy young lady hadn't given him a second look.

Two days after that, with Dan and Ernie Pro still out of town, he'd returned the originals to that box and put the phonies in his own box against the day when they might prove useful. Today was that day, and useful they'd be.

Back home again, Morley ran through the hazy plan taking shape in his head once more. Step one was to make the pickup in normal fashion and then disappear from Miami airport. He had some misgivings when he thought about how much the success of his plan depended on a number of assumptions. If even one of them was wrong, he was in grave trouble, and *grave* was the right word. He was assuming that Dan had left no records concerning him or this pickup. He was assuming that Ernie Pro had not identified him before or after the shooting to any of Dan's "friends." He was assuming the foreign clients had had no contact with the domestic boys; last of all, he was assuming the syndicate killers could not gear up their search too quickly. That was quite a packet, but he concluded that the odds were good enough to warrant a try.

That afternoon Morley made more phone calls from a pay phone, as well as a trip to Palm Beach Airport. Later he sought out a neighbor and dropped hints about a routine fishing trip, laying the groundwork for an alibi for Saturday. He had a superb dinner at a newly opened restaurant in West Palm and was back in plenty of time to buzz in Terry's man when he called from downstairs at ten on the dot. The disguise kits were as good as he'd expected them to be. He was glad; his life might depend on them tomorrow.

3

About the time Morley was making his arrangements at West Palm Beach Airport, some fourteen hundred miles to the northwest a man sat behind a large desk, chair tipped back, legs across the desk corner, staring out through a huge picture window at the snowflakes sifting lazily through the gray sky over Lake Michigan. His perch, eighteen stories up, all but eliminated the street noises of the late afternoon traffic below, but every so often he could hear the faint wail of a siren. He never had liked that sound, but there was a certain comfort in knowing that this time it couldn't affect him in any way. He remembered the not-too-distant days when a siren was a signal to run, hide, and shiver—to somehow get away.

James Matthewson "Jammy" to his friends—had been born Gennaro Giamatteo in the testing ground of Philadelphia's South Side forty-five years earlier. Now, on this dreary afternoon, he was a study in success, syndicate style. Jammy had done it all. He'd long ago stopped counting the people he'd had killed, killed himself, ruined, had ruined, stolen from, maimed, and walked over. He had never forgotten, however, anyone who had threatened or tried to do any of these unspeakable things to him. Jammy had been a hired thug at seventeen, a hired thug leader at twenty-one, and by the time he was twenty-five was hiring other twenty-year-old thugs to do it for him. He chose sides often and wisely during the shake-ups of the sixties, and when Mr. Henry, the top man of the new-look syndicate, the "Corporation," was making his power grab, Jammy was at his side at all the important times. The conquest was swift and the rewards spectacular. Mr. Henry gave Jammy Corporation control of the Midwest, running out of Chicago, and Jammy ran an efficient, tight ship for six or seven years. Then there'd been a hotel incident where Jammy and a couple of lieutenants had topped off an area Corporation meeting with a drunken party. There were some prostitutes involved, and one of them was badly beaten up. She got a smart lawyer and sued Jammy, because his cover firm was the registered renter of the party room.

This didn't cause much of a problem with Mr. Henry, since they were able to stifle most of the publicity and he expected his "boys" to be a little frolicky sometimes, but it was the beginning of the end for Jammy's marriage. That *did* bother Mr. Henry. Gina Matthewson (she'd gone along with the name change reluctantly) was the only daughter of Mr. Henry's best friend from his early New York days. He'd given her in marriage as substitute father and was the godfather of her first-born. Mr. Henry was unhappy with the way Jammy was treating his family, but he remained on the sidelines because he considered it their personal business; when it began to affect Corporation business that would be a different story. Mr. Henry watched the cash register closely, and he feared that this moment was not far away. It made him sad, but he was, above all, a businessman.

The conservative lettering on the hall door leading into the reception room of Jammy's office suite read JAMES MATTHEWSON ASSOCIATED. INTERNATIONAL INVESTMENTS AND SECURITIES. It did not seem important that neither the host nor most of the visitors to this office had even a nodding acquaintance with the subject. The three men who had just entered the reception area looked, at first glance, as if they might raise that average. They looked like businessmen.

Jammy stirred lazily as the intercom on his desk buzzed.

He punched a button without interrupting his snowflake inspection and mouthed a guttural, "Yeah?"

"Jammy, there's some guys here to see you."

His brow wrinkled with agitation and the fine red lines in his swarthy cheeks became more prominent. "You stupid broad. How the fuck many times do I have to tell you not to call me 'Jammy' when we got visitors. And who the fuck are these 'guys'?"

"Yessir. It's Mr. Banducci and Mr. Conners and Mr. Ragusi. Can they come in?"

"Oh shit, Sandy! Shit! Shit! Shit! Why'n't ya say who it was inna first place? And yeah, they c'n come in fer Chrissakes. What the shit would happen if I said 'no' after you've already told 'em I'm here? Dammit, you've gotta decide whether I should see somebody *before* you call me and ask right in front of 'em. I told you all this. Oh shit, send 'em in."

"Yes, Jam—Mr. Matthewson, sir."

The inner door opened and three men walked into his office: a short dark man, well dressed and barbered; a tall blond man, similarly groomed; and a medium-sized thug with curly black hair, long sideburns, and a flashy European-cut suit that was too youthfully cut for his age and his paunch. Jammy motioned with his hand, feet still up on the desk, and they sat down in chairs spaced around its front, waiting for him to speak.

"Well, what the hell's happening? The fucking cat got yer tongues?"

The well-dressed dark man answered without looking directly at Matthewson. "No sweat, Jammy. The soldiers got away. No strings."

"Yeah, great." Jammy's guttural voice dripped with sarcasm. "Now tell me about the fucking books—and the dough."

"No books yet, Jammy, but we'll find 'em, I'm sure. Same with the dough."

Matthewson looked hard and steadily at his impeccably dressed, college-educated nephew. He didn't much like what he saw. A nice kid, Mario, but stupid; he'd have been better off selling stocks or shoes or insurance. Took after his father, that useless bastard that filled Katty with five brats and then got himself killed in a goddam barroom fight. None of those fucking Banduccis had enough brains or guts to fight or figure their way out of a paper bag. If it wasn't for Katty . . . Shit, even the money he'd put up to send Mario to college was a waste. All it did was give him fancy ideas about what he was worth.

Mario Banducci was finding the carpet's deep pile very intriguing. Finally he looked up at his uncle's stormy eyes. Jammy spoke. "You're sure, are you? Tell me about it."

Mario looked down again. "I took the Chicago places—both his and the woman's; Conners took Florida; and Rags cleaned out the hotel in Washington. We went over cars, garages, storage lockers, everything."

"So why you so fucking sure you'll find 'em?"

Mario's jaw set. "I jus' know it, Jammy. Besides, Conners's got a key that we think is it."

"A key! Why the fuck didn't you say so? Key to what? Or is that one of your fucking secrets, too?" He turned to the tall blond man. "Well?"

"I found a key taped underneath a vegetable tray in his refrigerator. It looks like a lock-box key, and I'd imagine the box would be somewhere in that area—around Palm Beach. But I had a duplicate made and we'll try here, too. Krupa will be on it first thing Monday morning in Florida—can't get in 'til then anyway because of the time locks. Mario's contacts will check it out up here."

Matthewson raised his eyebrows and grunted. "First good news I've had today. Keep me posted—soon's y'hear anything Monday." He turned to the gaudily dressed thug. "Nothin' in the hotel, huh?"

"No, Jammy. We went over that place inch by inch. We took it apart." The curly-haired man spoke quickly in a surprisingly high, raspy voice, punctuating his sentences with lots of hand gestures.

Matthewson looked at him long and hard, then spit out, "And who in the name of shit is 'we'?"

"Tommy Winona helped me."

"And who the fuck tole you t'use Tommy Winona?"

"Hell, Jammy, Tommy was in all the way. He was the contact for the soldiers. He's solid as hell."

Matthewson stared, unblinking, until Ragusi's eyes dropped and his fidgeting stopped. "All right. You found nothin'?"

"Just some dough and some airline tickets. Nothin' else. I gave it all to Mario." Mario nodded and started to reach in his pocket, but his uncle's eyes stopped him.

"Okay. If it ain't there, it ain't there. Rags, get back to Washington and keep all the buttons on. Don't do anything, an' I *mean* anything, without you check first with Mario. Just go to the movies or play with yourself or whatever the fuck your bag is these days. Don't meet with Winona. Don't go to any of the hangouts. Cool. Cool. Cool. Got it?"

"No sweat, Jammy."

"And, Connors . . ."

"Yes, sir."

"Lemme hear Monday." He turned to his nephew. "Mario, stick around a minute."

As soon as the heavy door clicked behind the two men, Matthewson got up from the desk and walked to the window. The snow was getting heavier and the lights of the city were already blinking through it. His hands were clenched as he struggled to control his anger. Finally he turned, and in a disarmingly soft voice began to flay the oldest son of his oldest sister.

"Mario, you are a simple son of a bitch. You let Rags use that fucking hophead Winona on somethin' this important? Shit! We're lucky those soldiers hit the right people. Fer Chrissakes, with Winona tellin' 'em what to do, we're lucky they didn't drive away into the fuckin' White House garage. Mario, I got a good mind to make *you* hit Winona before he spills his guts all over that town. You know he's a crazy bastard—can't keep anything from his broads or his friends. Yeah, I oughta make you hit him, but you'd probably fuck that up, too."

"My God, Jammy, Winona's been clean for two, three years. He's one of our best boys. And contacts—man, does he have contacts. Honest to God, Jammy, Tommy's as solid as a rock."

"You'd better pray that he is, kid, 'cuz if he isn't, it's gonna be your ass and Rags, too. You know I'm not kidding."

"Yeah, I know. But, Jammy, Rags and Tommy are in as deep as anybody. They talk and it's their own ass. They're safe." He smiled. "You know what you always told me. 'The pay's good, but the punishment's swift.'"

"Okay. I hope so."

"And I got hold of the doc like you said. He's got the run of the whole place and he'll visit the broad tonight. There's no guard after visiting hours."

"You told him what we need?"

"Yeah, Jammy. I went over it with him—fine-toothed. The books, the dough, the code, the delivery, everything. And I told him to knock off the broad soon's he got it."

"Knock her off! In the hospital? Holy shit, Mario!"

"No sweat, Jammy. The doc's got some stuff he uses—he puts it into those tubes, y'know, and it acts slowly then disappears. It's the same stuff they use sometimes to knock you out for an operation."

"You sure you told this quack what we need?"

"Yeah. Of course."

"You sure he understands I want all that stuff more'n I want the broad dead?"

"Sure I'm sure. I told him myself."

"All right, when's he calling you?"

"Soon's he leaves the hospital."

"Good. I'll either be here or at the club. Call me tonight, whenever you hear from him. And, Mario . . ."

"Yeah, Jammy."

"We gotta get those fucking books. We gotta."

"I know, Jammy."

"Who'd've thought that old fart would be so fucking cute about it? Suspicious bastard. I'd'a bet he had those books in his suitcase."

This brought a smile to Banducci's face. Slowly Matthewson relaxed and returned it. He put his arm around the younger man's shoulders as they walked toward the door. "You goin' home for Sunday dinner?"

Banducci nodded.

"Give my love to your mother. Tell her I'll be out soon to see her and the girls."

"Okay, Jammy. See ya later." They walked through the reception area, and Banducci let himself out into the hall. Jammy snapped the lock, and turning to the secretary who'd been sitting quietly behind her big desk, beckoned her to follow him as he went back into his own office. Like two well-rehearsed actors in a long-running drama, they moved smoothly across the room. She locked the door behind her, then, going to the wall, opened the small service bar and mixed a lowball, heavy and dark with expensive bourbon. He went to the large leather couch, stripped off the cushions, and pulled the strap, converting it to a king-sized bed. He took off his shirt and T-shirt and tossed them on a nearby chair, kicked off his shoes, stepped out of his trousers and shorts, and sat down on the side of the bed to peel off his socks. She carried the drink to him and waited while he tasted it, nodded in approval, and then placed it on the end table. She knelt in front of him and raised her arms as he gently lifted her dress up over her head and tossed it carelessly toward a chair. She cradled his head as his face moved hungrily across her naked chest.

While Jammy Matthewson was exacting from his secretary the pound of flesh that was his due in lieu of professional services, Dennis Conners was sitting quietly at the bar of a fashionable

North Side hotel, sipping on a Scotch and soda, occasionally listening to the music of a live trio, but mostly just thinking. Dennis thought a lot. This, next to his blond good looks, was the thing that distinguished him most from the majority of his colleagues in the Chicago area. He had been working for Matthewson for over two years and had climbed steadily in the estimation and trust of his boss. It had been reflected in his pay, his assignments, and his status. But then, the competition wasn't very stiff in this nepotistically oriented organization. The family offspring, at least those Conners had met so far, were for the most part loyal and dependable, but they were devoid of imagination, initiative, and drive. He guessed this was the reason the superstar boss in New Jersey, Mr. Henry, had engineered the establishment of his Corporation utilizing the best talent and ideas he could get, regardless of the national origin or bloodlines. Conners remembered that that was why he had come into the outfit in the first place.

Jammy—or "Mr. Matthewson," as all the non-Italians called him—was not a bad guy, in a manner of speaking. He was smart and fair, and in his day must have been quite an operator. But now, something was bugging him. Mr. Matthewson didn't seem to care about business on a day-to-day basis, and usually only got interested in a deal after one of his boys had screwed up and it was too late to do anything but try a salvage job. It was no wonder the only real successful "moustache Petes" any more were those who had divested themselves of the liabilities of nepotism. Take Matthewson for instance. He'd probably earned the job in the beginning, and he was one of the very few "Italian legacy" types Mr. Henry had trusted to a significant degree but he was fast becoming just such a liability. Even worse, of course, was the next level. Regardless of what Matthewson was up to lately, or how many blank checks he had with the boss, he could not afford much longer the luxury of that thinly cultured and birdbrained nephew of his. Something had to give, and when it did, Dennis planned to be waiting in the wings. In a way he sort of hated to see Banducci get the ax—he was so easy to manipulate. Hell, he knew the key he'd found in the old man's Florida place was a safe-deposit box key, but he hadn't mentioned it to Banducci until just before they went in to Jammy's office. (Otherwise the simple ass would have tried to present it as his own find.) Anyway, the thing had turned out just as Conners had planned, and Mario didn't even know he'd been had. Now Krupa was reporting directly to Conners, and he was reporting directly to Matthewson. He had a feeling the news would be good on Monday, and he wouldn't have to pass it through Banducci.

Conners's musings were interrupted as a very pretty young woman, still brushing the snow from her dark hair, came in through the street door. She looked around, letting her eyes adjust to the soft gloom of the lounge, then spotted him at the bar, smiled, and started toward him. He watched her approach with apparent pride and affection. She stopped by the side of his stool, took off her coat, and shook it lightly. He spoke first. "Hi."

"Hi yourself."

"You look like you could use a warmer."

"Thought you'd never ask." She hitched herself up on the empty stool next to him as Conners ordered her a double Smirnoff on the rocks with a twist. The bartender brought it quickly, and she raised it in salute before taking a large sip. She made a face. "Oooh. I needed that. You're right, it's a real warmer."

"I've been prescribing warmers for cold ladies for many years. No complaints yet."

She raised her eyebrows. Her eyes were huge, sparkly, and smiling. "I'll *bet* you have, and I'll *bet* you haven't. Speaking of prescriptions what's new at the factory?" One of the Matthewson's principal cover clients was a large foreign pharmaceutical concern.

"Nothing and everything, if you know what I mean."

"I don't, but it sounds interesting anyway."

"It is. I mean things are popping, but it's nothing really

new. Are you still interested in changing jobs if the right opportunity comes along?"

"Oh yes. More than ever. I'm bored sick. Just make me an offer—anything that doesn't involve staying in Chicago."

"Well, we might have something before too long."

"Oh, Dennis, that'd be terrific. With travel and foreign deals, and all that?"

"Why not."

"And would we work together?"

"That's the idea, baby. You and me as a team."

"We'll knock 'em dead."

"I hadn't thought of anything so drastic, but I'm game if you are."

"I mean in a manner of speaking."

"Okay."

"What about your pal, Mario?"

"Funny you should ask. He's not really part of the picture any more. At least where I'm concerned."

"Hmm. That sounds good, I think."

"That is good, I know." He turned toward her, took her free hand in both of his, lifted it to his lips, then smiled. "How about some dinner?"

"Celebrate?"

"Something like that."

"I'm famished. Let's go."

They were a handsome couple, and eyes turned to follow them as they walked back toward the dining room, carrying their wet coats. They laughed and talked, arm in arm, looking like many other happy, healthy young lovers walking toward dinner tables all over Chicago that snowy night. But such was not the case. They were quite different.

4

Elizabeth Poppins, R.N., inevitably and affectionately known to her friends and colleagues as "Mary," closed the door of Room 512 very quietly. The patient was doing as well as could be expected, but she needed all the rest and quiet she could get. Those bullets had really torn up her insides. Damn! Such a lovely person to be mixed up in a gangland killing. It must have been a mistake. She just wasn't the type. Over the years in the nursing profession, most of them spent right here in Washington, Nurse Poppins had developed the habit of treating all patients alike, with equal parts of sternness and sympathy. But she was only human, and to some of them—those who were especially helpless or thoughtful or considerate—she weighted the treatment more toward gentle sympathy. Dorothy in room 512 was one of these, so she was enjoying dispensing that little extra care that was the patient's due.

Nurse Poppins stopped at the nurses' station to drop off the chart. Someone passed as she bent over to set the chart on hook 512, but when she straightened up, she saw only the back of a man retreating down the hallway she'd just come up. She started to go after him, since visiting hours were over, but his back looked vaguely familiar and he was carrying a little black doctor's bag, so she assumed he was one of the M.D.s who had privileges there but visited less frequently. The phone rang and

Nurse Poppins got involved in a change of medication for the patient in 527.

In room 512 Dorothy was dopily awake, listening to her visitor, one John Rayboldt, Jr., M.D., alias Dr. Forrest, which was the name he had just used with her. He said he'd been sent by "Mr. Cappacino's friends" to check on her well-being and see if there was anything she needed. This puzzled Dorothy enough to clear away some of the fog. She looked at him quizzically. "What friends?"

He hesitated momentarily, then said, "Mr. Henry."

"Oh. How nice." She didn't sound at all enthusiastic.

"Mr. Henry wants you to know that if there is anything he can do to make your recuperation quicker or easier, you have but to ask."

She mellowed a bit and some of the fog rolled back in. "That's very thoughtful. Please thank Mr. Henry, and ask him to find the people who did this to Dante and me."

"He said to assure you that this matter has top priority until it is finished, and that the punishment will be appropriate."

She nodded satisfaction, her eyes almost closed. The doctor went on. "Mr. Henry also asked if you could help him."

Dorothy was jolted awake again. "And how could *I* help Mr. Henry?" She gestured with her hands, indicating her own helpless condition.

"Well, Mr. Henry cannot find a large shipment of cash that was supposed to come in through Mr. Cappacino a few days ago, and then there were a number of notebooks, courier records, and code books that Mr. Cappacino was bringing to Mr. Henry. He thinks maybe the people who killed Mr. Cappacino also stole the books and the money. He wondered if you would know where Dante kept them, and if so, whether or not they'd been stolen."

Dorothy looked at the doctor more closely and didn't much like what she saw. He was a slippery-looking bastard, and it was apparent, even to her benumbed mind, that he was much more interested in those missing items than her physical well-being. "What day is today?"

"Friday the twenty-fifth."

"The money's not due in 'til tomorrow. It was delayed."

"Where and when?" This crisply businesslike and delivered in a not-at-all friendly tone.

"I don't know. I never do. Only Dante knows delivery details. Him and Santa. I only know about the transfers to Mr. Henry's people."

He was even brisker—almost shrill. "Santa? Who is Santa?"

Now she was alert. Something told her that it was important not to spill anything. "He's Mr. Cappacino's assistant, but I've never seen him. I don't know his name, except for 'Santa.' Mr. Cappacino always dealt with him alone."

"What does he look like? Where does he live?"

She shook her head. "I don't know. I told you."

"What about those notebooks? Where did the old man keep them?"

Old man, she thought. This creep is showing his true colors. Why, Dante was more of a man at seventy-one than this supercilious fucker was now or ever would be. But she would have to play along. "I don't know. I know he had some records or notebooks or something in his desk but I never saw them. Wasn't my job."

The doctor fought for control but couldn't quite master himself. When he spoke it was in a low threatening voice. "I think you do know, you little bitch. Now where are those books, and where is this Santa? Mr. Henry wants to know, and Mr. Cappacino wanted him to know. Now come on."

She turned to the wall, saying nothing. The doctor sat there silently, fuming. Finally Dorothy turned back, opened her eyes wide, and said, "I'm getting bad vibes from you, Dr. whatever-your-name-is, and if Dante Cappacino did *not* make arrangements to have those books passed on to Mr. Henry in case of emergency or accident, it was because he didn't want them to be. I can think of lots of interesting reasons why. So I wouldn't tell you even if I knew, but it doesn't matter one fucking bit anyway, Mr. Doctor, 'cause I *don't* know!" With this she turned again to the wall, pulled the covers to her chin, and mumbled, "Get out."

Regaining his composure, the doctor tried apologies, soothing talk, and promises, but Dorothy wasn't having any. She just kept mumbling "Get out" and finally threatened to call a nurse. He stood up and, keeping up a running chatter of entreaties, took a hypodermic out of his jacket pocket and tested it. Then, taking her I.V. feeding tube in one hand, he put the needle into it and plunged the contents into the tube. He got ready to leave, telling her he'd be back when she was feeling better. She mumbled something, either "Don't bother" or "Oh, brother," but didn't look up. He shrugged and walked out.

Nurse Poppins was standing in front of the station when the man came out of 512. She waited until he drew even, and when she saw he was preoccupied and not about to speak, took the initiative. "And how is Miss Dorothy feeling, Doctor? She didn't say anything about your coming."

He looked up, a bit startled, then took a closer look at the nurse. She appeared to be friendly and casual, so he lightly replied, "Oh, my visit was personal—family friend. I was in the hospital and just dropped in to say hello." He smiled. "I might as well have gone home—she's sleeping, so I didn't wake her." He continued to the waiting elevator and was gone.

He seems a pleasant sort, Nurse Poppins thought, but something about him bothered her. Then it hit her. Wasn't it unusual that a busy doctor would wait for over fifteen minutes in a room while the patient slept? She walked down the corridor to 512 and opened the door. Dorothy *was* sleeping soundly. Good, she needs the rest. Then, for reasons she couldn't explain then or later, Nurse Poppins walked over to the bed, reached under the covers, and grasped Dorothy's wrist. My God! There wasn't any pulse. Not a flicker. Nurse Poppins ran from the room to call the chief resident.

It was almost midnight Chicago time that same night when, unknown to Conners (who was at the moment in a soft, warm bed in a very compromising position with the soft, warm young lady he'd escorted to dinner), his master plan was advanced a giant step forward. A nervous Mario Banducci was talking to his uncle on the phone. Jammy was more than annoyed; he was almost apoplectic. "He what? You crazy fucking idiot! He killed her! And no books! You simple asshole, you told me you had that fucking quack on a leash, and I turn my back and he's wasted the broad and no books."

"I did, Jammy, and the doc understood, honest. The old broad got mean, and said she was gonna call the cops and that she didn't trust Mr. Henry, and Jesus, Jammy, the doc lost his head and stuck her. He was trying to protect all of us."

"Oh holy shit, Mario. You are somethin' else, kid. You weren't behind the door when they passed out brains, you were hiding on the fucking closet floor. Goddammit, there's a limit to family patience, y'know."

"Well, the doc did get the name of the guy that handled everything for Dante. This guy Santa."

"Sure, kid, and now all we gotta do is go to the fucking North Pole and pick him up."

"But, Jammy, I think the old broad was telling the truth. I don't think she knew."

"You think. Huh. That's a new one." Then Jammy stopped, relaxing his grip on the phone. "Hmm. Maybe you're right, the old broad *didn't* know. The old man *was* a cagey old fart." He began to talk rapidly, all business once more. "Mario, you get that asshole quack on the line right away—tonight—and tell him that this is his story, and if he fucks it up, so help me I'll cut off his balls myself and stuff 'em down his throat. Here's what happened. The broad said she didn't know anything other than the delivery was late and the bagman was called 'Santa.'

When the quack tried to squeeze her for more she got mean and said she wouldn't tell him anything anyway 'cause she recognized one of the soldiers and knew he worked for Mr. Henry. She got pretty wild and threatened to call the cops, so the quack had to stick her. But he did it so's nobody will ever know it was anything but natural. Now that's his story, and it's gonna be your ass as well as his if he fucks it up. Now get on it, kid."

"Yeah, Jammy, that's great I like it."

"Then I'm worried."

"What was that, Jammy?"

"Nothing, kid, get on that phone before the quack does anything else crazy. Wait a minute, one more thing. I want you and Conners to cover that delivery down in Florida tomorrow, and I want that sonofabitch covered like a blanket. I want that dough and I want that fucking 'Santa.' I think he's got the key to the whole shithouse. Got it?"

"Yeah. Got it. We concentrate on Santa and not worry about Mr. Henry's boys. Right?"

"Mario, you're getting to be a fucking genius."

"But, Jammy, how about me using Valletta instead of Conners?"

"Kid, you're trying my patience. I said Conners. I meant Conners. So take Conners. Got it?"

"Yeah, Jammy. We'll be there."

"You bet your ass you will. Now get the quack straightened out."

"Right. See ya later."

Jammy padded back to his bed, scuffed off his slippers, dropped his robe on the floor, and slipped between the warm covers. The girl moved in her sleep, clutching the blanket and turning sideways, giving him the provocative profiled arch of her unmistakably feminine behind. He started to slide his hand over it but stopped. It was too late for her to leave tonight. Gina probably had one of her fucking bloodhounds out there watching the building door. If they never left the office nobody could ever prove anything. So why not stay? Then they'd have plenty of time in the morning. Let her have her sleep tonight. She'd need it.

Poor kid, if it weren't for that fucking Gina, Sandy could have a decent life with him. They deserved it. Sonofabitching bitch. It all went back to Gina. Can he help it if his blood's hot? Shit no. Some is, and some isn't. His is. Everything was all right when they first got married. Shit, Gina liked it as much as he did, even though that fat-assed mother of hers had taught her that anything beyond one missionary position fuck a week was a mortal sin. Then comes the kids. Pop. One. Pop. Two. And three and four. And Gina starts puttin' her box off limits. Naturally, she won't use anything; that's against her religion. But it wasn't against her fucking religion to cut her old man's ass off tighter'n a drum. So what to do? Slip into the can and pull his pud like a fucking kid, or go out on the market? So he went looking, and finding—there was more ass in Chicago than even he could take care of in a thousand years. Comes along Sandy. No typing, no shorthand, but oh mother, mother, how she could operate a bedroom. Nothin'! Nothin' she wouldn't or couldn't do, and do better than any other fucking broad he'd ever met. He salivated just thinking about the morning, smiling for the first time that night. He still couldn't sleep, so he just lay there smoking and thinking.

5

Saturday. Morley was up early and had a leisurely swim in the heated pool before cooking and eating a light breakfast. He'd decided to leave for Miami about nine-thirty, as he had a number of things to take care of before the one P.M. deadline, things connected with the quick and inconspicuous departure he planned on making once he'd picked up the package. Maybe all these precautions were unnecessary, but if they weren't and he hadn't taken them, he'd be a long time dead.

He was rinsing the dishes when the nine o'clock news came on. One of the lead stories reported that Ernie Pro had died during the night at a Washington hospital. Morley felt sad. It didn't seem like long ago that Ernie Pro and he were having breakfast at the IHOP in North Palm. She was a nice person. He wondered if they'd gotten to her before she died. Surely they had a guard on her room—and the news item gave no indication of foul play. Well, there just wasn't any way to find out right now. There was one thing: with both Dan and Ernie Pro dead, they sure as hell had narrowed the field of people who knew Santa's identity. Dan had trusted Ernie to the hilt, and he was sure Dan was right. But who knows what she might have been conned out of on her deathbed—especially if she thought she was talking to a "friend"? This whole thing was getting stickier by the minute, and Morley almost had second thoughts about the deal, but some logic and a spurt of adrenalin kept him in line. The logic was that Dan's killers didn't know about the pickup from Ernie or anybody else, because neither she nor anybody else available to them knew. The adrenalin came from the challenge, and it told him he was living again, and he loved it. He set out for Miami.

About the time Morley was parking his car in the long-term lot at West Palm Beach Airport and putting on one of his light disguises, Banducci and Conners were stepping out of a cab in front of the Delta terminal at O'Hare Airport in Chicago.

Morley, traveling as Alfred Barron of Fort Pierce, Florida, was already in Miami Airport and had enjoyed a leisurely early lunch by the time the two Chicago travelers had arrived in Atlanta for a plane change.

A few minutes past noon Morley, whose closest friend wouldn't have recognized him, was seated in a waiting area near the Eastern Airlines station, shielded from the front by a newspaper, but with a clear side view of the whole area. For a long time nothing of interest to him occurred. He saw a few possibles, but none of them did anything appropriate or passed anything to any of the Eastern desk clerks. Then, at about quarter to one, a small, dark man, neatly dressed in a light-colored suit, white shirt, and tie, approached the Eastern counter slowly, looking from side to side as if he were expecting someone. He waited while a young woman attendant took care of an old lady's ticket problem, then he began talking to the girl. She listened attentively, nodded, and the man handed her a small envelope, smiled, and walked away. Morley got up and strolled slowly to the corridor exit nearest him. Once through the exit he moved quickly toward the one where the little man had gone out. He was gone. Morley walked on through to the outside corridor just in time to see the little man reach the taxi stand. There was a cab waiting and he got in. It took off and Morley's attention spread to the area around the cab stand. Nobody hurried out to get a cab; no cars pulled out to follow the little man's cab or to pick up someone who might have been watching him. Morley concluded after a few minutes that the man was clean—or that he was being tailed by some super-star pros, in which case it didn't matter what Morley did; he was already finished.

Morley retraced his steps slowly, decided there was no way to go but straight ahead, and walked in a manner he hoped was casual back to the area where he'd been seated for most of the last hour. He sat down and gave the place the same kind of casing he'd given the taxi stand. Satisfied, he waited another two minutes and then got up and walked to the Eastern counter. He was careful to choose a clerk other than the one who'd taken the envelope—it was too soon, and she might think it was odd. He waited until a young man at the other end of the counter was free. "Hello. I was supposed to pick up my ticket here. My cousin left it. Carradine—Earl Carradine." He spelled it for him.

"Just a minute, sir." He went to the center of the counter and started shuffling through a tray of papers. He came back with empty hands and a puzzled look. "I'm sorry, Mr. Carradine, there's nothing there in your name. Maybe your cousin hasn't left it yet."

Morley's mind raced. He knew he couldn't afford to get the clerk either curious or upset; these things had to be handled in a routine way so that the ID of the picker-upper never came under scrutiny. Still he knew it was there. Or did he? Hell, all he'd seen was a man he thought might be the courier, at the right place at the right time, with an envelope of the right size. Then it dawned on him. The man, the little dark man, looked like an eastern Mediterranean, and possibly, just possibly, he'd substituted a K for the C. Morley decided to risk it. "You don't suppose he used the old spelling?" He smiled at the clerk. "Sometimes my cousin's side of the family uses the old spelling of our name, with the K instead of the C. Would you check again, please, under the K's?"

"Sure." The clerk went back to that box of papers, shuffled again, then smiled triumphantly. Holding an envelope high, returned to Morley and handed it to him. Morley thanked him, and then politely brushed aside the man's offer of assistance on any ticket or reservation problems. Luckily, it was busy and the clerk's attention was quickly absorbed by another customer as Morley left. He walked casually to the nearest men's room, went into a pay booth, dropped his pants, and sat down. He opened the envelope, tearing the misspelled name, and took out an Eastern ticket from Miami to New York, also in the name of "Karradine." There was also a folded sheet of paper with a key taped to it. There was only one word on the paper, printed in small but clear letters. It read "lawu," which told Morley where the key would fit. He pocketed the key, tore the note and the ticket into small pieces, dropped them into the bowl, and with a flick of the wrist consigned them to the care of the Miami Sanitation District. He headed for the United area on the west concourse where the locker would be.

The locker was against the far wall, and as he sat quietly watching, nobody seemed to be paying any attention to it. He cased the place for fifteen minutes before he made his move. It *looked* good, and he figured he'd never be any surer, so he jumped. The key fit and the door popped open. There was a large briefcase in the locker. Nothing else. Morley slid it out and, steeling himself to walk casually, crossed the area and went out the door. He kept walking, now more briskly, until at last he was out in the sunshine. He was as certain as he could be that the pickup had been clean, but whether he needed it or not, he prepared to begin the intricate series of maneuvers he'd designed to make himself disappear.

West Palm Airport was crowded—too damn crowded—with bustling, noisy, happy winter-weekend people. Dennis Conners, looking like a successful young executive, and Mario Banducci, looking like a thug trying to look like a successful young executive, with Sal Krupa helping, had set up their coverage around the United desk area shortly after three P.M. It was almost five, and they were getting more worried by the moment.

Matthewson had received and passed on to them the procedures and recognition signals and had canceled the participation of the original bagman from New York.

On the click of five P.M. Conners approached the United ticket counter, identified himself to a wide-eyed, attentive young woman as "Mr. Merle Sandstone," and asked if his tickets had been left at their "will call" station. The girl went through the appropriate box slowly and carefully, but she came back shaking her head. Conners told her he'd check again in a little while and walked out of sight to the side of the United desk, where Banducci was waiting. "No dice, Mario. No envelope, no message, no nothing."

"Holy shit, if we don't get that package *and* that fucking Santa, Jammy will have our dongs in the meat grinder."

"We can't get what isn't here, dammit."

"Yeah. You know that, and I know that, but Jammy—he dunno that."

"Well, hang on. Maybe the guy's just late. You know this package comes from a long way off."

"Yeah, I know, but Jammy says that part's finished already. What we're waiting for is this asshole Santa, who Jammy figures picked the stuff up earlier today or maybe yesterday. Y'see, that's what worries me. Maybe this asshole gets smart and figures now Dante's dead, he'll skip with the dough. You don't suppose, Dennis, that little prick has run off leavin' us holdin' the bag?"

"I hate to say it, but that's just what I was thinking."

"Oh no! If we lose him *and* the package I can't go home."

"Mario, dammit, we can't lose what we never had. Maybe that broad didn't really know anything. Maybe the whole package deal aborted when Dante died, and there never was any pickup by Santa. Yeah, and maybe the word just hasn't got here yet. Huh?"

"And maybe the sky's a big fucking blue balloon. Thanks, Dennis, but if we don't get 'em both Jammy's gonna pin the whole business on me for that stupid quack wasting the broad before she could tell. I never told Jammy, but the doc admitted he lost his temper and the broad really did get pissed off and wouldn't even tell Doc the time of day. She *was* about to call the nurse when Doc gave her the joy juice. I think he did the right thing, but Jammy'd never see it that way."

Conners nodded sympathetically. He was amused and elated, but careful not to show either. The simple shit had really dug his own grave this time. Uncle or not, Jammy could not sit still or cover for Mario's stupidity much longer. Mario was right. Jammy *would* pin the whole business on him.

While the two Chicago "businessmen" and their local representative waited for Santa to show for the delivery, they in turn were being watched by an elderly gray-haired fellow with horn-rimmed glasses and a gray mustache, dressed in slacks and a sports shirt. The old man was on the mezzanine, seated so that he had an oblique but uncluttered view of the whole United ticket area. He'd been able to pick out the two Chicagoans rather quickly, although he admitted to himself that the blond one might have fooled him if he hadn't had frequent conferences with the more obvious dark one who was looking around worriedly all the time. The third man was even tougher to spot. Nice looking, like a young professional athlete, he stayed seated unobtrusively off to the side, dressed casually in a nicely coordinated conservative sports outfit. The old man had considered the third one a remote possibility only because he had been sitting there too long, until the blond guy, obviously the leader of the detail, had gone over and had a chat with him. The attention and deference the third man had given to the blond one stamped him as lower echelon, but with his smooth appearance and movements he had to be a comer.

The old man watched the threesome only long enough to sketch their faces on his memory, then he got up slowly and walked to the far stairway down and out into the late afternoon sun. He crossed the perimeter road and the parking area to his car. Once outside the airport grounds, he breathed a long sigh and relaxed. Watching closely for following cars, he turned left on Belvedere then right on Congress. He made a U turn and parked, watching. Nothing suspicious. He waited, counting slowly, timing his entry into traffic to be the last car through the left-turn light back onto Belvedere. Nobody rushed or cheated to follow him. This time he continued to the I-95 ramp and headed north. He got off at the Blue Heron exit and, following a circuitous route, stopped at a little fish market on the mainland side of the lake. He bought two good-sized groupers, unwrapped them after getting into his car, and put them in a pail on the back floor next to his pole and tackle box. Off came the wig and mustache, and combing his hair with his hands, Morley proceeded over the bridge, the "fisherman" home from a successful foray on the deep.

When he got up to his floor, Morley knocked on his neighbor's door. The wife answered and he offered her one of the fish. She accepted gladly. He'd known she would—they were declared fish fanciers.

Whew! Morley sat on his balcony holding a very large and dry martini, relaxing for the first time that day. One more big item to take care of and stage one would be over, apparently successfully: the storage of whatever it was—money, he assumed—in the briefcase resting in the trunk of his car. He hadn't even looked at it yet. He'd just put it there quickly and left it, planning to wait until well after dark to bring it into the building. He didn't want his neighbors to remember him walking in from his "fishing trip" with a briefcase. He could not do anything about safe storage until the banks opened on Monday, but he'd feel a lot better with it up here than sitting in that parking area with just a thin steel trunk lid between it and disaster. By this time he was convinced that Dan's killers really didn't know who or where he was.

Morley was glad now that he'd taken the chance and made the stakeout at the delivery point. At first the added risk had been against his better judgment, but he knew his disguise was good—that had always been one of his strengths—and he figured that if they knew who he was, he was finished anyway the minute he didn't show for the delivery. His idea was that since this was, in Dan's terms, an unusually valuable package, there'd be a "first team" effort on the part of the old man's killers to get it. Presumably, he now knew three of them on sight, which gave him a small but significant advantage; he needed all he could get. He was also pleased that his basic assumptions concerning Dan and the syndicate seemed to be valid. This helped convince him that his longer range planning was pretty solid too. Sunday he intended to devote to convincing neighbors and friends that everything was routine and normal; Monday he'd go to work in earnest.

6

Jammy was surprisingly calm when Mario reported by phone from Florida that Santa and the money were still missing. It was as if he'd known all along that this was how it would turn out. When he didn't even want to see them until Monday morning, Mario began to believe he'd lucked out again. He couldn't have been farther from the truth.

Mario was quite jolly in his ignorance as one of his men, who'd picked them up at O'Hare, dropped Conners at his North Side flat. They drove off with Mario waving and telling Conners he'd see him on Monday. Wrong again.

When Conners let himself into the locked lobby of his apartment building, a man who'd been sitting quietly in one of the overstuffed chairs got up and came toward him. Conners recognized him as one of Matthewson's leg men, but he didn't know his name.

"Mr. Conners?"

"Yes."

"I'm Paul Agrico from Mr. Matthewson's office."

"Yes. How are you?"

"Okay. Mr. Matthewson would like to see you. Now."

Conners didn't hesitate or look at his watch. He just said, "Okay, let's go."

Fifteen minutes later, at almost midnight, he was seated in Matthewson's office. Agrico had remained outside with that pleasant but rather dull receptionist. Matthewson was pacing back and forth from desk to window, obviously concentrating and agitated. Finally he stopped, sat on the corner of his desk, and looked at Conners like he was seeing him for the first time. "Dennis, I'm glad you could come tonight."

Conners nodded, waiting silently.

"We gotta problem that won't quit and I need your help."

"Yes sir."

"Just between us, Dennis, I don't think this is Mario's kinda job, so I'm sending him back East for a month or so." Matthewson was all serious business in a concentrated way that Conners hadn't seen for months. "I want you to handle this Santa business, Dennis."

Conners again nodded silently. Matthewson got off the desk and started to pace. "I gotta have that motherfucker, Dennis. I gotta have him bad. The dough's important but that little bastard has some notebooks that are dynamite. We gotta get 'em. The sonofabitch is standing between me and some damn big deals, and if you help me on this one I'll remember it for a long time."

"I'll do my best."

"I know you will—that's why I'm asking you. Now this Santa, he's got over two million in fresh, top rate, clean green and those books, and we don't even know who he is, much less where he is. Mr. Henry seems to find this pretty fuckin' hard to understand. We gotta do something and do it fast. I think this is your kinda job—you got the kind of experience we need for finding this little shit. I don't even know where to start. I'll be honest with you, Dennis, I dunno where the hell to start looking. You got any ideas at all?"

"Yes sir. I do. I've been thinking about it."

"Good. Lemme hear about it."

"Well, I think Santa is a local Florida man Mr. Cappacino picked up as a bagman. How he got the books I have no idea— yet—but the money's easy. When he learned Cappacino's dead, he just picked it up and went to ground with it."

"Why you think he's local?"

"A bagman who'd be unknown to other parties, be able to blend with the scenery, all that. He'd best be a local man."

"Makes sense, I guess. But what the fuck is he up to? Supposin' he's just halfway smart, how's he figure he's gonna rip off our green an' live to spend it?"

"Yeah, that point bothered me too. I figure he has to be smart, so then he has to think he can get away with it or he wouldn't have tried. To me this means Santa is a guy with some kind of background or experience in our business. I mean he's gotta know something about heists, getaways, passports, money changers, and all that or he wouldn't have started on this caper."

"Yeah. I think you're right. Maybe that'd be why that old fart picked him up in the first place."

"Exactly. Cappacino would have been attracted by these same qualifications. Right. That's why I say this Santa figures he can outsmart us. He thinks he knows the game."

"He's been right so far." Conners looked closely at Matthewson, but the remark seemed to have been just wryly innocent, in no way personal.

"Yes, he has, but he's had the advantage up to now of having information we didn't have. From now on I figure we're even."

"So where do we start, Dennis?"

"I'd start with everybody and everything connected with Cappacino and the woman in Florida, and everything I learned I'd run against what I think has to be; sooner or later both lines would meet right in the middle of this Santa." He saw Matthewson frowning in puzzlement, so he went on quickly. "I mean there *must* be some clues. Somebody who knew the old man *must* have seen him sometime with this guy. And when we get a description and other clues, they're gonna lead us to some specific guy, and my bet is that'll be Santa."

"Do you think he'll just sit there on all that dough?"

"No sir. I figure if he's got the guts and confidence to steal that much money from you, he's gotta have a plan for getting away. But I think we got some time if we work carefully and don't scare him off before we're ready to grab him. I mean he's got to make a lot of arrangements if he wants to get away with that much dough—new name, background, and all that—and then he'd probably plan to leave the country. He's gotta be a very busy as well as smart guy."

"Yeah. I guess you're right. That's why I want you on this job."

"Thanks. I'd like to do it."

"What first? Whadda you need?"

"First, I'll go back to Florida—early tomorrow. I got a feeling we'll find some good stuff in the old man's lock box—maybe the notebooks and the jackpot on Santa."

"Really?"

Conners hesitated, and then grinned sheepishly. "No, sir. I'm afraid to hope for that. Maybe the books—maybe. But I got a feeling Santa wouldn't have risked the heist if he thought there was any chance we could get his identity very easily."

"How could he figure that?"

"My guess would be the old man told him. It could be one of the reasons Santa took the job. If it was, it was also the main reason he'd think he could rip us off and get away with it. But I'm just guessing."

"Makes sense to me, Dennis. What kinda help you need?"

"I'd like Sal Krupa full time."

"You got 'im."

"And one other man. A good one."

"How about Ragusi?"

Conners looked at him. He seemed serious, but Conners sensed better. "No way, no sir, not this job."

Matthewson cracked a smile. "Good. If you'd said yes, I'd have known ya weren't serious about the job, and I'da called the whole thing off." Then he actually laughed for the first time. "I'll leave that asshole with Mario—they deserve each other. How about young Agrico, outside?" He motioned with his thumb.

"I don't know anything about him, but he looks more the type I want. We'll have to pass for some kind of government investigators. Is he good?"

"I recommended him, didn't I?"

Conners looked straight at him, no hint of humor. "Yes sir. You recommended Ragusi too."

Matthewson looked long and hard at the younger man, then decided that it was an honest, not a smart-assed remark. Finally he saw the humor in it and smiled, then chuckled as he saw Conners relax and return his smile. "Yeah, so I did. Agrico is young, but he's good and he's tough. He's got more fucking brains than Ragusi and Mario put together." He chuckled again. "Which I'll admit ain't no fucking big deal. Anyway, him I do recommend and it's serious."

"Good. He'll be fine."

"How many more?"

"None right now."

"The three of you! C'mon, Dennis, ya got half a state to look through. You gotta be kiddin'."

"No sir, I figure there might be lots of people—cops, government, whatever—interested in Cappacino about this time. I don't think we want to make much of a splash down there. We gotta be soft and quiet, and I think three of us is the limit."

"Well, okay, if you say so. But won't it take a long time with just the three of yuz?"

"I don't know, sir, but I do know we can't risk any more people—at least at first—in that area."

"How'll you have these guys operate?"

"We'll pretend to be feds."

"Yeah? Ain't that dangerous? What if somebody blows the whistle? Ya know, calls the real feds? How you got that covered, Dennis?"

"Well, sir, we did this type a' thing in California last year.

Right in L.A., too, where you know the people are awfully ticklish about feds and questions and privacy. Had no problems. I think we can do it easier in Florida where the people are more sophisticated and much less suspicious."

"Whaddaya use for show?"

"I've got some credential folders for an outfit called the "Interservice Investigative Unit." They've got official-looking seals and signatures—you know, eagles, admirals—and we'll put in Agrico's and Krupa's pictures, relaminate, and they're in business. Of course there *is* no such outfit."

"I see. But what if somebody ya already questioned wants to get in touch with you later?"

"No trouble. I'll hire a local answering service, pay in advance, and use a phoney government address in Washington. We'll all have cards with our phoney names—the ones on the credentials—and that answering service number. Of course we won't hand out any cards unless somebody insists."

"Sounds awright, I guess. I still wonder what happens if somebody complains to the real feds; ya know, the FBI or somethin'."

"Well, sir, I guess the truth is we don't know. They never have, and it's our job to see that we don't bug 'em or spook 'em to that point. My feeling is that we'd be aware while we were talking if somebody was that upset; then too the local FBI is busy as hell and has hundreds of complaints every week. I know it takes them quite a few days to get moving where there is no big crime or no immediate danger to anyone. You see, we never will actually *claim* to be feds."

"Hmmm. Sounds like you got this thing pretty well thought out, Dennis. Guess that's why I chose you to handle it. Okay, go ahead the way you plan to. If ya need more help just gimme a buzz and tell me what kind and how many. You'll get 'em."

"Good."

"Anything else?"

"No sir."

Matthewson walked to the door, opened it, and said "C'mere, kid." Agrico came into the room. Matthewson put his arm around the young man's shoulder. "Paolo, I want you to go with Mr. Conners on a special deal. It may take a few days or a couple months. We don' know yet. But however long it is, I want you to give it all ya got. And, Paolo, Conners is the boss, no questions, no shit, an' you do what he says just like it was comin' from me, or you'll sure as shit wish ya had."

"Yes sir, Jammy. No sweat."

"Okay. Sal Krupa will be working with you and he'll be taking all his orders from Conners too." He went to his wall safe, opened it, and took out a package of bills. He riffled them quickly and tossed them nonchalantly to Conners. "Here's ten big ones. I'll put ten more in that Palm Beach bank we use. If you run low let me know. I ain't skimpin' on this one. I want that bastard on toast. Dennis, I want telephone reports at least twice a week, say Tuesdays and Saturdays, and special calls whenever somethin' deserves it. We ain't got no more important business at the moment than this."

He turned to Agrico. "See, Paolo, you're in the big time. This is a numero uno deal. No shit. Do it right an' I do right by you. Okay?" He patted Agrico on the back, shook Conners's hand, and said, "Call me Monday if the key fits."

The younger men left, and Matthewson went back and sat down behind the big desk. He sat there for a while, deep in thought. Then he made a decision. He reached for the phone, dialed a number, and waited. "Mario. Yeah, yeah, I know it wasn't your fault. No, of course not. We'll get the little asshole. Don't worry. Listen, Mario, I got a top-level job for you in the big city. Yeah, I think you'd better pick up Rags in D.C. and take him with you. Yeah, of course it's important. Bet your ass. Now, don't worry about that Santa business. No. No. Of course we'll get him. No sweat, baby, no sweat. That's an easy one. Now, the one I got for you, that's a tough one. Here's what I want you to do."

7

Monday morning. Morley was in West Palm and then Palm Beach shortly after the banks opened. He visited his new lock boxes, leaving a number of packages in each of them, wearing his black hair and mustache disguise as on Friday. As he was getting into his car around the corner from the second bank, a white LTD pulled up at the bank's front door. Morley would have recognized both the blond man at the wheel and the smooth, dark young man who got out and went into the bank as people he'd seen at the airport Saturday. He would have been surprised at their presence; in fact, he would have been shocked.

Morley drove south on U.S. 1, happy that that task was out of the way. Despite his confidence, he'd been nervous with the contents of that Carradine briefcase in his place. All it would have taken was a bold and lucky burglar. My God, he'd been prepared for something valuable, but it still shook him up. There had been $2,220,000 in that briefcase! Neat stacks of bills cramming the thing full. The sight was unbelievable; one side was thirty-two packages of tightly packed hundred-dollar bills, five hundred to a package—$1,600,000 in cold cash. The other half had thirty-two packages, mostly of fifties but with some twenties, totaling $620,000. This kind of money had been unthinkable to Morley until two nights ago when he opened that case. Suddenly all the money in the world was right there in front of him, and now it would be up to his wits to hang on to it, as well as his health. Since five P.M. Saturday those two items had become inseparably related.

About an hour later Morley pulled into the entrance area of a large hotel in Fort Lauderdale and turned his car over to the parking attendant. He walked confidently through the crowded lobby and down a hallway behind the desk to the hotel phone operators' room. He asked the nearest girl for Molly Carrero. She pointed toward a brunette on the far side of the room who was busy talking and taking notes. When she finished, Morley moved quickly to her side. She turned her pretty, dark, small-featured face toward him with a pleasant but openly curious look.

"Miss Carrero?"

"Yes."

"I'm Lloyd Patterson, a friend of Mr. Rourke. Did he call you about me?"

The magic name earned a big smile. "Oh, yes, Mr. Patterson, of course. Mr. Rourke said you would make some calls to be billed to him. Of course. May I help you?"

"Yes, thank you. I want a person-to-person overseas call to Bern, Switzerland. The man I wish to reach, this is his name." He handed the girl a slip of paper and pointed to the last line. "And this is the number of his office. I believe the office will have a number where he can be reached, if he should happen to be out at the moment."

"Very good, sir. Let me check with the New York overseas operator and see if there's a delay on Switzerland. Monday can be a very busy day."

"Please." Morley stood silently as she queried New York, then listened. She turned, smiling. "Only a very short delay, sir. I hope to have a circuit in just a few minutes, then it will just be a matter of locating your party. If you'd care to wait in a booth—take number three—to the left outside, I'll ring as soon as I have him."

"Thank you. I'll be there."

It was almost ten minutes before the phone in booth three jogged Morley into action.

"Hello."

"Mr. Patterson, sorry for the delay, your party was not in his office. The Bern operator has located him and he will be coming on any minute."

"Thanks, I'll hang on."

"Good—oh, here he is, sir. Go ahead."

A deep voice came on. No discernible accent, but a hint of good humor and even more of curiosity. "Mr. Patterson? This is Wilhelm Stehrli in Bern. How may I be of assistance?"

Morley waited for the successive clicks that told him the New York operator and Miss Carrero had closed their circuits; he couldn't tell about Bern. Oh well, not to worry; if they listened, they listened. "Willi, this is Pat."

"Pat! My God! It *is* you. You devil, where are you? Why didn't you let me know you'd be calling? How are you? What are you doing? Why—"

"Whoa, Willi, hold up. One at a time. I'm in Florida. I'm still living here. I work for a travel agency now, and I'll be visiting Europe next week."

"That is great news, Pat. I am truly delighted. You will come to Suisse and you will be my honored guest. It is true? Ilse will be delighted."

"Yes and no, Willi. I *will* come to Switzerland and we can surely get together if you're free, but I can't be your guest, not this trip."

"Oh. I am sorry, Pat."

"So am I, Willi. Truly I am, but I'm on a terribly tight schedule; I will only be in Zurich for a few hours. I'll miss seeing Ilse. I know you'll understand."

"Of course. Of course. When will you be coming?"

"Swissair from Paris, Saturday morning, ten-fifteen your time, Zurich airport. Could you meet me, Willi? I know you're busy as hell, but it's important."

"My good friend, I will be there. Now what is it you wish me to do?"

"Willi, you're as perceptive as I remembered. I'm embarrassed to be calling you after these many months just to ask a favor, but I do need your help."

"My friend, you must never be embarrassed to ask me for help. It is what friends are for to each other. Besides, to you I will always be indebted as well as grateful. You know that, Pat."

"Yes, I know Willi, but it is not so. Your friendship has repaid me many times over for anything I did for you."

Willi started to protest, then stopped and began to chuckle. Then he broke into a deep and hearty laugh. "So! We are acting like your famous English comedians—'after you, my dear Gaston'—is it not so? Yes, how foolish. What do you need, Pat?"

"I will be carrying a briefcase which I do not wish to have opened in customs."

There was silence, so Morley continued. "The contents will be legitimate, Willi, no contraband of any sort but I don't want to be noticed, and I don't want the contents noted, or rather, I don't want any record or remembrance that *I* brought them in on that date."

"Hmm. One question only—it is money?"

"Yes, Willi, it is; that is, most of it, along with some few papers and records."

"And you simply wish me to see you through customs."

"That's it. Yes."

"It will be done, my friend. Consider it done. I will meet you in the customs waiting area soon after landing. It is okay?"

"It is perfect, Willi and I assure you no Swiss law will be broken with what I bring in."

"Do not say more, my friend. It is done."

"Many thanks. Now to more pleasant things. Can you join me for a large wet lunch? I will have an appointment in Zurich at eleven-thirty and should be free no later than noon. I must catch a three-forty-five flight back to Paris, but it will allow us to hoist a few for old time's sake. Can you possibly make it?"

"Delighted. It will be a treat I shall look forward to. Delighted! Now, I shall not waste your money talking; we can catch up on Saturday. Not so?"

"Yes, Willi, it is so. I will see you then—after ten-ten—in the customs area. And, Willi—"

"Yes?"

"Thanks again."

"Not to be mentioned, my dear friend. See you on Saturday. Good-bye."

"Good-bye."

Morley then used the same procedures, via Miss Carrero, to contact and arrange an appointment with the senior vice-president of a prominent bank in Zurich for Saturday morning. After he'd hung up, he beckoned the young operator out into the hall and transferred a crisp twenty-dollar bill from his hand to hers. She nodded knowingly when he suggested she forget these calls ever took place and assured him that in the billings they would appear as two routine overseas calls from the offices of Rourke Associates in Miami. They parted with mutual pleasure over the exchange of courtesies.

Driving back north Morley smiled widely as he imagined Willi's stern, handsome, almost Nordic face when he'd been asked to look the other way on a customs regulation. Or maybe customs "practice" would be better terminology; they were not obliged to search every bag, they just had the right to do so if they wished. Good God, it'd been almost ten years since that night in Geneva when he and Willi had become close friends. Willi, a fast-rising junior officer in his country's security service, had been assigned to work with the U.S. Army on the Swiss aspects of a sabotage case centered in Germany but with tentacles into Austria, France, Switzerland, and Denmark. He and Willi had hit it off from the start, and when in a critical moment Morley's fast action had enabled them to stop an almost successful attempt to blow up a Swissair passenger plane, Willi became his friend for good. Not only had they saved many lives, but the action had saved Willi's career—he'd have been blamed had the disaster occurred. Morley felt badly about cashing one of his "blank checks" with Willi, but then, he rationalized, Willi was a proud man who always seemed delighted when presented with an opportunity to return a favor. And after all, it *wasn't* illegal in Switzerland to bring in money to put into Swiss banks. Hell, everybody should be happy. Everybody except those three hoods and their bosses, that is.

It was late afternoon by the time he got back in the Palm Beach area. He decided to drop in on Roger and see if he could firm things up a bit. Roger was there, looking harassed, as if he'd been too busy to get away for one of his continental lunches. He jumped up smiling when Morley came in. "Patrick, my lad. Good to see you. You're just in time for some business discussions, but we must adjourn to more comfortable surroundings, *n'est-ce pas?*"

Morley smiled back, amused as much by the obvious correctness of his own guess as by Roger's levity. "And why not, my good friend? 'Twould appear you have already wasted too much of this glorious day in the pursuit of Mammon."

"How true. How true. Let us away to yon public house while we are still able."

"Lead on."

Safely ensconced in a padded booth in a cool dark corner of a nearby cocktail lounge, Roger lifted his glass in salute. "I'm glad you decided to come to work a bit early, old man. I was about to parch away."

"This is work?"

"Well, yes and no. You'd be surprised how many big deals I've swung in places like this."

"No!"

"Whaddaya mean, no?"

"No, I wouldn't be surprised."

"Aha, my boy, see how fast you are learning the travel business."

"I like it, I like it. Is it payday yet?"

"You need some dough?"

"No, just kidding, Rog."

"Okay. But you know—anytime."

"Yeah, I know. Thanks, but everything's solvent, honest."

"Good. Hey. I talked to Campeau in Paris yesterday."

"And?"

"And he's anxious as hell to see you. He's got some terrific ideas. One of 'em is a World War Two tour that sounds terrific. You know, all the battle sites and lots of history and schmaltz."

"I haven't seen Campeau in five, six years. How's he doing?"

"Great. I told him you'd be coming over soon to firm up some deals for us. He was delighted. He said he wants to show you that Paris hasn't changed, not in the really important things."

"That means broads and booze to Campeau."

"So what do *you* think is important?"

Morley smiled at his friend's mock seriousness. "Lost my head for a minute. Sorry. I'll be glad to see Campeau again. By the way, Rog, since you and he are as anxious to get going on this thing as I am, I think I'll leave Friday on that new Paris-Miami flight. Sound okay to you?"

"Great. Perfect. I'll call Campeau first thing tomorrow."

"Yeah, but tell him I'll be at his place Monday morning, or I can give him a call Sunday if he'd like."

Roger's eyebrows raised fractionally, but he didn't comment. Instead, he said, "He'll want to meet your flight, you know."

"I know, but I'd prefer not. Okay?"

"Sure, okay. As you wish. I'll tell him you're coming in by local flight, time uncertain, and you'll call him Sunday. How's that?"

"Perfect. Same old Rog, fast on the uptake."

Again Roger held his comment. He signaled the waitress for a refill, and when she'd brought it and departed again, he pulled out a small note pad. "Now, Pat, here are my ideas on the kinds of things we might be able to do with Compeau and Gianella in Rome. I think those two will be enough on your plate this trip." He started ticking off notes he'd made on the pad. Morley listened carefully, tossing in a question or comment every so often. They were still sitting there when the after-work crowd descended on the place, still absorbed in their wet business meeting.

Morley would have been even more pleased had he been able to sit in on another business meeting that was being held at about the same time in a large motel in downtown West Palm Beach. This meeting, which had started on a triumphant note, had finally degenerated into frustration. Dennis Conners was the principal purveyor of both moods.

Krupa's contacts, with only a modicum of unfriendly persuasion, had come up with the location of the lock box for the key, and then with some illegal administrative assistance from a suborned official of the bank, they were able to get the contents of the box. The bank official was pretty nervous, but Krupa convinced him not only that his action was in his own best interests, but that he'd never get caught because the record owner of the box, the ex-owner, was a nonperson.

The box did indeed contain seven spiral notebooks that in size and content appeared to be the code, contact, and procedure books for Cappacino's courier service. One was even marked "Santa," but it was only a ledger of dates and payments. Conners's immediate reaction was delight at being able to tell Matthewson that they had the books, but while he was waiting for Matthewson's man to arrive and pick them up, he took a closer look at them, and his optimism started to wane. At first he thought maybe they were too complicated, or maybe just too simple. Anyway, he couldn't make any sense out of them. Then he wondered if maybe there was a code key book missing. Finally, he reluctantly concluded that Cappacino, even in death, had reached out to give them one final frustration—the damn books were phoney! He didn't say anything to his men or to the courier who arrived in midafternoon with all the right passwords from Matthewson and left with the package of notebooks a few minutes later. The courier told Agrico "off the record" that he was taking them directly to the "big boss in Jersey." Conners hoped he was wrong, that he just hadn't found the key, but in his heart he was convinced the books were phony.

And this guy Santa was making the day even more frustrating. Conners's optimism on this one was fading fast too. They had started out with all the obvious angles: people with Saint or Santa in their names, Cappacino's records and household accounts, neighbors, storekeepers. They had ended up with nothing.

Conners and Agrico had started with Cappacino's apartment and then branched out into the rest of the building and started on the other nine condominium buildings in the area. They had not gotten very far today, but a disturbing pattern was already emerging: Cappacino had really played it cool. There was no clue in the apartment, everything was routine, and there was nothing in his building. His neighbors and the resident manager were friendly and cooperative with the "federal officers" conducting the "very confidential investigation," but it was clear that Dante had successfully avoided any social contact with them. They all assumed Ernie Pro had been his wife, and of course neither Dante nor she had ever done anything to disabuse them of this assumption. The neighbors had not considered Dante's standoffish attitude or conduct offensive or even unusual, because so many absentee owners of Florida condominiums were similarly cool about relationships with other owners or tenants.

Conners left Agrico to work on the other high rises in the area while he went back to meet Matthewson's courier, and it was too late to do any more that day. Krupa had a more interesting, but no more productive, afternoon. He'd used another of his contacts to get at the telephone records. Conners was really impressed by the strides this young man had taken in his year in this area; he'd really laid his lines out like the pro he was. He'd made a listing of all Cappacino's toll calls during the last year. There were quite a few intrastate calls, mostly to Miami and Tampa, and many more to Chicago, New York, New Jersey, L.A., Honolulu, San Pedro, San Francisco, and Seattle. They could all be checked out, but Conners decided it didn't make sense to spend much time on them now. Same with the less frequent but still numerous overseas calls, mostly to France, Turkey, Lebanon, and Morocco. It was the local calls that would tell the tale, those nontoll calls in the Palm Beach area—and of course, there was no record of these. No attempt had ever been made to bug Dante's phone or either of his apartments, not even the broad's, because Dante was too smart. Hell, he'd written some of the books on *that* subject.

So the meeting ended on a falsely hopeful note, with predictions all around of happier days ahead. Conners joined in the optimism, but he had trouble believing in it.

8

Morley woke to a beautiful sunshiny morning Tuesday. He walked down to the ocean for a prebreakfast swim, a practice abhorred by natives in January but one that he found particularly invigorating this day. He dawdled a bit over eggs and toast and still made it to Hurst's Global Travel for the opening bell. Roger took obvious pleasure in introducing him to people and showing him around the office, finally leading him to a small but tastefully furnished room that had his legend on the door: PATRICK MORLEY, ASSOCIATE.

Roger had already talked to Campeau and got him working on the Paris meetings, but he suggested that it might be better if Morley himself called that "crotchety old bastard Gianella" who might or might not respond to anyone else. So Morley called and firmed up his Rome appointments for Tuesday evening and Wednesday. Gianella, who was in a good mood, seemed genuinely delighted to hear from Morley and even passed on his regards to Roger. Roger was so pleased with the way things were shaping up that he suggested an early and long celebration lunch; Morley, similarly pleased, did not refuse him.

Before he went home that evening Morley phoned Terry Rourke in Miami. Terry sounded happy. "How's it going, Patrick? That merchandise okay?"

"Super, Terry, but then I expected it would be."

"I know that's some of your Irish blarney, but say it any way."

"No crap, the stuff is first class."

"Good. Good. What next, me boyo?"

"Well, I'd like to put a couple of stops out, if I can."

"Tell me where and what kind, and *I'll* tell you if ya can."

"One's at the Pentagon. I'd like to be alerted if anybody comes around or if there are any mail or phone inquiries from somebody wanting info on my service record. Any kind of nibbling would be of interest."

"Can do. Got a few contacts there. Sure one of them can handle it. Where's the other one?"

"Santa Barbara. I'd like the same kind of coverage for anyone snooping around the courthouse—birth records especially—yeah, very 'specially."

"No problem. Got a good man in L.A. who can cover that. But, Pat, you don't really want 'stops' do you?"

"No, you're right, not 'stops,' just alerts. Let the bastards look if they want to, but let me know as soon as possible when they start looking. And of course I'd be interested in knowing exactly what info they got, *if* it can be determined without spooking the 'lookers.'"

"Gotcha. I'll instruct my boys just that way. Any other problems? Those were easy."

"I don't want to give you any hard ones, Terry, though I know you could knock 'em off easily."

"Yeah, yeah. Thanks a lot. You've got my curiosity up about twenty-five feet high, but I know better 'n to ask what it's all about."

"You're right, Terry, you do." They both laughed, then Morley continued. "In due time, lad, in due time. All I can do at the moment is assure you that you won't go to jail for anything you're doing for me. Now I don't know what the hell else you're doing that might be jailbait, but my stuff isn't. Okay?"

"Yeah, I guess. You're a regular frigging fountain of information, pal, but mine is not to question why. Okay, Patrick, I'll be in touch soon as I get anything. Take care."

"You too. And thanks. Tell Barb her husband's a nice guy even if he doesn't deserve her."

"Yeah, I'll do that."

"Oh damn, Terry. One last thing—incidental, but maybe important. Can you get me some background—I guess I mean organizational background—on the syndicate's Chicago setup? The current one, the one they call the 'Corporation.'"

There was a long pause before Terry came in. "Yeah, I can get background, names and numbers stuff, but I'm not sure I should. Are you playing around with those cuckoos? That's big league stuff, buddy. They play for keeps."

"Not to worry, Terry. It's just that it'd be interesting to see if a couple names match up."

"What're the names? I'll see."

"I don't have them yet."

"Hmmm. You are a close-mouthed bastard, Patrick. But all right, I'll see what I can do."

"Thanks again."

"Don't mention it, pal. Watch your rear end."

"Sure. Sure. Good-bye."

Later that afternoon, Conners and Krupa were sitting in lounge chairs near a corner of the motel pool, going over the events of the day. The atmosphere was heavy with disappointment.

Krupa had been working at the banks today. Cappacino had two different checking accounts, one in Palm Beach and another in West Palm. Using the same scared and cooperative official, he was able to arrange access to "friends" in these other banks and had obtained all the Cappacino records, duplicated them (on the banks' machines, of course) and brought the copies back to the hotel along with the canceled checks Conners had taken out of Cappacino's apartment office. After a long and grueling session they had come up with zilch. There were lots of "cash" checks and quite a few made out to D. E.

Prohaska. All the others were pretty routine, nothing to raise any doubts. The only "unusual" ones, using the term loosely, were a one-time payment to an attorney in North Palm Beach and a couple of sizable checks made out to a financial consultant firm in Miami. There was nothing that could be construed as payments to a bagman, nothing concerning any names or persons unknown or not easily explained. The records seemed to be a dead end.

Conners had spent part of his day in the shopping centers at both ends of Singer Island, using the pictures of Dante and Ernie Pro to try to jog memories. It was no dice. People were friendly enough, but they just didn't recognize the man or woman, not even a TV repair shop that had made two service calls to Dante's apartment and been paid by check. Conners talked to the serviceman who'd handled one of those visits—the other one was made by a former employer, whereabouts now unknown—but he couldn't even place the man or the apartment. It had happened almost a year before, and the man was very busy and *not* very interested or bright. Bars, nightclubs, and restaurants were equally sterile. It was almost as if Dante had never left his apartment when he was in Florida. Maybe that was the answer.

Agrico came out of the hotel into the pool area, wearing the closest thing to a smile that Conners had yet seen. He came over to their table and sat down, pulled out a cigarette, tamped it, put it in his mouth, and finally lit it. Conners just looked at him, straight on. Finally Agrico spoke, and it turned out that his grin was genuine. "Think I hit some pay dirt."

"Good, tell us about it."

"Y'know the old man's next-door neighbor? The one was out of town yesterday? Well, he got back and the manager told him I was lookin' for 'im, so he called me and left a message. This guy, his name is Farber, I think it's probably 'Farberg' if we was to know, anyways he's a talker. And nosy. We should hire this asshole to work any apartment we need covered. He's better'n a hunnerd bugs. Anyways, Farber says the old man and 'his woman,' he knew they wasn't married, don't ask me how, never had much company. In fact he didn't remember seeing anybody who visited them socially. Farber said the old man, 'old Casper' he called him, was pleasant enough whenever they met, but made it clear he didn't want to get chummy.

"Now the woman, 'Dorothy,' was somethin' else. Farber said he'd talked to her quite often in the hall and at the pool, and a couple times she'd accepted his invite for a drinkie at his place. She was friendly as hell, but still cool, Farber said, like maybe she wanted to play but was scared to. Anyways, I'm sure Farber was tryin' to get into Ernie Pro's pants, and according to him she was about to drop 'em for him one time when something scared her off. Farber says he 'spects that 'somethin' was a guy who came lookin' for Dante. Farber didn't see the guy full on that time—oh yeah, they were in Ernie's place, so she answered the door—but a couple weeks later the guy came again when Farber and Ernie were at the pool, so he got a good look. The guy was about thirty, five ten or eleven, one sixty-five or so, slender, brown wavy hair, medium length. He was tanned like a native, that's Farber's words, looked well dressed. He didn't have any particular accent, not foreign, not Southern, not anything, but Farber says he talked like a well-educated man. Farber was sure he and Dorothy knew each other, but when he asked her right out, she said no, she'd never seen him before. Farber says he knew this was a lie because he'd got enough voice and back of the head that other time to know this was the same guy who'd screwed up his piece of ass that other day."

"This Farber—what's he do?"

"He's some kinda big landlord up in Jersey. Lives down here mosta' the winter. I figure he's gotta lotta dough and property he didn't earn, and he just sits around and drinks and chases pussy."

"Is he sharp?"

"I dunno, Dennis. I guess so. He took a good long look at my phoney ID card. I almost shit. He seems to be smart enough. From what he told me, this guy made enough impression on him that he remembered a lot about what he looked like."

"You said Ernie Pro seemed scared of this guy?"

"Did I? I don't think 'scared's a good word. I'd say more like 'embarrassed.' Yeah, I think Farber said just that, that Dorothy seemed kinda embarrassed at this guy showin' up and findin' her playin' 'kneesies' or whatever with the old man's neighbor."

"Now, Paul, what's your own judgment of this guy Farber and his story?"

"I think Farber's leveling, Dennis, 'cause I don't know why he wouldn't. I think he's a flag-waver who figures he's helping out the feds, who will forget the whole thing the next time a twitchin' ass bikini goes by. But I do think he's smart and I think his description of the guy—the visitor—is probably pretty good. Now whether the guy is Santa—who knows?"

"Yeah, I agree with you. It's sure as hell worth following up." Turning to Krupa, Conners said, "Sal, check with Chicago and New York, and get New York to okay a check with Miami on the names and descriptions of 'official' visitors to Dante— over, say, the last year. Yeah. Paul, when was it this guy showed up?"

"About six or seven weeks ago, Farber thought."

"Yeah, Sal, have 'em check that time frame especially."

"Okay."

"And, Paul."

"Yeah."

"Good work. Any more missing people out there who might have known the old man?"

"No. Not that I know of. But I think it might be good to have another go at Farber in a few days. He might remember more. I told him to try and he said he would. I'll hit him about Friday."

"Good, but make it tomorrow, and when you see him I'll have a guy I want you to take along."

"Yeah?"

"Yeah. He's an artist. I want him to do a sketch to the tune of this guy Farber's description of the visitor."

"Hey. Great idea. Yeah. I'll tell Farber he's one of those cop artists like on TV."

"Paul, you tell Farber nothing more. Let him do the talking. But make sure my man keeps drawing until Farber says the picture looks like Ernie Pro's visitor—*then* we'll get to work in earnest."

Agrico was taken aback but adjusted quickly. He was used to obeying commands; it was just that it was the first time he'd seen this crisp, authoritative, steely-eyed side of Dennis Conners. But then very few people in the organization had. Agrico nodded assent rapidly. Krupa said nothing but was inwardly amused at Agrico's discomfiture; he was one of the few who *had* seen Conners in action before.

The artist gimmick worked great from a technical point of view. Farber was fascinated with the concept and played with this new toy 'til he was sure the results were perfect. He said the sketch looked "almost like a portrait" of Dorothy's visitor.

The next move was the slow and thorough recanvassing of all the island areas they'd been over with the other pictures, trying to find somebody—just one—who could name the man in the sketch. Conners had impressed on Krupa and Agrico the need for subtlety, care, and tact in this second go-round. He sure as hell didn't want anybody's feathers ruffled so they'd go calling the cops. Nor did he want to alert this guy Santa and scare him back into his hole. His men understood and followed Conners's instructions to the letter, using an agreed-upon set of questions and explanations that clouded their objective rather neatly.

After two unproductive days, Conners got the phone call that changed everything. It was Matthewson, a different Matthewson, puzzled, petulant, and deflated. "Dennis, I just had a call from Jersey, Mr. Henry. I don' unnerstand it and I don' like it. He wants to know what's happening on this Santa business. I tell him, an' he don' like *that* either. Anyways, he says he wants to talk to you. Yeah, you. He says you should take the Eastern flight to Newark tomorrow, that's at nine-fifteen from your end. You go to the Eastern ticket desk when you get there and his man Savilli will find you. You can't miss that creep, he ain't got no blood. He looks like a fucking checkerboard with all that white skin and black hair. Anyways, Savilli will know you. You go with him. Okay?"

"Sure, okay, but what's it all about, Mr. Matthewson?"

Jammy's voice took on a sly tone. "Hey, Dennis, you're not shittin' me, are you? You haven't been talkin' to Jersey, have ya?"

"No sir, no way. I've never met him. In fact I don't even know anybody from up there. No sir."

"Okay, Dennis. Good. What's the man want? Hell, I don' know. All I know is ya better do like he says."

"Right. I'll catch that plane. Be back as soon as I can. We've got some pretty good leads working here and the boys'll be pushing them all out."

"Anything hot?"

"Not hot, but we got a couple flickers on that sketch."

"Good. Doesn't look like he was an official visitor?"

"Not so far, anyway. I don't think so."

"Well, keep at it. I hope it ain't too late. Gimme a call when you get back if the old man don't swear ya to secrecy." Matthewson laughed drily as he said it, but even over the phone Conners could sense the feeling of very unhumorous despair with which it was said.

"Yes sir. Good-bye."

9

Conners felt like he'd died and gone to heaven. He knew he hadn't because he felt too alive, and he had no illusions about the kind of hereafter he merited. But this place looked like he imagined heaven would look. He'd been brought into the room by a butler after driving what seemed like miles from the huge iron gates, through a wonderland of a park to the huge mansion. The entry hall was bigger than a tract house. The room he was in, a library, bespoke quiet, solid luxury and he assumed from the size of the building that there were probably twenty or thirty rooms this size or larger. Three-quarters of an hour's drive from the squalor of Newark's airport area and he'd changed worlds.

The door opened and a man came in. He was of medium height, slender with neatly trimmed gray hair combed straight back without a part, clean shaven, and impeccably tailored in gray flannel slacks, a smoking jacket of a subdued plaid, a soft wool shirt, and a matching ascot. The man's back was ramrod straight, and he walked with a spring in his step, but as he came closer, Conners revised upward his first impression of age; the man was well preserved, but he had to be in his seventies. Then the man focused his eyes on Conners's face. They were ageless, deep set, and unblinking; they seemed to have an existence apart from the rest of him. Conners's overall impression was of a degree of presence and command beyond anything he'd ever experienced. The old man broke the spell by displaying a row of perfect white teeth in a half smile and holding out his right hand. He spoke in a beautifully modulated voice, soft yet strong. "I'm Albert Henry, Mr. Conners. Very pleased to meet you."

"My pleasure, sir." Conners took the hand. It was slender, but the grip was firm and warm.

"Would you have a glass of wine with me? Yes? Then we'll have a sandwich while we talk. I'm sure you're famished after your long trip. Perhaps the terrace would be best today."

As he talked, the old man pressed a buzzer on the wall and then opened French doors leading to a raised flagstone terrace enclosed in what looked like heavy thermal glass and shaded by a deeply overhung roof. The three glass sides looked out on a gently sloping lawn and a curving flagstone walk that lead down to a large swimming pool. Beyond and off to the side Conners could see a tennis court and two gazebos. A glass table on the terrace was set for two, with white linen, gleaming silver, and sparkling crystal. A number of comfortable chairs were scattered about. The old man pointed to two of them separated by a round serving table. Conners waited until his host was seated, then took one himself. The butler came through the French doors and stood politely in front of the old man's chair.

"Yes sir."

"Oliver, please bring us some *Chateau d'l' quem*. And we'll have lunch at twelve-thirty."

"Thank you, sir." The butler retreated through the library.

The old man looked at Conners again. "Tell me, Mr. Conners, how long have you been with Gennaro Giamatteo?"

"About two years, sir."

"You've learned a lot?"

"Yes sir. I believe so."

"And what is your opinion of Gennaro's operation? I mean does it seem organized, efficient, well directed, and so forth?"

Conners was taken aback, more with the timing of the question than with its bluntness. He tried not to show it.

"That's a difficult question, sir."

"Why?"

"Because I've not had exposure to all of Mr. Giamatteo's operation, only to those parts in which I've been actually working. When I first began, I was told not to be inquisitive about what other people were doing."

"I can't argue with that statement, but let me rephrase the question: what do you think of those parts of his operation to which you have been exposed, those in which you do have personal experience?"

Conners had been prepared for Mr. Henry's superb diction; the stories about his private "culture tutors" were too many and widespread to all be false; nevertheless, he was impressed with the fluidity of the man's excellent English. He was certainly a far cry from the stereotype of the old "Mustache Pete." He answered. "Sir, I could give you my opinion, but I wouldn't presume to say I know more about his operations, these particular parts, I mean, than Mr. Giamatteo. He has been very fair with me, and I feel I owe him the same treatment."

"So you feel you *could* comment on the Gennaro's operation, but that if you did it would be presumptuous, or disloyal, or both. Is that right?"

"Yes sir. That's it."

Conners was thankful that the butler knocked and then entered the room. He set the wine bucket near the table, handed Mr. Henry a goblet, and poured a sip into it. He tasted, nodded approval, and Oliver proceeded to fill the goblets. He left.

The old man sniffed the bouquet, took a sip, then looked squarely at Conners. His eyes were almost hypnotizing in their unwavering intensity. All at once Conners found it easy to believe all those heretofore incredible stories about the pile of skeletons on which the old man's rise to the top had been effected. He spoke softly, but his words had a steel edge.

"Mr. Conners, I will make one point clear, then I will not mention it again—ever! Giamatteo works for me. He exists, Mr. Conners, by my sufferance. His operations are *my* operations, and if they are bad, I suffer; if they are inefficient, I am unhappy; if they lose money, I lose money. Mr. Conners"—the eyes blazed—"I do not like to suffer; I do not like to be unhappy; I do not like to lose money. You understand?"

"Yes sir. I do."

"Well?"

"Sir. I think Mr. Giamatteo is, intrinsically, one of the very best people I've met in the business. I mean that when he *does* put himself into an operation personally it is always done in first-class style. But I think something has happened to him. It is sad, sir, to see a good man lose interest, to stop caring about his work and that, I think, is what happened to Mr. Giamatteo. He is not the same man he was two years ago. He's lost touch, lost control; worst of all, sir, he doesn't seem to care."

Mr. Henry nodded seriously. "And specifically, Mr. Conners, what has been the result of this, this lack of interest on Gennaro's part?"

"He's lost day-to-day contact. He stays in his office and tries to run his operations by delegating all of the decisions and responsibility."

The old man jumped on that one. "But delegation of responsibility and decisions is certainly no sin in itself; in fact, there are those who will argue that it is the benchmark of good management. Is there more to your comment?"

Conners smiled inwardly at the old man's insight. Damn, he thought, I'd sure have hated to have crossed this old pirate in his day. Look at him and he's gotta be seventy-five at least. Sharp as a bright kid. Conners answered slowly. "Yes sir, there is. Mr. Giamatteo has delegated to the extent that his supervisory control is gone. He doesn't know what's going on until one of his men tells him, and they never tell him until the flap is so big they can't handle it alone."

"Still, this is a problem of degree, is it not?" Mr. Henry's eyes belied the seriousness of this question, but Conners decided to treat it as if he hadn't noticed.

"Yes sir, I suppose it is, but there's an additional problem, one of judgment. Mr. Giamatteo delegates important responsibilities and decisions to incompetents whose only qualification is blood relationship, and then assumes that they'll do it right, although even his own experience tells him otherwise."

Conners almost bit his tongue on that one! He knew Giamatteo was the son of one of Mr. Henry's loyal and trusted capos from the old days, and that Jammy himself had earned his spurs many times over in Mr. Henry's service. He also knew of the traditional sanctity of the bloodline in the families that had been the basis for the old man's rise to power and for his current status. But something in the old man's line of questions—his attitude—told Conners that this was the right kind of answer, so he'd shot the wad. He was right.

The old man didn't even raise an eyebrow. "Like Mario Banducci?"

"Yes sir. He's the best case in point."

The old man swished the wine in his goblet, watching carefully as the film ebbed from one side of the glass and then the other. He looked up at Conners, his eyes stern but not cold. "You got balls, son. You know I've got nephews and friends and friends' nephews and sons all through my organization? You know we were *built* on bloodlines? Are you telling me that's all horseshit?"

Conners thought he detected an absence of rancor, maybe even a hint of approval in the old man's tone, although he certainly still couldn't prove it by his looks. But the die was cast, so he went on. "Yes sir, I know about the tradition, and no, sir, I *don't* think it's all wrong but I'm sure you are very objective about your own delegation of responsibility."

"Maybe. But still, don't you believe loyalty, especially family loyalty, blood ties, blood loyalty, such things, are important?"

"Yes sir, within reasonable limits. I mean that blood and loyalty and efficiency don't necessarily come as one package. The Bible tells us not only that the first murder was committed by one brother on another, but that it was botched up."

Mr. Henry slipped into his half smile on that one, but took up the cudgel once more. "Life is a compromise. Nobody's perfect. You have to take the best you can get."

"Yes sir. I agree fully but I don't believe you should settle for less than the best person available because he happens to have a desirable bloodline, when he may or may not be loyal or efficient."

"Well said. I'll buy that. Let's go back to specifics. You think you'd have handled the Cappacino business better than Banducci, which means better than Gennaro?"

"Yes sir. I do."

The half smile again. "I believe you would have." He fixed Conners with that gaze. "That's why I *told* Gennaro to have *you* handle this Santa business. Which brings me to my point for asking you here today."

The butler knocked and announced lunch. It was exactly twelve-thirty. They moved to the table and Oliver served them thick, steaming soup from a tureen. It was deliciously filling, and as they spooned it up, the old man talked about his estate—the problems, the advantages, the seasons—nothing personal. Oliver appeared silently, took the soup dishes away, and brought salad bowls and two plates with huge open-faced turkey sandwiches. After he'd served the salad dressing, the old man told him to leave the coffee carafe and said he'd ring when they were through. He ate about half his sandwich, pushed the plate aside, poured coffee for himself, and passed the carafe to Conners. He continued to chat until Conners had finished his sandwich and poured himself a coffee, then sat back in his chair and began. "Now, Mr. Conners, do you feel disloyal for making those, shall we say, honest but uncomplimentary, statements about Gennaro Giamatteo?"

"No sir. I now understand I owe an overriding loyalty to you."

He really did smile on this one. "Well said. May I call you 'Dennis'?"

"I'd be honored, sir."

"Fine. Now, Dennis, this Santa job, you must know, this is a job for me personally. A most important and most personal job. I will give you some facts, facts very few people know, and you will understand *why* I want this job done right, and *why* it is so important to all of us that it *is* done right. Understand?"

"Yes sir."

"Good. But before I start, I need to know one thing. You must be honest. Are you happy working with my organization?"

"Yes sir, I am."

"You wish to stay? No hard feelings if you don't, Dennis but you must tell me now."

"Yes sir. No question. I'd like to stay."

"Good—because once I tell you all this, all these facts, I would be very upset if you were to leave us. Okay?"

"Yes sir."

"Now, Dennis, you have heard of the European brotherhood called the 'Union Corse'?"

Conners nodded, and the old man continued. "The Corse, as such, is practically nonexistent at present but a very well organized and managed business syndicate was fashioned out of the old Corse. It is known as the 'Company Corse,' and it is very much alive, very strong. This new Corse was begun by old Corse leaders, but, with very few exceptions, it is now controlled by businessmen with new ideas, much as our own organization is. Three of the top men, say three of eight, are old friends of mine, and one of them—in fact, he is the man who designed this 'new look'—is a former close business associate. The other five top men I have no contact with. I seek none, and they, too, seem to desire it this way. Although we have, of necessity, a number of joint ventures, they have made it clear that these arrangements are temporary and not really desirable."

The old man stopped to refill his goblet, took a long draught, and went on. "This was the situation as it existed, say, a year and a half ago. We were all aware of it, and we did not like it, but it was better than a war. Besides, my three friends were still strong enough to keep the pot from boiling over. Then comes along Dante Cappacino. Dante—who once saved my life, who has always been like a younger brother to me, whose mother was like my mother, rest her soul—Dante contacted the Corse and made a proposition that he knew would be favorably received by at least those five businessmen. Now, Dennis, make no mistake about it, Dante was a genius. No question. He designed and built and operated the system of money flow and courier service from all our overseas operations. Now this money is very important to us. It is clean and clear, and it's used for security—all kinds—and for starting new smaller businesses and many other things. We let Dante run his own show, even let him take on some outside courier jobs, even some for the Corse, as our only interest was in continuing his safe, efficient operation. Then, Dante began to service certain other of our international 'laundry' mechanisms. I think it could be said that Dante came to control the flow from operations totaling over a billion dollars a year."

Conners let out a breath, and the old man nodded approvingly. He continued. "But Dante, poor Dante, he was not satisfied somehow. About a year ago, ten months maybe, he contacted the Corse secretly. He offered to sell the Corse a deal that would have, shall we say, 'unionized' his whole system under the total control of the Corse. As I say, he was a genius, and the gradual takeover he proposed was foolproof. We would have awakened some day and the Corse would have been milking us for a billion plus a year, and we wouldn't have had one fucking line of recourse." The old man was furious just telling about it. Conners had heard that when his store-bought grammar slipped back to the street—beware. Especially if you were the object of his anger.

"And what did Dante want for this, this many pounds of his own brothers' flesh? Money! Can you believe it? And status! Yes, status. He would be rich and a Corse leader. That was it. Never mind that the Corse would eat him up and spit him in the Mediterranean after they milked him dry. Dante had a clever arrangement worked out whereby they would not have all the parts of his operation until almost five years later. You see, Dennis, only Dante had the overall knowledge of the systems, the hundreds of airline, customs, immigration, police, and government officials all over the world who were on his payroll. We know that he kept this information well documented and up to date in six or seven notebooks. His place in Florida was like a fortress, and we figured this was why.

"But Dante made one foolish, and for us, lucky mistake. He picked as his Corse contact a man, a good man, who'd been his close friend for thirty years. Dante forgot one thing: this man has been *my* good friend for *forty* years. My friend told me the whole story shortly after Dante approached him, which made us both extremely sad. Our old friend. To think he would do this kind of thing.

"What could I do? I tell you, Dennis, it was like the cancer. Even though it was part of your body, you must cut it out before it kills you. But this cancer, it had to be dissected, so to speak, first. We had to have those books, Dante's records, before we permanently removed this cancer.

"And so I called Gennaro Giamatteo, who for so many years—even as a very young man—had been a strong right arm for me. You see, with Dante headquartered in Gennaro's territory, even though he lived half of the time in Florida, he was Gennaro's responsibility. His treachery was against Gennaro, and the vengeance belonged to Gennaro. I told Gennaro exactly what I have told you. I know him well, he is a very smart man. Oh, Dennis, he was so quick and so smart and so dedicated, shall we say, ten years ago. It pains me to see him now.

"Anyway, I have to assume that Gennaro knew how important it was. I even told him that if Dante's records and what was in Dante's head got into the wrong hands anywhere in the world we, the organization, would be in very bad trouble. Actually, I always felt in my own heart that Dante, may his troubled soul rest in peace, did not wish to destroy us. I do not think so. He would rob us for this large money and this 'leadership status' that he considered so important and that he must have felt we had cheated him out of somehow. But, no, I am sure. He would not try to destroy us.

"Gennaro understood, but Gennaro failed me!" The old man spit out the statement. His voice was as cold as his eyes were hot. "The fool! He stayed in his warm office fucking that stupid oversexed secretary of his and turned over this most important job to some of his stupid relatives. I do not think that even today, Gennaro has got his head far enough out of that bitch's crotch to realize what a monumental mistake he has made."

The old man took a long sip of wine. It seemed to cool him off. His voice was lower and sadder as he went on with his story. "Poor Gennaro. You have analyzed his problem well, Dennis. He has lost interest, lost his judgment, and lost all the qualities that made him such a good man. I have noticed, but I have been patient. One does not forget soon all the good things a friend has done." His voice rose in volume and intensity. "But there must be a limit, Dennis. There is a point beyond which one can no longer excuse or forget. I do not know, even yet, how big a mistake Gennaro made. I cannot tell, but I do know it was a terrible thing. Yes, Gennaro bet his wallet on one stupid throw of the dice, and he lost without even staying to see what he rolled. Now he must pay the price. It is our law and our custom. I cannot change it."

Conners nodded, straight-faced, but a chill flickered down his spine. He realized he'd just heard the commander-in-chief condemn to death one of his trusted generals.

The old man got up and started to pace the far side of the terrace. "But that is not why I'm telling you all this, Dennis. That is not why I want you to do this job for me or why it is so important. Can you guess *why* it is so important?"

Conners didn't hesitate. "Yes sir. I believe I can. I figure those notebooks we got in the Palm Beach lock box are fakes, and so this man Santa is the number-one suspect for having the real ones stashed away."

Mr. Henry just looked at him for a long moment, then nodded his head. He smiled. "Why did you not finish the law school?"

Conners answered quickly, but he knew from the sudden crinkle around the old man's eyes that he'd shown surprise at the question. He shouldn't really have been surprised at the depth of the man's knowledge of his background. "I wanted no part of their system, sir. They were hypocrites who pretended to be honest. I didn't want to play their game the rest of my life. Their idea of justice made me sick."

"And we? How do you find us in this regard?"

"Well sir, I find your organization's rules understandable, and with few exceptions at my level of experience, fairly administered. I am always satisfied if my progression in a job is dependent on my performance; I've found it to be that way so far in your organization."

"Fair enough. You're quick, son. I need people who are quick. And I liked your feeling of loyalty to Gennaro, whether or not he deserved it." He smiled, then continued.

"You're right, the notebooks are fake, and our best bet for finding the real ones is this Santa man. But the real problem is that we don't know anything about this Santa man. We don't know what he wants to do with those books. If he's smart, and I believe he must be, he will know their value, but I can't believe Dante would have gone so far as to tell this Santa man about the Corse deal, much less about the way Dante planned to work it. Now what would you do if you had those books, Dennis?"

Conners answered crisply, the humor touching only his eyes. "Why, I'd bring them personally to you, sir."

The old man laughed aloud. He had a good laugh, deep and sincere. "I asked for that, son. Good one. Now seriously, I mean *if* you were this Santa?"

"Well, sir, to start with I agree he must be smart, just from what we know so far. But I also think he is a man with some kind of experience in our business, I mean, at least in some related line of work." He smiled. "Like maybe an ex-cop or ex-customs or treasury man."

Mr. Henry returned Conners smile, but his answer was a crisp question. "Why do you say that?"

"Because I think that would have been a necessary qualification for Mr. Cappacino to have selected him for the job, and I think also for his decision to try the heist."

"I see. I like that logic, even if I don't like what it means. Yes, I see. You feel he was more than just a local bagman for Dante?"

"Yes sir, though it probably started that way. I figure Dante had to have told him about those books or he wouldn't have known. I don't think, from what I know about Dante, and you'd know this far better than I, sir, that he'd *give* the books to this Santa to hold but the fact that the fake ones were in the lock box and we figure Santa has to have the real ones indicates some sort of an emergency plan for these books, in which Santa was included."

"So maybe he was Dante's confidant—this Santa man—as well as his bagman? Yes, I like that. Go on, my boy."

"I figure, sir, that Santa was an important part of Dante's scheme, with the Corse, I mean. I don't mean that Santa knew about it; I mean that Dante was planning to use him in some important way when it came down to the wire. I figure this is why Dante took such pains to conceal Santa's identity. I understand even Dante's girl didn't know."

"Who knows? That lying quack that killed her says she didn't know. But we'll never know that story either. But go on. I'm very interested."

"I believe that Santa had a bigger piece of the action than we thought at first, especially with Dante dead. I think Dante must have left him a note, instructions, location of the books, something like that. Otherwise, why the phoney books in the lock box? But I also believe that this is good."

The old man cut in sharply. "Why?"

"Because the more this guy knows, the more he realizes that his only sensible way out is to deal with us. He's got to be scared because he doesn't know how much we know about him."

"So what kind of a deal would this Santa man be making with us?"

"Money."

"He's got two-and-a-quarter million of ours already. He will want more for the books?"

"I think so. I'm afraid so, sir. But I also think we have two jobs: first, to get him before he's ready or able to deal; if that's not possible, to get him when he tries to deal."

"I like that better. You think along the right lines, Dennis. I like that. Yes. Get this Santa man and the books and the money. That's what we must try for. But why do you say it's good that he's so smart?"

"Because, sir, he's smart *and* greedy, so even if he gets scared, he knows the worth of the books and won't do anything panicky like try to sell them to the feds, or, say, to the Corse. A smart guy has to know we're his best prospect, and a greedy smart guy has to know we're his only one. He knows we'll keep looking for him 'til we find him, so why not bet his wallet and make one big deal?"

"You make a persuasive case, Dennis. What would you have us do? Not just wait for him to come to us, books in hand?"

"Oh no, sir. I'm just theorizing about his motivation and plans. I think we have to go all out to identify Santa, and when we're positive we have him and know all we can about him, we move in and squeeze."

"Hah. I like that better too. But why do you say we must know him so well before we pluck him up and squeeze him dry?"

Conners thought he recognized another "test question," but that didn't change his answer. "Because, sir, I don't want to be in the same bind that Giamatteo got in. I don't want to see Santa dead *before* we've got the books and the money in hand. We have to know what kind of a man he is and what kind of 'insurance' he might have arranged before we can plan how and when to pluck him and how to squeeze him dry."

The old man chuckled throatily, nodding deeply as he looked at Conners. Those fiery eyes were almost benign for a moment. "I am now very sure I've picked the right man for this most important job. I liked what I knew about you, your background, military investigation experience, your stint with Spalstein in Las Vegas, all that but I wanted to see for myself. We needed a new face on this job so the feds and the Miami brothers wouldn't know immediately what was going on, but as you said earlier, Dennis, I didn't want to sacrifice anything in efficiency for a little speed or an edge in blood loyalty. Now I'm sure we are on the right track."

"Thank you, sir."

"Now, Dennis, what to do?"

"I believe Santa is still in the Palm Beach area, still carrying on his daily routine, planning his approach to us and his getaway. But I do think time is important because my theory may be wrong, or it may be right at this moment and the man change his mind tomorrow. So speed is essential."

"You need help?"

"Yes sir, but not too much and just a certain kind. We don't want to publicize our search."

"Right. Name what you need."

"I think two good men, sir. They should be in the thirty-to forty-year-old range—no older, not younger—and they should be smooth, well-dressed types, college background if possible, so they can pass as federal investigators when necessary."

The old man smiled. "No young 'Mustache Petes,' huh?"

"No sir."

"Anything else?"

"Yes sir. I'd like the capability for some local investigations—employment records, courthouse, police, that sort of thing—whenever we need it, and probably anywhere in the U.S."

"You got it." The old man pulled a small note pad out of his jacket pocket and wrote on it. He tore off the page and gave it to Conners. It was a name, area code, and telephone number. "This is my, uh, personnel chief. I will call him and tell him that you will be in touch. He will give top priority to any requests you make."

"That's perfect, sir."

"And I'll have those two men you want on their way south today. They'll report to you personally at your hotel. They will take orders from you personally from now on. Anything else?"

"Not that I can think of at the moment, sir."

"Well, if anything comes up, let me know. Savilli can always be reached on my number, and I have already told him to service any request from you immediately. Now, Dennis, I imagine you would like to get back to Florida and find this Santa man. You understand that you are in sole charge of this operation and that the facilities of our organization are all available to you. You will report to me, not to Gennaro, although I have no objection to your keeping him posted; in fact, I think that's a good idea. Do it. And Dennis, I will be watching closely. I do not expect the impossible, but I do expect the maximum possible. I am sure you will not disappoint me."

"I'll do my best, sir."

"I know you will, Dennis. I'm counting on it. It has been a pleasure lunching with you. We must do it again soon."

"I hope so, sir."

"Good. Good-bye and good luck."

"Thank you, sir. Good-bye."

The flight back to Florida was anticlimactic. After that lunch almost anything would have been. Conners's mind was racing faster than the jet streaking its way down the coast. He'd wanted a chance, and man, he had it now. Sink or swim. He wasn't intimidated by the responsibility Mr. Henry had bestowed on him. No, exhilarated would be a better description. That Mr. Henry. Man, he was something. Like seeing a living legend, only the real thing was better than the stories. He knew most of the stories well, and although many of them were just that, stories, some were undoubtedly true. The man could be cold as ice or hot as fire, and either way he exuded strength, command, presence, charisma, whatever you wished to call it. He was second-generation American, unlike so many of his peers, but he had grown up in the bustling squalor of New York's Little Italy, and he had suffered through most of the same rough road to stature that most of the old dons had, although his father had developed a successful legitimate business, moved to Jersey, and staked him to two years of college. Nobody seemed to know where he'd acquired the name "Alberto Henrici," from which his current title had evolved; consensus was that it was the best of a number of aliases he'd used over the years. His family name was said to have been Malfalcone, but no one had ever found any records on that either.

Family economics and his own ambitious impatience had cut short his higher education, but this taste of the arts and sciences had whetted his appetite and given him an insight into things his colleagues neither considered nor understood. He became a stickler on English and a fancier of exotic wines, expensive art, and baronial estates, but more importantly, he had acquired a business acumen second to none in his peer group. It was he alone who realized shortly after the postwar crime hearings in Washington that the age of brutal "family" gangsters was over and he alone who did anything about it. Certainly, he'd used the old families, the old ways, the old connections, to build his new organization but the real foundation was a number of new ideas; the legitimate holding companies; the laundry systems; the intricate structures of small business (real and cover); the foreign operations, some owned, some just contracts. But most importantly and innovatively, he'd built most of his organization on the shoulders of a few key outsiders. It was the contemplation of this last fact that gave Conners a feeling of exhilaration. This was the new syndicate, not the old brotherhood: the payoff was based on performance and the sky was the limit.

Conners had a sandwich in the grill with Agrico and Krupa that evening, eating contentedly while they excitedly plied him with questions. He told them as much as he thought necessary and appropriate. They were duly impressed. Later he called Matthewson and gave him a sketchy rundown, emphasizing that Mr. Henry had told him to keep Matthewson posted fully. Jammy was pleasant but monosyllabic, and Conners assumed that the smart but lazy guinea had pretty well figured out the whole pitch. In a way he felt sorry for the man, but not too much.

About nine P.M. the two men from New Jersey arrived. Conners was impressed; they were exactly the type he'd needed and requested. One, a handsome, surprisingly blond and blue-eyed Italian named Landini, had known and liked Agrico a few years ago in New Jersey, so they had immediate and solid rapport. The other, a pixie-faced redhead with a Brooklyn accent, Arnold Mastick, was sharp, pleasant, smooth, and a real extrovert who hit it off quickly and easily with the group. Conners felt good. His first real "staff" appeared to be composed of first-class people, which was unusual in any league. Of course, Mr. Henry knew this too and would be expecting them to produce accordingly. Speaking of Mr. Henry, those new boys really had the word. Obviously they'd been told in no uncertain terms that Conners was Mr. Henry's personal designee for this job, and they showed it. Conners put them on an informal, first-name basis, but made it very clear that he was Mr. Henry's choice and was in complete charge.

Lying there that night waiting for sleep to ease the nervous tension of the eventful day, Conners wondered if he'd been too rash that afternoon in the great man's presence. He decided he had not.

10

That afternoon, while Conners was basking in the rarefied air, and his men, busily trying to find a name for the man in the artist's sketch, were anxiously awaiting the return of their leader, Morley was boarding a flight to Paris in the Miami airport. He had a small carry-on bag that had gone through the X-ray machine unscathed and that he shepherded tenderly every moment. A larger bag he had checked through to Paris. Morley's first tour business appointment was, as he'd insisted, with Campeau Sunday evening; Roger had assumed, as Morley had intended, that he was getting there early to have a weekend of lotus eating around his old haunts. Morley would have loved to do just that, but regrettably his busy weekend would have to involve Swiss finance, not French nightlife.

He transferred to a Swissair flight to Zurich Saturday morning without leaving Orly or going through French customs, met Willi, did his banking business, and returned to Paris Saturday evening. After four days on a whirlwind schedule in Paris and Rome, he arrived back in Miami, pooped but perky, on Thursday night. He'd lined up some super tour deals, especially one with Gianella, that Roger'd been trying to get for some time, so Roger was delighted and already urging him to go again. Morley too was pleased: his numbered Swiss account now contained $1,600,000 U.S. green.

□ □ □

By that Thursday night, Dennis Conners was totally and embarrassingly frustrated. The sketch might as well have been that of a man from Mars—nobody recognized it. He'd gone himself, finally, to see if he could shake Farber's story or description, but the guy told it the same as ever and was adamant about the sketch being a perfect likeness. As Conners had suspected, there had been no known "official" syndicate or Corporation visitors to Cappacino during the past year, and certainly not during the critical period specified by Farber. In fact it had become apparent during the course of these inquiries that Cappacino just hadn't had "official" visitors down here—anytime. It was this point that had first convinced Conners that the visitor had to be Santa; later, after all these fruitless days, he'd remembered Mr. Henry's story of Cappacino's contacts with the Corse and became just as convinced that Ernie Pro's visitor was a Corse contact. That explained everything—everything, that is, except who Santa was and where he was hiding with all that beautiful dough and those lethal notebooks.

So here they were, back at go, with not a damn thing to show for all those heavy days and nights. Okay, if he had to start over again, so be it. That's exactly what he'd do. He went to his room, called in Krupa and Agrico, had some sandwiches sent up, and they started reviewing the packets of notes they'd kept concerning every bit of their investigations. The men had grumbled at first, but gradually had come to see the value of this procedure and to respect Conner's judgment in requiring it.

Conners set the ground rules. "I suggest we make some assumptions before we start. If you guys feel they're wrong or overstated, speak up. I want us to be in agreement on these points. Okay?"

The two men nodded silently.

"Okay. Let's assume Santa was a local man."

"Why?" This from Agrico.

"Because we'd've got some kind of ripple if he was imported—either around here or from some one of the Corporation offices. Mr. Henry would have heard. Dante couldn't chance it."

"Yeah, and because Dante would have wanted somebody low profile and clean with the law here in Florida as well as unknown to the Corporation. Right?"

Conners nodded. "Exactly, Sal. I think he had to get a clean man and a local. It had to be. Okay, Paul?"

"Right. I agree."

"Okay. Now I think we can also assume that Santa had to have one more qualification—he had to be some kind of a pro. He had to have some kind of experience in the business."

"I gotta ask why again." Again from Agrico, this time tentatively.

"Don't hesitate, Paul. If you're not satisfied with anything, say so. I think he had to be a pro because there was too much dough and too many lives involved for Dante to risk using an amateur. And, yes, I think Dante intended for this guy to be more than just a bagman."

"You mean because he had the books?" Agrico interjected.

"Exactly. Whether or not Dante gave them to him, he still was able to get them. He had to be involved in Dante's business way beyond running errands."

Krupa was excited. "Dennis, if Dante was gonna hire some local dude to be his—sort of—partner, wouldn't he get the guy checked out? You know, to see if he's some kinda plant or not? Especially, if the guy has that experience you talked about— ex-cop, ex-rackets, whatever. Right?"

"Sal, you hit the nail right on the head. I think you gotta be right. Of course. Dante would have to run a check on the guy. Good. Damn good! Tomorrow, I'll start back over all Dante's records looking for this. It's gotta be there somewhere. He had to have somebody to do it, and he had to pay them."

Then it was Agrico's turn; his words came in an eager torrent. "Yeah, and if Dante took the risk and expense of having this Santa guy checked out, he must've first known the guy was a pro, and dammit, Dennis, if the guy was local and Dante knew it, then shouldn't other people around here know it?" He ended triumphantly.

Conners smiled widely. "You guys are becoming ace investigators. Absolutely, Paul. You're dead right. Let's work this idea into our 'question package' for the next go-round. By all means. Damn good idea. We're looking for somebody whose background includes law enforcement or the rackets—even con games—or maybe investigative work, or maybe even a spy. Somebody with a particular past, and one that is not *too* well hidden."

"But what if the guy told Dante himself?"

"I don't think it matters, same logic applies. If he told Dante, then he must have told others."

"Yeah, I see. Yeah." Agrico again nodded.

"But that's a good question, Paul. It reminds me of something that's bothered me from the start: Santa seems to be a step or two ahead of us all the time. Suppose, just for starters, that he's always ahead 'cause he's following a very carefully devised plan that anticipated our reactions."

"You mean the heist could have been Santa's caper from the beginning?" This from Krupa.

"Right. Suppose he was the predator from the start. Suppose he spotted Dante, got a general idea of the operation, and let himself be picked up and used."

Agrico chipped in, "But he'd still have to have that pro background, wouldn't he?"

"Yeah, of course."

"And Dante would've still had to check him out?"

"Right. But he'd have taken precautions to make sure Dante's check, or any check, ended up with the right information."

Conners stepped in. Time to cut off speculation. "Only trouble is that if this angle is the true one, we're all in deep trouble. If this was a long-planned caper and was just triggered by Dante's death, then Santa was ready to leave and should be long gone by now. There wouldn't be much sense in looking for him around here. Even if we identified him, or I should say, the cover identity he was using, we'd have nothing. We'd just have to wait, hoping he'd contact us about the notebooks looking for more dough."

Krupa and Agrico looked deflated. Conners went on. "No, I don't think we can assume that it was Santa's caper from the start. There are too many holes in that theory. I think common sense and all the facts we have point to a bagman who saw a golden opportunity and took it. I think he's still around here, scared shitless, and wondering if and how he's ever gonna get to use all that bread."

"Then we go on as we have been?"

"Yeah, we have to. It's the only way to fly, except we will be especially alert to the kind of background we figure Santa's got."

"Right."

"Now, let's start back over these notes. I think we should be looking for leads to anyone—neighbors especially—that we didn't squeeze hard enough before, or who seemed the least bit reluctant to talk. Okay?"

"Right. Let's go." This from Krupa; Agrico nodded.

The leads turned out to be meager, but they did indicate that another canvass of Dante's high rise and its immediate neighbors might be worthwhile. It was on the second day of this chore that Conners and Agrico got a break. A little mail jeep pulled into the porte cochere of the building, and the uniformed mailman got out, opened the master mailbox panel with his key, and started to fill the various slots. A couple came out of the building and stopped for a moment to talk to him. Conners mentally snapped his fingers. Nobody had talked to the mailman! A notorious source of information on residents, and nobody had talked to him. He waited until the man had finished and locked up, then approached. "Good morning, do you have a minute?"

The mailman grinned broadly. "Sure. Got a couple if you need 'em."

Conners opened a small card case and showed it to the man. He looked, raised his eyebrows, but didn't say anything. Conners put the case away and started his pitch.

"Mr?"

"Bryant. Will Bryant."

"Mr. Bryant, we're conducting a routine investigation. This is not a criminal matter, and while I am not permitted to tell you exactly what it is, I can assure you that anything you tell us will remain confidential, and that there is no chance you would ever have to repeat it in court."

The man, now serious, nodded several times. Conners continued. "We're trying to identify an associate of Mr. Casper— apartment four C—who used to visit him here. You knew Mr. Casper?" The mailman nodded. "The man we want is younger, in his thirties or early forties, and was probably a frequent visitor. Did you ever see Mr. Casper around here?"

"Sure, lots of times. He used to meet me here quite often. Lots of people around here wait for the mail every day. He did it too." He stopped, appeared to think, then continued quickly. "Oh yeah, I used to see him walking over there—on that bike path, and sitting. Yeah. He used to sit on the benches along the path. It's sunny there. He seemed to like the sun. Yeah, I saw him lots of times along there."

"Ever with anyone?"

"Hmmmm. Usually alone. But wait—there was a man used to sit with him sometimes. And walk too. Yeah. I remember. A young guy. I'd say no more than thirty-two or thirty-three. I saw him quite a few times. But not lately. Maybe three or four months ago."

"Dark? Light? Hair and complexion, I mean."

"Light side. Yeah, definitely. Light hair. Tan skin though— looked like a native."

"Tall? Short? Thin? Fat?"

"Hmmm. He was much taller than Mr. Casper. I'd guess

over six feet, maybe six one or two. And slender—not skinny, but definitely not fat. Yeah, slender: Looked like a pro half-back—that kind of build."

"Over six feet and maybe one hundred eighty or one hundred eighty-five?"

"I'd say my best guess would be six one, one eighty-five, slender but not skinny. Well built, athletic looking."

"Mustache? Hair?"

"No, I don't think so, no, I'm sure—no mustache. Hair? I don't remember anything particular, so I guess it must have been regular length. Quite blond, especially against his tan. Yeah, I'd say not short, not long."

"What kind of clothes? Business suit? Sport?"

"Definitely sport clothes. Yeah, as I said, the guy looked like a native—tan, casual clothes, all that."

"Where did you see him, Mr. Bryant, and how often?"

"Oh, let's see. Saw him walking with Mr. Casper, on the path over there, three, maybe four times, maybe more'n that. Then I saw him, I guess half a dozen times, sitting there on one of those benches talking to the old man."

"When was the last time? You said three or four months. Right?"

"Yeah, it's been all a' that—I'd guess maybe around Thanksgiving at the latest."

"You ever see the young guy anywhere else—say on your delivery route or anywhere around here? You wouldn't know where he lives or who he is?"

Bryant chuckled. "No. Sorry. I'd've told you earlier if I did. But I do know, I mean I think, he's from around here, this part of Singer Island."

"Why?"

"Well, I remember one time. He must have been saying good-bye to Mr. Casper, and then he started to walk away down the path. I mean, no car."

"Which way'd he walk?"

"South, of course. The path ends about a block north of

here, and then there's nothing but narrow road all the way to Lost Tree, three miles or so. Nobody walks along that road. So I'd suspect your man lives on south, that end of the island."

"You ever hear them talking, I mean close enough to maybe catch a name or what they were talking about?"

"Nope. Never got that close."

"Well thank you very much, Mr. Bryant. One more thing. I'd like to bring one of our staff artists to see you and see if he can come up with a sketch that looks like this man. Okay?"

"Sure. Anytime. I'll always be by here about this time every day but Sunday. Or you can get me through the Riviera Beach post office. Just leave your number if I'm out, and I'll call you back."

Conners was happy all the way back to the motel. He got the artist lined up and arranged a session with Bryant the next morning.

Within three days they had reworked all the old ground with the new sketch and had unearthed half a dozen "possibles" in the more congested southern end of the island. In three more days they'd washed out those six and turned up three more. These three went the same route, and here it was, damn near a week later and they were still spinning wheels. Conners was discouraged. All the things that should produce weren't producing. He began to suspect all sorts of things: the artist was a bum; his men were incompetents; his theories were all crap; Santa never existed; Farber and Bryant were setups thrown in to confuse him; and on and on.

Then Conners remembered: he hadn't really followed through personally on the idea about Dante having Santa checked out. Damn! Chances were that Dante would have paid by check—cash wouldn't have looked right. He took Krupa's record box and began poring over all the checks and bank records. And of course, there it was. The incompatible item he should have looked for from the beginning. Dante Cappacino had consulted and paid a Miami financial advisory and investment firm! My God. That was like having the Miami Dolphin's coach ask the Coral Gables High coach how to handle the Pittsburgh Steelers pass rush. How the hell had they failed to catch this before? Damn it, all this time wasted. He picked up the phone. "Can you get me a Miami number?"

"Yes sir. What is the number?"

"I need the number. I don't have a Miami book. The listing should be under Biscayne Financial Advisory and Investment Company."

"Yes sir. Please hold."

A few clicks and buzzes later it rang in Miami, and a female voice answered "Biscayne Services."

Conners was ready; he'd decided to shoot the buck. "I need a quick and confidential financial investigation. To whom should I speak?"

"Let me see if Mr. Fosgrove is free, sir. I'm sure he can help you." There was a pause. "Yes sir, he's free. I'll transfer you to his secretary."

That was it! Of course. The Biscayne Company had a connection with a national investigative service. They could arrange a financial investigation of a person or a company and have it broadened to whatever extent the client desired. Mr. Fosgrove was most accomodating and very frank in discussing this; obviously the whole operation was aboveboard. He assured Conners, in answer to his question, that both the fact and the results of any specific investigation were entirely confidential and so held by the company, adding that even the record of this phone call would be confidential. Conners had thanked Fosgrove and said he'd be back to him at a later date. He gave him a phoney name and number in West Palm Beach, not caring whether Fosgrove checked or not. He'd found out what he wanted, but that had merely created another problem: he had to get the file on Cappacino's investigation. Maybe it had nothing to do with Santa but all his instincts told him differently. It made too much sense. Maybe getting it would be more trouble than it's worth. Burglary is never a picnic, especially in those modern office buildings with all their security devices. It would undoubtedly be a touchy operation, but Conners had a feeling it would pay off. Somehow he knew this was the lead he'd been looking for.

Krupa cased the Biscayne Company's office over the weekend and moved in on Monday. It was a much smaller outfit than they'd anticipated. By the simple ploy of applying for a job, Krupa got in the place long enough to note most of the essentials, and on that basis, Conners decided they could probably do the job soon, without the long buildup and complicated operation he'd first envisaged. So it was only two days later that a window-washing team hit the floor of the Biscayne Company, timing their arrival to coincide with the departure of Messrs. Fosgrove and the two other men who constituted the male staff of the company. Krupa had determined that two days in a row the men had gone to lunch together. This left two girls, a receptionist and the secretary and the latter had left within minutes after the men on both days. She followed the same script this day, leaving the two window washers and a receptionist who was preoccupied with her lunch and her nails. The window washers split up; one washed, and the other searched files. They both did a good job; when they left the windows sparkled, and four slim manila files rested in the bottom of the washer's equipment kits. The receptionist nodded absently, waving her nail file as they said good-bye. She didn't know or care that they had finished washing windows for the day.

Conners permitted himself one long "son-of-a-bitch." Wouldn't you know. Nothing in this damn case was simple. Cappacino had hired Biscayne to investigate three—count 'em, three—men. So back to the mailman. But Bryant couldn't be sure. He'd never seen the guy really close. He was sure the dark-haired guy was not the man, but he was sorry, it could be either of the other two. Sorry. Sorry. Sorry. But that was the best he could do.

Okay, so Coleman was out; the other two, Patrick Morley

and Daniel Roamer, damn it, one of them had to be the man. The Biscayne Services files were not that great; their "investigators" were more record searchers than they were investigators, and their production, compared with that of real pros, was notable for what it *didn't* have. Still, there was enough meat in the files to give Conners something to chew on. (The fourth file had been "Mr. Casper" and was completely administrative. Hell, they didn't even have an address for him, only a post office box. Some investigators!)

Morley was thirty-five. Born in California. Lived Terre Haute, Indiana, from 1960 to 1969. Attended Northwestern University, Evanston, Illinois, graduating 1972, Bachelor of Arts in History and Romance Languages. Received ROTC commission, served with U.S. Army, Europe 1973 to 1976. Employed Special Services Detachment, Department of Defense, Washington, D. C. 1977 to 1985. Morley married Monica Ralston June, 1978, she died in December 1983. Morley now single, unemployed, residing Ocean Drive, Singer Island.

Roamer was thirty-four. Born Zanesville, Ohio. Graduated number forty-nine in his class at the U.S. Naval Academy in 1973. He'd done his five years service, including a stretch on a carrier in the Pacific and a stint at the Pentagon, and then resigned from the navy. He lived on Gulfstream Way, Singer Island, and was the proprietor and manager of the Monday Marina in West Palm Beach. He married Susan Cotlett in 1979. She lived with him at the Gulfstream Way residence. They had no children.

Conners went through both files again. He was happy. Both these men were exactly the kind he'd have looked for if he'd been Dante Cappacino looking for a solid bagman and assistant. In fact it wouldn't surprise him at all the learn that Dante had put 'em both on the payroll. Be that as it may, only one of them could be Santa. But Conners was happy; one of them had to be Santa.

Conners couldn't blame the mailman too much. The two men's pictures were similar, and their general descriptions were even closer. Offhand he liked Roamer best as his candidate—navy, boats, access to the ocean, the Bahamas and all that. But the guy had plenty of dough. That marina business was lucrative as hell. But Morley too. A thirty-five-year-old beach bum? Didn't make sense for him to be retired so young. He appeared to have sufficient means, but they didn't appear inexhaustible. And that Pentagon service the guy had. Sounded interesting. He'd better find out more about that. He decided it was time to use Mr. Henry's name and get some help. He dialed the area code and number the old man had given him for his "personnel chief." The reaction was beautiful and fast. Less than thirty-six hours later he had a phone call from the personnel chief's "number one."

"Mr. Conners, I have an interesting answer to your requirement."

"Yes?"

"Yeah. My man ran into a buzz saw, but, luckily, he knew how to handle it as he'd been there before. Anyway he—"

"Wait a minute. What's that mean? Buzz saw?"

"I mean when my Washington man passed your requirement to his Pentagon contact, the contact almost shit. It seems he'd had the same request for the same check on the same two names a year ago. Y'see, this guy at the Pentagon—the contact—is old; my man is new, and his predecessor simply passed the contact on to him. The earlier checks were ordered by that predecessor—who's no longer with us, if you know what I mean."

"Yeah. I follow you. But what's that about the buzz saw and why were there no Corporation records of that earlier Pentagon check?"

"One at a time, Mr. Conners. The buzz saw was his description—the contact's—of what happened when he floated an inquiry last year. All hell broke loose. He was called into a top headman's office and chewed out. Lucky this guy can talk as fast as he can think and did a pretty good job of spinning a cover story, so they bought it."

"But then there was no buzz saw this time?"

"No, that's right."

"Well, did he check?"

"Sure, but he did it on his own. Didn't ask anybody. He got at both files, but there wasn't anything there but biographical data; nothing about their Pentagon assignments; nothing dated beyond their entrance on duty date at the Pentagon."

"So what's it mean?"

"The contact says it means that these two guys were probably assigned to a top secret task force in the Defense Department. From very little fact, some rumor, and some educated guessing, the contact says it might well be 'Squad C,' which is an action unit that works on foreign terrorists, hijackers, illicit munitions traffickers, and the like. It's a real hush-hush outfit."

"Squad C?"

"Yeah. It originally was the 'CRAF Squad.' It stands for Counter Revolutionary Attack Force, or something like that. Anyway, that's as far as it was safe to go. Our contact won't be able to get anything else, although he could figure out from the records that one guy, Morley, was with this Squad C over five years. The other guy only about two years. He said Squad C was a real elite outfit, whatever that means."

"Any indication they knew each other?"

"My man asked that very question, and the contact said there was no way he could tell. He didn't know how many people were in it or how well they were compartmented. He just couldn't say."

"Not to worry. I think you've given me just what I need. One more thing, though. Why, do you think, was there no Corporation record of that earlier Pentagon check request?"

"That's easy, Mr. Conners. The Washington man who's no longer with us—well, he was a close friend of Dante Cappacino."

"I see. Yeah, I see. Well, thanks a lot. You've really been a big help. I'll be in touch if there're any loose ends."

"Anytime. Ciao."

Conners was still staring thoughtfully at the phone he'd put down, when it rang. "Mr. Conners?"

"Speaking." The other voice was familiar, but before he could place it, the mystery was solved for him.

"This is Savilli. 'He' wants to talk to you."

Mr. Henry came on, the strength and magnetism of his personality evident even through the miles of wire and microwaves. "Ah, Dennis, how are you?"

"Just fine sir, and you?"

"Fine." He hesitated, then continued with just a hint of good humor. "I hope I'll feel even better after you tell me how things stand."

"I believe you will, sir. We've narrowed it down to two men. Incidentally sir, your personnel chief and his staff have been most helpful, as you said they would be."

"I'm delighted to hear that." He sounded as if he really were.

"These two men, sir, both live and work around here. They both have exactly the kind of background we figure Santa has to have; both had access to Dante, and both fit the description of Dante's young friend. Dante spent money and time checking them out, and I think he hired one of them to be his bagman partner."

"Why not both?"

"No reason, sir. I mean he *could* have hired them both, but still only one is Santa. But I don't think he hired two of them, sir, because he only needed one, and he was a stickler for security. Why tell another man your secrets if you don't have to?"

"So now you have to pick one. Which one is this Santa man, huh?"

"Yes, sir."

"What about taking both of them for a 'boat ride' and persuading them to open up?"

"I think that should be our last resort, sir. They're both professional intelligence and counterintelligence officers and we have no idea of what they might have in the way of plans, contacts, 'special arrangements' in case of disappearance, all that sort of thing. If we spook them or 'dispose' of them too soon we may wind up like we did with Dante—two corpses and still no books and money. I feel strongly, sir, that we should know a lot more about them before we decide which is which and how to handle it."

The old man chuckled. "You sure you don't want to go back and finish the law school, Dennis? You would be murder, so to speak, in front of the jury."

Conners laughed too. "No sir, I think I'll just stay out of courtrooms."

The old man really belly-laughed at that. "Yeah. See that you do. Now, how are you approaching this Santa man problem with these two?"

"Penetration of their personal lives. We've bugged both their homes and phones. I've got a maid into one guy's house three times a week, and I've got a girl working on the other one."

"Who are these people?"

"The maid's a girl Sal Krupa has known for years. She's very good, and she's done exactly this kind of job before. The other girl I brought in from Chicago. She's new, but very smart and very beautiful and very reliable."

"How'd you set them up?"

"Well, sir, this guy Roamer has a maid—his wife is not home much. Sal persuaded the maid that she should 'have to go to California' for a couple months and that she should recommend a 'close friend' as her substitute. You know the routine, sir. It worked like a charm."

The old man chuckled. "Yeah, I know. It's old but good. How about the other one? What's his name?"

"Morley. Yes sir, I guess this routine's as old as the other one and just about as good. Morley is a lonely bachelor and the girl's a beauty. We just arranged to have them meet and let nature take its course."

"And you're sure of both girls."

"Yes, sir, all the way."

"Good. Good. Yes, I like that. Now, Dennis, have either of these men given any signs that they have our money and our books? You know, any indication they're getting ready to leave town?"

"No sir, not really. But that's another funny thing. One guy, Morley, just recently went to work for a travel agency in Palm Beach, and what does he do as soon as he goes to work? He makes a business trip to Europe. We're checking back through the airline company but I'll take odds he went to Switzerland. And the other guy! He's made five boat runs to the Bahamas in the past month, and at least twice he's anchored in at a little private, deserted island overnight. So you see, sir, they both still qualify. I'm hoping the girls can solve the riddle for us soon."

"I hope so, Dennis. But you're right, I do feel better after talking to you. Sounds like you're running an efficient and sensible operation. My experience is that these usually succeed. And Dennis—"

"Yes sir."

"Remember this is a personal favor for me. I will not forget your hard work." Then he chortled ever so slightly. "Especially if it's successful."

"Yes sir."

"Good-bye, Dennis."

"Good-bye, sir."

11

Jammy was worried. In his business, no news was bad news, and he hadn't heard a peep from Jersey since the phone call from Savilli telling him to have Conners come North. He'd asked Conners to call him on his return and Conners had done it. At the time Jammy thought this was a good sign—at least Mr. Henry hadn't cut him off to that extent—but as the days wore on with no communication from the top, his concern increased. Conners, in accord with the instructions Jammy had given him, was regular and prompt in his telephone reports, and they seemed to be on the right track. Jammy hoped it wasn't too late, but his instincts told him it was. Because of the territorial lines he'd had to go to Mr. Henry—via Savilli, of course, that fucking zombie—to get an okay to hit that doctor in Washington. Tommy Winona—maybe Mario was right about him—had learned from a contact at the hospital that there was a stink brewing over the Ernie Pro hit. Some nurse had smelled a rat, and then they'd done a quick autopsy. Winona's contact said they had discovered who the doctor was. He'd been seen by the nurse coming out of the old broad's room just before she croaked. So he'd had to tell Jersey the whole story, admitting that the doc was a weak sister who wouldn't stand up to very much, if any, pressure, and asked for the okay to shut the simple asshole up permanently. He hadn't heard about that yet either.

The phone buzzed. "Jammy?"

"Who the fuck ya think it was?"

"I'm sorry. There's a long distance call from Tommy Winona in Washington. Shall I put him on?"

"Of course, you simple bitch. Put him on."

A click, and Tommy's guttural voice came on. "Jammy. How ya doin' out there?"

"Okay. What's up, Tommy?"

"Just thought you'd wanta know, the doc is gone."

"What the fuck you talkin' about? Gone where?"

"I mean dead! Gone! He was killed last night when his car went through a guardrail and hit a tree on the G.W. Parkway."

"An accident?"

"Yeah, Tommy, some timing." Jammy could smell that one from Chicago, but let Tommy accept it at face value. He'd never understand, anyway. They chatted a few more minutes, then Jammy closed it out. "Okay, Tommy, thanks for keeping me posted. Appreciate it."

"No sweat, Jammy. See ya later."

Now Jammy was more than worried. He was close to panic. He knew as well as he knew his father's name that the Jersey guys had wasted the doc, ignoring him completely. This was the final insult. His stock was at rock bottom and it was time to cut and run. He buzzed on the intercom. "Yeah, Jammy."

"C'min here a minute."

The door opened and Sandy entered. An uncharacteristic wave of affection, totally without passion—at the moment, anyway—swept over Jammy. She was a sweet kid, not heavy on the smarts, but loyal and honest, at least with him, which was what counted now. He made his mind up. "Honey, I want you to go to the bank next door and draw out our business account. Don't close it—that'll take too much time—leave fifty bucks in it. How much we got?"

"Right now?"

"Right now."

"Thirty-seven thousand, four hundred six dollars and fifty-eight cents."

He smiled for the first time that day, reaching out to pat her rosy cheek affectionately. "Now how the hell do you know that?"

"I write it down every morning and subtract checks at the end of the day. I don't want you to get mad again."

He chuckled, and gave her a light kiss, remembering the time she'd made the five thou mistake and they'd ended up with a check bouncing, which was a number one no-no in Corporation cover business practices. She'd been damn careful since then. It had taken a couple weeks for that black eye to heal to the point where she was presentable again. No way did she want another outburst like that.

"Okay. Take out all but fifty and get it in big bills—half hundreds and half fifties. Then take five thou of that and get traveler's checks in your name. I'll meet you in the lobby coffee shop in thirty minutes. That should give you plenty of time. Okay?"

"Sure, Jammy. I'm on my way."

"And, Sandy . . ."

"Yeah?"

"Don't phone anybody, don't go anywhere but the bank, and don't get in any conversations in the bank or the coffee shop. Just do what I said and wait for me. Got it?"

"Yes, Jammy. We leaving for good?"

He glanced up sharply. The sweet broad wasn't all dumb. "You bet your ass, honey, as far and as fast as we can."

"Good. See you at the coffee shop," She picked up her coat and boots and left. Matthewson just stood there shaking his head for a minute. He'd just seen a new Sandy. He wasn't sure whether he liked it as well as the old one.

Matthewson opened the wall safe and shoveled everything in it into a briefcase. He took a small suitcase out of the closet and started throwing in nightclothes and underclothes (his and her office supplies), along with the contents of the medicine cabinet in the bathroom off his office. Then he did the hard part. He called Savilli in New Jersey and told him about the doc, saying with a laugh he hoped didn't sound *too* forced that they could cancel his request for a hit. Savilli said okay, he'd pass on the word, and rang off. Jammy grimaced to himself. Those assholes really had a high opinion of his smarts, didn't they. The fuckers didn't even give him credit for figuring out the doc's "accident." Oh, well, shit! At least it would get them a day or so start before that fire-eyed guinea fucker from New Jersey set his bloodhounds after them. A day might be all he'd need. He had the two phoney passports and over seventy-five g's in cash, and they could go a long way before tomorrow morning. And then, when things cooled off just a little, he could slip into Switzerland and get at that beautiful "retirement fund" he'd been building for so many years. He smiled to himself. Sometimes it's good if your enemies don't think you're too smart. He'd show those cocksuckers. In a couple days he'd be down on some South American beach with a new identity, watching those gook broads with the big tits, just like in the travel folders. And they'd be sticking their noses into passenger lists an' wondering why he wasn't on 'em.

And then there was Sandy. He salivated and touched himself at the prospect of all that free time to ride that gorgeous pony. No more hiding in motels or office fucking. Hell, he might even marry her if that's what the sweet, dumb little broad wanted. Fuck Gina and fuck her private eyes. Let those mothers find him now.

Jammy was sitting in the coffee shop when Sandy came in from the bank. She was all business, but she showed breathless excitement when she recited how she'd followed his orders to a T. Jammy kissed her cheek right there in public and didn't give a damn who saw it, then he picked up the suitcase and they took an elevator down to the parking garage. They got to Jammy's car quickly and he put the bag in the trunk. He admired the car as he uncharacteristically opened the door for Sandy, who was standing by it and waiting, also uncharacteristically, in ladylike fashion. God, how he was gonna hate leaving this beautiful hunk of metal behind. Thirty-seven thou' worth of the best European craftmanship. Drove like a dream and rode like a limo. He loved it. Maybe he should leave it. Take a cab. No, hell, that wouldn't work. He planned to drive to Milwaukee, leave it in a lot somewhere downtown, take a cab to the Milwaukee airport, and disappear from there. This might even buy them another day or so. Besides, even if he left it here—safe in this garage—how the fuck would he ever get it back again? Yeah, let's go as we planned. He went around to the other side, got in, put the key in the ignition, and turned it.

Martin Garrett stopped to relieve himself in the men's room before going to his parking place. He told all his friends later (as many times as they'd tolerate) that he'd been just one little piss away from eternity that day. As he came out of the lavatory door he could see that chubby dark guy who parked next to him getting into that flashy foreign car, then before he could take three steps the world became red, white, orange, and yellow, and a massive wall of sound and hot air slammed him back against the wall, knocking his glasses off and his wind out of him. Writhing and gasping on the floor, Garrett could see the burning, smoking mass of twisted metal that seconds ago had been his car, then he realized with a shock that the car next to it had almost disintegrated. The chubby man! Garrett struggled to his feet, still gasping for breath, and ran for the elevator.

12

That same Thursday afternoon Morley walked along the beach, heading north into a breeze that threatened to become a brisk wind. It was far from chilly, but his light sweatshirt felt good. The mass of Canadian air that was giving ulcers to the citrus and vegetable growers up in the northern part of the state was putting a little bite in the breeze even this far south. But Morley scarcely noticed the weather; he was too busy running his mind at full speed. He had a lot to think about, and he feared that time was getting short.

The second European trip had gone off as smoothly as the first. To Paris, on to Switzerland, again without going through French customs; Willi's boys at Zurich waved him through airport formalities with lots of smiles, and then he had made the final deposit in the Swiss bank. He could afford to relax with a walk on the beach. Morley smiled to himself as he remembered Willi. Same as ever: coldly formal on the outside, warm and generous on the inside. Willi had seemed truly pleased to see him, and, as Morley had figured, even happier to be able to do a favor for him. Morley had almost forgotten how rank functioned in most European countries. A friend of Willi's was an immediate VIP. Willi himself was obviously a highly respected and well-liked officer, but he left no doubt as to his expectations regarding the perquisites of his station in life. His subordinates reacted accordingly. And never a question! Willi took a friend on faith alone.

And then the bad news. Terry had called yesterday. He'd just received an alert from his contact in the Pentagon. Somebody had rustled the leaves around Morley's old cellar door—not enough to cause a problem, but sufficient to show a coincidental interest that turned on lights in the contact's head. He thought it might be the same guy who'd made some more open inquiries about a year before, using some trumped-up reasons to explain his interest in Morley's unit and records. The "rustler" was more subtle this time, and if the man hadn't been warned to be on the lookout, the sniffing around might well have gone unnoticed. As far as Terry's contact knew, the guy didn't get anything, but of course that was something in itself—he did learn that Morley's personnel file was unavailable.

Morley wasn't too upset by this—he had expected something of the sort sooner or later—but the fact that it was so soon had put a few of his hackles in a state of permanent erection. He had figured that the opposition was good and that they'd eventually tighten the list down to a few solid suspects, one of whom would be him, and then they'd go to work on these suspects. But he sure as hell hadn't figured they'd accomplish it quite so fast. It was a bit scary. Of course, he didn't know how many others were still in the running or how much meat they had to feed their suspicions concerning him. But this he knew: if they were willing to take risks like redoing that Pentagon check, then they were damn serious about him already, and his time was running out fast. He decided he'd better step up his timetable a bit, but not too much, because he'd felt from the start that it was important to maintain a slow, easy, and routine type of existence and not startle anybody with sudden moves until the big one.

Morley looked up. He was about to walk right up the heels of a lady walking in front of him. He was that lost in his thoughts. Then he became conscious that the heels led up to a pair of beautifully shaped legs and a scenically rounded bottom, the latter shielded from the sun, breeze, and Morley's eyes only by a narrow triangular band of dark material. By this time, Morley had pulled out properly to the left and passed her. She was looking out toward the ocean, and since she made no effort to look at or greet him, Morley just walked on, resuming his cogitation.

He felt he had to have about two weeks more to complete all his arrangements. Earlier than that, or without some of the facts he was still awaiting, he stood too much chance of botching the deal. There was too much at stake to let himself be panicked into any premature motion. He was not making the mistake, again, of underestimating his opposition; on the other hand, any premature move against him on their part risked goofing up their objectives, too. They needed him alive, well, and rational—*after* they decided that he was their man. Morley wondered what kind of person was running this show for them. He was smart, no doubt about it. And methodical. He moved quickly to the heart of problems. And he was probably highly trusted by his top management. This was a very important and sensitive operation, of that Morley had no doubt, so the boss had to be first team.

The wind started to pick up, so he decided to turn around and walk with it. He'd covered only about a quarter mile when he saw the lady with the lovely legs—it had to be her, there were no others in sight—sitting on a palm trunk that had washed up on the beach. She was looking alternately at a bunch of shells at her side on the log and at the whitecapped surf of late afternoon. The rest of her was a worthy complement to those legs, and when she looked up as he approached he saw the face get better and better as he got closer. She was a very pretty lady, so he figured "what's to lose." He smiled his friendliest neighborly smile and said, "Hi. Gettin' a bit chilly."

She returned his neighborly smile. "Feels great to me."

"You must be from Alaska."

She chuckled. It was musical. Really musical. "Not quite, but you're getting warm. Or should I say cold."

She loosed the throaty chuckle again, and this time Morley joined her. "Minneapolis?"

"Warmer; now don't say St. Paul."

"Hmmm. Lemme see. You've got that 'big city look.' How about Chicago?"

"The young man on the beach wins the box of bonbons on his third try." She turned her smile into an exaggerated "stage" frown. "What's a 'big city look'?"

"Oh, not to worry. It's good. Very good. It's just clothes and hair and grooming. You know, all those kinds of things. They do 'em better in the big cities, and their ladies show it."

"I think you made that all up." She glanced down at her bikini. "Especially the part about clothes."

"Scout's honor. Besides I used to be a Chicagoan myself and I can spot the Chicago 'big city look' quicker'n most old men."

She raised her eyebrows in a saucy way that was more effective than any of the vulgar vernacular expressions of disbelief popular these days, but Morley only noticed those huge dark eyes, with laughing lights deep inside, that looked right at him. "Guess I should say 'small world,' but I've always met so many people from Chicago when I'm on vacation; it must be that we all go to the same places whenever we leave home. But you look like a native Floridian. I might say you have that 'big beach' look."

"Okay. Fair is fair. What's the 'big beach' look?"

"Oh, it's just the casual look: tan, windblown, fresh, relaxed—all that."

"Fresh?"

"Yeah. Fresh. Did you really live in Chicago?"

"Well, no. I did live in Evanston, went to school there, but I lived a lot in Chicago."

"I'll bet you did. I won't ask why you left. I can think of a lot of reasons, all good."

"I won't ask why *you* left in February. Even I can figure that out."

"You're right. Chicago froze to death last week and slipped under the ice into Lake Michigan. I got the last sled out of town."

This time they laughed together again. It was easy and friendly. Morley queried, "Where're you staying?"

"The Rutledge Inn." She turned and pointed, unconsciously giving him a profile that made his pulse pick up a few more numbers. She turned back. "It *is* getting a little chilly, though it hurts me to say it. Guess I'd better get back." She stood up. Barefoot, she came to a point almost even with his chin. About five six, he thought. She was some pretty lady. Again, what's to lose? "Mind if I walk with you?"

"It's a public beach," she teased. Then the smile came on stronger. "I don't mind at all."

By ten o'clock that night Morley had discovered two items of monumental importance: one, he loved baked stuffed pompano; two, the girl came to just above the tip of his nose with heels on. The first he'd discovered in the Rutledge dining room when he let her order both dinners; the second when they danced to a little combo in the Rutledge lounge.

Her name was Dana—soft a's—Kelly. She worked as a secretary/receptionist for an insurance firm in downtown Chicago and shared an apartment with two other working girls on the near North Side. She was in Florida for two weeks with another secretary from her office, and they'd picked Singer Island and the Rutledge out of a travel folder. They'd arrived two days before, and Morley had just missed meeting the "roommate," who was having dinner with friends in Palm Beach. Morley thought that the "roommate" might be nonexistent, a "security" invention, but he went along with the gag.

He'd been impressed when they'd arrived back at the Rutledge that afternoon and he'd asked her to have dinner with him; she hadn't hemmed or hawed or been coy. She'd just said she'd like to very much. She had insisted that they have an early night and suggested dining at the Inn, and Morley was glad she had. When he'd offered an after-dinner drink in the lounge, she'd accepted, and then the rhythmic and talented combo had enticed them into dancing.

She was light as a feather. Morley had heard the expression for years, but he'd never really known before what it meant. She was pleased when he mentioned it and explained that she'd worked as a professional dance instructor when she was in college. This brought on some personal talk and he learned she was originally from Ventura, California, northwest of L.A. She had gone to UCLA, but dropped out in her third year to get married. Then she was widowed eighteen months later by a Vietcong mortar shell and left California and its memories to come East. She lived for a while with an aunt in Racine, just up the interstate towards Milwaukee, but Racine was no job heaven, so she'd eventually ended up in Chicago, hoping (delivered with a coy smile) to acquire that "big city look."

Dana liked Chicago and liked her job, but she didn't want to spend her life in *that* city doing *that* work; on the other hand, she admitted that she wasn't sure what she did want to do, much less where she wanted to do it. Before there could be any deeper discussion on that subject, she insisted that she'd been monopolizing the conversation. How about him?

Morley complied with an honest but sketchy background, underemphasizing his years of military service and over-emphasizing his interest in and acquaintance with the travel business. Shortly after eleven she said she must say good night and asked him to escort her to her room. The roommate wasn't back yet, so she had to use her key. She opened the door, brushed her lips lightly across his cheek, thanked him for a lovely evening, and went inside.

Morley couldn't sleep. He kept seeing that perfect face framed by that casual black hair and lit by those luminous eyes. He kept feeling the soft warmth of her back and hand as they danced and her subtle exotic perfume, which was almost narcotic. But most of all he kept wondering whether she was for real or whether she was syndicate bait. Was she Dana Kelly, Chicago secretary out of Ventura, in Florida on vacation or was she somebody, name unknown, whose only interest was to set him up for a syndicate killer? In just a few hours, she'd awakened in him ideas, desires, and needs that he thought had died forever with Monnie. He hoped to God that somehow she was real but damn it, the odds were long. Timing, coincidence of place, availability—the whole schtick reeked of setup. But that's just it: wouldn't they be more subtle? Maybe they relied on the girl's attraction to deaden the victim's reflexes, and maybe they were right. If she couldn't do it, nobody could. He found himself hoping again, almost but not quite praying (he hadn't done that for some three years) that he was wrong. And that was why Morley couldn't sleep: he was too anxious to see if he could prove himself wrong.

In the morning, after a quick visit to the office in Palm Beach and a phone call to Terry to request Chicago and California traces on Dana Kelly, he drove back to the Rutledge and called Dana's room on the house phone. A woman answered, and after finding out who he was, identified herself as Felicia Martin, Dana's roommate. She said Dana was down on the beach.

Morley was annoyed with himself. He felt elated as a schoolboy after his first kiss, elated simply because he'd found that his girlfriend hadn't lied to him on the minor point of the roommate. He wasn't even sure that was why he was elated; he was only sure that he *was* elated.

Dana was lying on her front on a huge beach towel, reading a book that was propped up on a mound of sand at the tip of the towel. Her bra strap was undone in back for full tanning exposure. Her figure was superb. Every time he looked at her he saw two or three other things he liked. Her skin was smooth, unblemished satin, and there wasn't a line, bulge, curve, or angle that was out of place. The tiny strip of material across her bottom could hide no faults; obviously, there was no need for it to.

He came up behind her. "It is two below zero in Chicago at this moment."

She answered without looking around or even moving. "Liar, I saw the TV news this morning. It was two *above*."

"I was close."

"Counts only in horseshoes."

"Come on. Haven't you ever watched your friendly, over-paid TV weatherman? Close is the name of the game."

"In Chicago it's called hindsight—consists of long explanations of why yesterday's forecast never happened."

"Anyway, it's nice here, you have to admit."

She reached back, snapped her bra strap together, and rolled over, braced on one elbow. Any doubts that her womanly charms were anything but real were dispelled forever, as the motion of her torso tested the scanty bra cups and bikini bottom. She smiled her big smile. "I give up. You must be a frustrated ambulance-chaser. Ever consider it?"

"Only as a callow youth. Decided the money was badly outweighed by the hours, which just ain't my bag."

"Hmmm. Speaking of hours, you get fired?"

"No. The boss thinks I'm out drumming up business, trying to entice lovely young ladies into a harem cruise ship down the Nile. Or is it up the Nile?"

"Who cares? Up or down. If it's the Nile I volunteer. Has to top secretarial work."

"You wouldn't like it. The women bathe in olive oil and the men not at all. I've got a better idea for you."

"If it doesn't involve bathing in olive oil I'll probably agree. What is it?"

"How about lunch and a tour of Palm Beach?"

"Sounds enticing. Sure you haven't been fired?"

"On a day like this, who cares? What about it?"

"I'd love to. Let me change—say, half an hour. Meet you

down front. No, better yet, why don't you pick me up at the room and I'll introduce you to my roomie. Okay?"

"Okay."

So started day two. It ended, or more correctly, blended into night two, with a few long embraces at the door of her room, but Felicia was home early so they didn't go inside. Morley was infatuated; he knew it, but he didn't care. It had been so long. Lunch at an exclusive Worth Avenue restaurant, with Roger's phone call paving the way for a super table in the most picturesque corner of the garden area. Then a tour of the unbelievable world of Palm Beach. Dana shared his wonderment that so many people could have so much money, and they played a silly game of guessing how the various owners had prospered. They went down A1A all the way to Pompano, then had dinner on the way back and ended up at the Rutledge again for after-dinner drinks and dancing. When he drove home that night, his mouth still savoring the feel and taste of hers, he was convinced she had to be for real.

The next day was even better. By now, she said, she was certain he was either unemployed or blackmailing his boss. He had explained that he had considerable time off in repayment for some recent European business trips on which he'd worked through weekends, and that, besides, they only worked a half day on Saturday. She had nodded, raising her eyebrows, but he wasn't sure she bought it. They swam and sunned for a while, ate a late lunch, toured up north for miles, and returned at dusk. A little later, still not hungry enough for dinner, they decided to have a stroll on the beach. It was a gorgeous night with the almost-full moon scheduled shortly to rise. First they stopped at the Rutledge, where Morley shed his jacket, shoes, and socks and mixed a pair of drinks while Dana changed into slacks and a cotton pullover. Then on to the beach.

The night was fantastic. The moon was just coming up off the water, huge and bright, bathing the sand and the trees in a pale, silvery glow. There was hardly any breeze, and the whole place seemed unearthly still and quiet. They walked north hand in hand, past the hotels and an outcropping of beach where the sand had almost covered what had once been an offshore reef, finally stopping and laying a beach towel on the sand in the shelter of a dune. Then they sat, hips and shoulders touching, looking, fascinated, at the rising moon, the surf, and the night. She turned her face toward Morley, catching the light on one side. He thought she was the most beautiful woman he'd ever seen. He told her so. She lowered her eyes demurely. "I'll bet you say that to all the girls on the beach in the Florida moonlight."

"No, I usually just mumble nonsensities."

"Yeah. I'll bet. It is a gorgeous night, Pat. Chicago was never like this."

"Well, not in February anyway."

"I could name a few more months."

"Eleven?"

"Yeah."

"I thought so."

"It really is spectacular. I mean it. Balmy breezes, swaying palms, whispering surf, moon-washed sea—and all the magic of a South Sea island."

"That sounds poetic. You could write travel brochures, as well as pose for them."

"Hmmm. You sure know how to turn a girl's head, Mr. Morley, don't you? Guess I've always been fascinated by tales and pictures of South Sea islands. When some place looks like this, I get all melty. I saw *South Pacific* five times."

"I know what you mean. I feel the same way. Guess I'd say I'm ape for islands, oceans, boats, and all that stuff. 'Spose that's why I settled here—closest thing to a South Sea island, where you can still afford gasoline, see pro football, and have supermarkets."

"I'd really love to see one, some day, and I'm not sure I'd miss the gas or the football, or even the supermarkets. I really would."

"Let's do it. Let's go tonight."

"Sure. Give me ten minutes to pack." She giggled at the thought, while Morley filed it away under future reference. They watched the surf and the heavens and talked about life and places and things, but mostly about each other. Dana's maiden name was Hayes; her black hair and brown eyes came from her Italian-American mother. She'd studied languages and international relations at UCLA and had hoped to get into some kind of foreign service with the government, but Raymond Kelly had changed all that. Then, after the telegram that told her she was alone again, she tried going back to school but it didn't work financially or academically, so she came east. Her aunt was still fluent in Italian, so Dana had been able to keep it up—the foreign service idea was still in the back of her mind—but the Spanish went down the drain pretty fast. Chicago. Fun at first, but then the routine of work and the cold, cold months got boring, until she felt like screaming. There were times when she would have taken almost any job, as long as it was out of Chicago.

Dana didn't pump or push in any way, but Morley soon found himself talking about personal things he hadn't even thought of for years. They were both intrigued by the many similarities in their backgrounds. South-central California origin; early loss of parents. Her father had died when she was twelve, and although her mother had remarried, it had never been a happy situation for Dana. She admitted that she was partly to blame, having never been able to reconcile herself to the good but colorless automaton who replaced the warm, successful father she'd adored. Then too, both she and Morley had moved to the Midwest, both of their marriages had ended tragically, and both had started that search for an unknown "something" they wanted out of life.

Although Morley had skimmed through the marriage section of his life, he had told her the essentials: how he'd met Monica in Washington shortly after his first military tour in Europe, the whirlwind courtship, the society marriage, the struggle against his rich father-in-law's effort to tie him to a brokerage desk in New York. Monnie had been on his side all the way, and it had become an unreasonably bitter bone of contention between the two men. Then Monnie had been killed in an airplane crash in Europe on the way back to join him for Christmas. They were stationed in Beirut at the time. She'd been visiting her sick mother, and her visit had been prolonged by the old lady's death and funeral; she'd left despite her father's entreaties to stay for Christmas. Of course, the father would never forgive Morley for this final wound.

Morley explained that he'd come into some money about that time and couldn't see staying in Washington, where he'd been transferred after the tragedy, so he decided to take that indefinite sabbatical in Florida. He loved it. It had become his "South Sea island," and he didn't plan to leave it, ever, at least for anything less than the real thing.

Dana listened quietly to Morley's recital. When he had finished and was staring thoughtfully out to sea, she impulsively leaned over and kissed his cheek. Morley turned slowly to look in her eyes and then gathered her in his arms. The kiss was long and searching, gradually changing from tenderness into mutually demanding passion. His hands explored and caressed the exquisite softness of her breasts under the loose pullover and ventured under the waistband of her slacks. Suddenly there was no turning back. Another kiss and two zippers later they were making violent love, oblivious to the moon, the surf, the sand, and everything but the rising crescendo of their excitement.

They lay back on the towel, sated, she still secure in the crook of his arm. Dana kneeled at his side, looking down at his face. She smiled and quickly lowered her face to his, resting her palms on the sides of his face. "Wow! Guess we got carried away with that South Sea island bit. I forgot this is Florida, where the natives are sometimes restless. Hope we didn't have an audience."

Morley laughed. "I don't think so. Didn't hear any clapping." Then he reached up and pulled her down for a kiss. "I've got an idea, though, that there might be some jealous suitors or local voyeurs around, so we'd better have more privacy. I know a place. Interested?"

"Hmmm. Maybe. Just what did you have in mind?" She grinned widely.

"Oh, I thought maybe we could, mmm, dance."

"But I'm not dressed for dancing, love."

"Just for love, love?"

She looked coyly at herself. "Maybe you're right. Maybe we should go where it's—well, warmer." She reached for her slacks and pullover and slipped them on. "Not that it's really too chilly on our South Sea island, lover, but that damn moonlight makes me feel like I'm on center stage."

Morley laughed, the mood of passion deferred, not dismissed. They dressed quickly, and adjourned their meeting to a location with a higher and more secluded view of their island. He returned her to her ground-level quarters at the Rutledge shortly before dawn. Lisha was still not home.

Morley was really in a quandary now. He couldn't even sleep it off because sleep wouldn't come. Man, did he ever want this girl to be the McCoy. But moonstruck infatuated as he was, he'd played the game too many times not to recognize all of the danger signals. Of course there might be an explanation, or better yet she might be straight as a ruler, but he had to admit that the odds were against it. But dammit, the least he could do was give her a chance. Her life hadn't been easy either. She hadn't said so but he figured she'd had to work pretty hard to finance those three years of college since she wasn't getting much attention, much less support, from home. He also figured that she'd become persona non grata with her family when she married Kelly and had been left pretty much on her own after he died.

She was smart and clever, without being a smart-ass; sunny and pleasant, without being a giggler; beautifully feminine, without being cheap or coy; but most of all she was great, great fun to be with. Yeah, fun—and games. Sex. She was something else. His Indiana religious upbringing, even his marriage, had not prepared him for this girl and her honest and unabashed delight in the wonders of the human body. She treated everything so naturally, in a relaxed and joyful way; she had no inhibitions about any aspect of sexual relations or intimacy and no compunction or embarrassment about discussing it. She was indeed a new and exciting experience for Morley, and she seemed to know it and to revel in his obvious delight in her. He found himself emulating both her wide-ranging tastes and her unbounded satisfaction in the results.

Was he falling for this lovely free spirit? Of course. But "free spirit" was not a fair description; it implied some aspect of irresponsibility, and this did *not* fit her. She believed in marriage and family and blueberry pie and all that, but she just felt that in the meantime some healthy expressions of affection—displayed and dispensed on a very selective basis—were natural, enjoyable, and excusable. But back to the problem: he *was* falling for her. No question about it. Maybe *was* was the wrong tense—he'd already fallen, hard and some time ago. What to do about it? He didn't know. He really didn't like to face the problem because it was extremely unpleasant. But he had to find out about her before he got in any deeper. (He found himself smiling at the expression.) Maybe he'd think of something tomorrow. Tomorrow! That was all he needed to start him counting the hours until he would see her again, and he finally went to sleep on this happier note.

The phone rang at nine-fifteen, racking Morley out of a nightmare into the brightness of morning. He'd been dreaming that he was chasing a beautiful naked girl, and when he caught her she'd turned into a huge gorilla and started biting and clawing him. He'd let her go, and she'd become the beautiful woman again, he'd start chasing again, and so it went. Where are you, Freud, when I need you?

It was Terry Rourke. "Hope I got you up."

"You're one up for the day. What's your next hope?"

"Hope it's raining harder there than it is here."

"You're back to scratch. Wanta stop?"

"Never have quit when I'm even, but I guess it's never too late to learn. I got a report from California and thought you should have it soonest. Nobody with you, is there?"

"How you talk. No, unfortunately, I'm solo. Tell me about California—the part that was worth your getting up so early on Sunday morning."

"We never sleep, y'know."

"C'mon, get the friggin' commercials over with."

"Okay. Dana Hayes Kelly. Born Ventura, California—May 6 is the day to remember. The first child of Elena Magnelli Hayes and Melvin James Hayes. She attended high school in Ventura from 1977 to 1981 and then UCLA from 1981 through June, '83. B minus average, language minor, international relations major. Married Raymond Charles Kelly, January 1983, L.A. That was about it in California. You told me not to have any live interviews run. No police records on any pertinent Hayes or Kellys."

"What about Wisconsin and Chicago?"

"About the same degree of exciting. Dana went to Racine August, '83, residing with Mr. and Mrs. Lyle Carstairs, relationship unknown. She worked as a receptionist in a medical clinic in Racine until November '84, when she quit and moved to Chicago. Clinic records indicate she was a good employee— two raises in less than two years—and her reason for resigning was desire for better advancement opportunities more in line with her educational qualifications. Only thing odd to me, Pat, and not further explained, was that the clinic records indicate she gave them a specific forwarding address in Chicago when she left. She knew right where she was going."

"Uh-huh. Would it be that Delaware Avenue address I gave you?"

"You're psychic!"

"Not really, but thanks anyway."

"What does it mean?"

"Only that she knew one or both of her roommates before she came to Chicago."

"So?"

"So let's check them out, okay?"

"Will do."

"Incidentally, who are they?"

"Angela Mornay, age mid-twenties, works as an account executive at a Michigan Avenue brokerage house. Private life still private. No police record, Chicago or federal. Good credit rating. Couldn't get anymore on her without live interviews or deeper record search. Will do if you request."

"Hmmm. I think we have to dig more, but first, how about number two?"

"She's Marjorie Banks Ferris, age twenty-eight or nine, exec secretary at a large wholesale produce outfit downtown. All pertinent records clean. Same problem as Mornay with private life."

"So we don't know which one knew Kelly before?"

"Not yet, but we can find out. Want me to?"

"Yeah. I think it's important enough to risk some live interviews—with your usual discretion."

"Okay. I'll set it in motion today."

"No problems with the time and energy I'm taking up?"

"Nothin' we can't handle—long as you pay the tab. Any other wishes, sire?"

"Not particularly. Hey, did you get that info on the Chicago hood setup?"

"Yeah, and I don't like it very much."

"You mean you weren't gonna tell me?"

"No, not that, Patrick. Just that I didn't quite know how."

"What do you mean?"

"Well, the setup there isn't too clear at the moment. It seems that the Chicago chief was bombed into hood heaven a few days ago. So I don't quite know all the names and numbers at the moment."

"Yeah, I think I read a small news squib on it. What was his name, Masterson?"

"You're close, it's—or rather it was—Matthewson, James Matthewson. An investment broker they called him, known to his friends, of whom there were not many, as 'Jammy,' and to his parents as Gennaro Giamatteo. Oh yeah, his secretary-girlfriend made the mistake of being in the car when old Jammy turned the ignition key. Name was Cassandra Porter. Also, it would appear from remnants found in the blast area that Jammy and Cassandra may have been planning a trip. You know, luggage, passports, and lots and lots of scraps of U.S. green."

"Very interesting. Any comments on significance?"

"None that haven't occurred to you, I'm sure. Got my lines out, and I'll let you know if I pick up anything."

"Do. It might be useful."

"Thought it might, but I won't ask why."

"Good. Well, thanks a million Terry, ole man. Don't know how I coulda got up this morning if you hadn't called. Love to Barb and the kids. I'll be in touch."

"Okay. 'Bye."

Morley was thoughtful as he hung up the phone. He knew he should be happy that Dana had checked out so well—so far—but he had a nagging, intuitive feeling that something was out of kilter. He didn't know why he felt that way, but he did, and it bothered him. He knew that sooner or later he was going to have to brace Dana with some very unpleasant accusations. He had to find out, but he wasn't looking forward to the prospect.

The next couple of days went like gangbusters. They rented a boat and went deep sea fishing. Dana got a large kingfish and insisted on cooking some for them that evening. Morley was gratified but not surprised at the scrumptious meal she whipped up. This brought up the subject of domesticity and they agreed it was the natural way of life. Dana was serious throughout the discussion. She said she would get married "in a minute" whenever she and the man were sure and when she did, it would be for keeps and "exclusive." She liked kids and hoped to have some some day, but wanted to be sure first that they'd get the best possible start in life—"not money, but love and guidance." Morley listened and agreed, and then he kissed her and the toboggan ride started while the dinner dishes were still on the table.

Another day they went athletic: waterskiing in the morning, tennis in the afternoon, and a dip in the ocean to cap the day. By this time Morley was convinced it was more than infatuation. He couldn't believe anything bad about this woman. He came close to not giving a damn about anything she'd done or been before right now. Now was what counted. Was it love? What else? He'd loved Monnie very quickly, very much, and very faithfully, but it wasn't the same. Monnie had been the "girl of your dreams" type, on a sort of pedestal, who never let you get too close to her. Oh, she loved him too, no question of that, and she was loyal and faithful in every way, but Monnie's privileged upbringing, her status as the center of her parents' attention since birth, had coated her with an almost impenetrable veneer of reserve that extended even into the intimacies of their marital relations. Morley shook his head. But sex, wonderful as it was, was not the main attraction with Dana Kelly. There were other things. He looked in the mirror, combing his hair, and commented, "All right, asshole, shape up. You know this girl is a plant. She's here to set you up for a long ride. You know it! Get hold of yourself." But the guy in the mirror looked him right in the eye and said, "But I love her. What are *you* gonna do about that?"

13

Ash Wednesday. And it was at the top of the ride when the bottom fell out. That morning, much as it pained him, Morley had had to leave the delectable Kelly charms and maintain the semblance of job routine. He had driven down to Coral Springs, fifty-odd miles away, to work out the details of a large group tour, "Europe from Paris to Petrograd in twenty-two days." Everything was resolved, and he was on his way back, happy that he had a bone to toss to Roger, but mostly because now he could move up the time of his date with Dana. Just thinking about it gave him a schoolboy feeling again.

He smiled to himself, thinking it would undoubtedly be a long and lovely but strenuous night and maybe he should prepare for it with a good lunch. He turned, still smiling, into the parking lot of an excellent little Italian place near Deerfield. Then the smile vanished. For the first time in a week he was all business again, and it was a good thing, as it eased the pain just a bit from the kick in the guts he got. There, standing in the half-shielded entryway to the restaurant, in close and obviously serious conversation, were Dana Kelly and the tall blond man he'd last seen at the United counter at West Palm Airport that fateful Saturday!

Morley drove on through, came out on the next block, and paralleled the highway for a couple miles before rejoining it. He wasn't hungry any more. What a stupid lovesick ass he'd been. He'd followed the script just like it'd been written. How naive can you get. Oh hell. He'd known it all the time; he just hadn't wanted to admit it. He was having too much fun playing house with this beautiful girl and convincing himself it was love.

Then he came out of shock and began to think more rationally. He'd suspected from the start that Dana was too good to have just happened along. But he'd convinced himself that that didn't necessarily mean she was a syndicate lady—until he saw her with that soldier, that is. But damn it, he'd been making judgments about people for quite a few years as to whether they were loyal, truthful, trustworthy, etc., and he'd had damn good success at it. Could he be a hundred percent wrong on this girl? She'd have to be not only the greatest actress since Bernhardt but heartless as Jezebel to be setting him up for a kill by pretending to love him. Of course, the annals of espionage, as well as crime, were full of just such maneuvers. But not Dana. Not him. It couldn't be!

Morley stopped at the office in Palm Beach, gave Roger the happy part of his trip south, said he had some personal things to take care of, and left for the day. At home, he made a tall libation and went out on his balcony to drink and think. He went over it all again, with no brilliant conclusions other than the one that had been dogging him from the start—he was condemning without a trial somebody he'd held, just a few hours ago, above everybody else in this world. Now he'd admitted it and he felt better. Hell yes, Dana certainly deserved the basics, and a lot more, like the benefit of the doubt. How to do it? The shock treatment? He might lose her. So be it. He couldn't have her and not trust her—not ever know. That made even less sense. He had to bring it to the surface, clear the air, and soon.

His phone rang, startling him into reality again. It was Dana. She was downstairs. He buzzed her in, then waited at the door while she came up in the elevator. She looked lovelier than ever in the tailored suit she'd been wearing when he saw her a few hours ago in Deerfield. When he'd released her, she slipped out of the suit jacket and plumped onto a couch. "Playing hooky, love?"

"Not really. Just had a few personal things to take care of. Left a little early."

"Hey, I'm sorry. Didn't mean to interfere. I'll get out and let you work."

"No way, baby, you never interfere. Work period's over."

She hooked her finger and Morley came obediently to the couch, leaned over, and kissed her. She pulled him down beside her, then reclined back against the pillows as he followed. Morley, now lost in his desire, with no reality but those soft lips and that softer body, was at once gentle, rough, demanding, and compliant. Inevitably, when the arm of the couch was draped with fragile blouse, an even more fragile bra, and a slightly wrinkled skirt, Morley picked up the gorgeous, warm, naked girl and carried her into the bedroom.

The afternoon sun painted stripes of light and shadows on the wall as it poured through the balcony doors into the bedroom. One of the light stripes moved a fraction of an inch and centered on Morley's right eye. The eyelid twitched and opened. He woke slowly but fully, still reluctant to release that drowsy, satiated feeling that he remembered so well and had missed so long and so much. He turned his head. Nothing had changed. Dana Kelly, or whatever her real name was, all satin-tan five feet six of her, slept quietly on her back, one arm hooked over her head, the other resting across her middle, the shadowed indentation of her navel peeking out between splayed fingers. My God, she was lovely, every inch.

Dana stirred, turned, and opened one alert and sparkling eye. She saw Morley unabashedly admiring her curvaceous form and turned toward him. "You like, meester?"

He answered by kissing the nearest parts, the soft round of a shoulder and the pert coral of a nipple.

"Fresh!"

"Yeah, sure is."

They laughed, but before the natural evolution could begin

again, Morley raised up on one elbow to face her more directly. It was now or never. "Dana."

"Yes, sweetheart." Her fingers were making traces on his chest and stomach.

"Why are you here?"

She looked up with the same pixie grin that had accompanied the earlier banter. "Like the man said, love, ever' body gotta be someplace."

He smiled thinly but said nothing. She became serious, and the fingers stopped. "Why am I here? Funny question. I guess I'm here 'cause I want to be—here—with you. Yeah, and because I think you want me to be here. What else? Guess I don't know what you mean."

Morley was still unsmiling; the first lights of annoyance replaced those of puzzlement in Dana's dark eyes. Finally he spoke. "I mean here in Florida."

The brown eyes got even brighter and a frown began to darken her face. "You're serious, aren't you. My God, you are. Okay. What should I say? What do you want me to say. I'm on a quote well-earned vacation end quote? Okay. That's it. I've been thinking it was my best ever vacation and a lot more, but all of a sudden, I'm beginning to wonder. What is it, Pat, what's wrong?"

She too was deadly serious now.

"I don't know, Dana, why don't you tell me?"

"My God! I don't know what it is you're after. Suddenly you think I'm different, or you're different, or what? You tell me. Damn it, you're scaring me. You're not like you. You're different. Why? What's wrong?"

"I guess I am different."

"Why, for God's sake. You weren't different an hour ago, or five minutes ago. What happened? What's changed?"

"Five minutes ago my head wasn't in charge. Now it is."

"What the devil are you talking about?"

Morley's eyes got steely, almost cloudy, and his mouth was a tighter line than she'd believed it could be. He spoke flatly with no intonation of friendliness, much less affection. "C'mon, Dana, you know fucking well what I'm talking about!"

She pulled back as if he'd slapped her, mouth dropping in disbelief. Her dark eyes started to harden, then misted over, and she instinctively clutched at the edge of the sheet, pulling it up over her legs. Her voice was emotion-clogged but steady. "I see. I mean, I think I see. All at once you talk to me as if I'm a whore, so all at once you must think I'm a whore. But why? I still don't know why. What's changed? What have I done?" She looked quizzically at him. A tear slithered off the corner of her eye and rolled down her cheek. "Five minutes ago, I thought I loved you," she continued. "Maybe I still do. I don't know. I thought you loved me. Guess I was wrong on that too. You've got me so damn confused, I don't know what I'm thinking. I don't know what you want." She turned away, pulling the sheet farther up on her body.

Morley's look softened. He reached over and took her hand. She started to pull away, then didn't, holding tight instead. He touched her cheek with his other hand. This time he spoke softly and the steel had gone out of his voice. "I'm sorry. I really am. But I've had a shock too. You asked why I was playing hooky from work. Well, I got sick! That's why."

She just looked, unblinking, the tears still oozing out one by one. He went on, seeming to make up his mind about something difficult. "I got sick because I saw you at a restaurant in Deerfield this noon."

Dana's whole body relaxed, starting with her face and working down. She laughed with relief. "Oh honey, honey. Why didn't you say so? Today. Thank God! I was just having lunch with—"

He interrupted, but not harshly. "Don't lie, Dana. I couldn't take it."

She bristled. "Why should I lie, damn it. I was having lunch with a fellow I know in Chicago. He called me this morning, and since you were working, I agreed to meet him for lunch. That's all."

"In Deerfield?"

"Yes, damn it, in Deerfield! He's on business near there—Boca Raton, I think—and he couldn't get away long enough to come up here, so I agreed to meet him there."

"For lunch?"

"Yes, for lunch. What do you think? He's a nice guy, but we're just friends. No romance. No assignation. No crap. No nothing."

"What his name?"

"Dennis Conners."

"What's he do?"

"He's with a brokerage outfit." She had answered without thinking. Now she hesitated, and then began to fume. "Hey! Wait just a minute! What's with the quiz? Dammit, you don't own me. If I want to date somebody else, or-or-or even sleep around, it's no concern of yours!" She was really close to tears now, but she beat them back and continued. "What the hell gives, Pat? One minute you're all love and kisses and the next you're pouncing on me like a D.A. I thought at first you were jealous, and I was flattered, but now I know that's not it, is it?"

He had softened perceptibly again, but he didn't try for the hand she'd taken away. "I know I've got no right to dictate who your friends will be, or when you do or don't see them." He decided to take the plunge. What the hell, if they knew who he was, then they knew. If she knew, then she knew. But if she didn't—well, he'd never have a "shock" opportunity like this again. "But you see, my dear, this guy I saw you with, he's not just another guy from Chicago like you said. He's a syndicate hit man, and I think I'm his target!"

"What *are* you talking about. He's a broker. A harmless business man—not even a rich one. He doesn't even know you."

He noted that she didn't ask what the "syndicate" was or what a "hit man" did, but he didn't know whether to file that fact under "prior knowledge" or "emotional upset." Man, she was really upset, either that or she *was* the new Bernhardt. He decided to press the advantage, whatever it was. "Broker my ass, and harmless, double my ass. Dana, that guy's a hood and I think you know it!"

She was so taken aback she just spluttered. "What do you mean? Who do you think I am? What're you trying to say?"

"Dana, Dana. C'mon sweetheart. You set me up like a kid in a candy store, and I jumped everytime you waved a tootsie roll at me. I can't deny I loved it—any man in his right mind would have—but I do resent being had. Dammit to hell, lady, I wish it weren't this way. I'd give anything if it weren't, but I know it was all a put-on. You and this hood Conners took me for a ride all the way, didn't you?"

She stopped sputtering. Her eyes were wet, but they blazed defiance. She looked straight at him. "My God! You're either crazy or sick-kidding. For the last time—Conners is a broker, I'm a secretary, and I'm in Florida on vacation. I don't know anything about a 'setup' or a 'ride' or whatever you're talking about. I thought I'd met a wonderful guy and that we'd fallen in love; I didn't know where it would lead and I didn't care, 'cause I thought it would be good wherever it was. All of a sudden, I just don't know any more."

She was so serious, and looked so hurt, that Morley had to steel himself to keep from taking her in his arms and forgetting there was anything else in this world. But he didn't waver. He decided it was time to show an ace and bluff that she'd think there were more of them in the hole. He shrugged. "Sorry, but it won't wash. I have a friend who saw this guy Conners coming out of your place on Delaware Avenue at four A.M. on the night of January twentieth." She just looked at him, didn't even raise an eyebrow, so he went on. "But the real kicker is that earlier that same evening he was closeted for over an hour with his boss, Jammy Matthewson, who's the syndicate boss for the Chicago area!"

She still looked at him silently. He continued. "Incidentally, Matthewson was blasted to death last week—along with one Cassandra Porter, by an automobile bomb."

This did get a reaction. Her fist went to her mouth, her eyes opened even wider. "Oh no! No! I know Sandy Porter. And Mr. Matthewson. My God! Sandy. I'm sorry. I don't know Mr. Matthewson, but I know he's Conners's boss." Then she pounded her fist on the headboard in frustration. "But it's a brokerage, foreign investments, I know it! I know companies that do business with them. What is this bomb business? I suppose you want me to believe the syndicate, whoever *they* are, killed Sandy and Matthewson? Well, I don't. And I won't believe it! I don't care. What's it to me anyway?"

"No, Dana Kelly, you don't *have* to believe anything you don't want to, but then neither do I. Do I?"

She shook her head, balled hand still touching her lips. He went on. "You see, facts are facts and your not believing them or my not believing them doesn't make a damn bit of difference. It is a fact that Matthewson's company is an organized crime cover business. It is a fact that he and the Porter girl were wiped out in typical organized crime fashion. It is a fact that Dennis Conners is one of Matthewson's, or his successor's, chief assistants. And it is also a fact, my dear, that whether you know it or not, you've got yourself in with a pretty sleazy bunch of animals!"

She just sat there and looked. Defiant, startled, rattled, and naked. Then she seemed to pull herself together. She straightened her shoulders, oblivious of the libido-boggling things this did to her magnificent bust, and said in a soft but controlled and cool voice, "Who *are* you?"

He accepted it as a question, but decided to downgrade its seriousness. "Pat Morley, travel agent and would-be man-about-town. That's all."

She retorted in kind, now fully in control of her voice as well as her emotions. "To quote you, 'my ass' that's all. And why, mister travel agent man-about-town, is this, this syndicate"—she spat it out as if it were a distasteful morsel of food—"after you? What the hell is it I'm supposed to be setting you up for? Whatever that means. And what the hell's in it for me? And incidentally, who's your big-eyed friend in Chicago who hangs around peeping in girls' apartments?"

Morley recoiled just a bit from the ferocity of her attack. Inside he was all admiration—she was superb, guilty or not. Outside he resumed the "more in sadness than anger" attitude and mounted a counteroffensive. "Touché, my dear. You're right—those are perplexing questions. Maybe it's true that neither of us can answer them all. But this I do know, love: you're in Florida for Conners, you were on that beach for Conners, and you dated me for Conners! From then on I don't know. I'm conceited enough to think some of it was for me. It's true, I don't know if you know the whole story. I thought for sure you did at first, but I'm not so sure anymore. I hope my second guess is right, but that's really not too important at the moment. Anyway, the syndicate thinks I have something of theirs. I *think* I know what it is, and I *think* I know why they think I have it, but the fact is that I don't. I don't now, and I never did. I suppose that whatever they told you about the reasons, your job was to find out if I had it. Well now you know. The answer's 'no.' Go tell 'em!"

She took this without flinching, with even a cool, cynical half smile that stopped just short of her eyes. "I see. Here's your hat and what's your hurry." She slid off the side of the bed. "Hope you won't mind if I use your living room to get dressed before I bug out of your life, which is obviously what you're after." She walked straight and saucy out of the room. Morley watched, fascinated. Insulted, beaten, naked, shocked— she still exuded class and dignity. What a woman. If only . . .

She came back to the doorway, buttoning her blouse, jacket under arm, bag over shoulder, and stood there tucking the blouse in. Morley couldn't help himself—the stirring started, and all at once he didn't care much anymore whether or not she was a phony. Then she spoke, calmly and quietly. "Good-bye Pat. It was fun 'til you spoiled it. I hope some lonely night you'll miss me, and then maybe you'll remember that I share that apartment on Delaware with two other girls, and that thousands of people, lots of them secretaries, come to Florida from Chicago every winter. Maybe, Mr. Smart-ass, just maybe you've been wrong. So think about it, Patrick, my boy, think about it." She turned on her heel and walked out of the apartment. She shut the door softly and was gone. Morley, still lying in bed, shook his head. "Class, real class. What an exit." He got up and walked toward the bathroom. She hadn't even given the door a womanly slam. Sheer class!

It was six o'clock the next evening before she called him. He'd begun to lose his confidence. She'd had a good point—how did he know Conners had been visiting her that night? Hell, he didn't even know Conners had been on Delaware Ave. in January. He'd been bluffing. Still, Dana had never really addressed herself to his statement. Suppose she was telling the truth. It would make sense if she were, that she didn't know when Conners might have visited her roommate. But then the phone rang. "Hello."

"Pat, I'd like to talk to you."

"Any time."

"Tonight."

"Sure. My place or yours?"

"How about a neutral corner?"

"Had dinner?"

"No."

"Like to?"

"Yes."

"Ready in half an hour?"

"Now."

"I'll be there in ten minutes."

"I'll be waiting in front."

"See ya."

As he drove to the Rutledge, Morley mulled over last night in his mind. He'd parked in the Rutledge lot about half an hour after Dana had left his place. He could see the front of the Inn, including the pay telephone booth. He'd been there about half an hour when Lisha came out dressed and coiffed fit for the bandbox, got into the brown Pinto, and roared off down A1A towards the bridge. He waited in the car about an hour, and when nothing happened, he got out and went into the lounge. He had a drink, then went through into the inside courtyard of the Inn. He could see the small balcony of Dana's room. Someone was sitting there, feet propped on the railing, smoking. He went a little closer, and as the smoker drew on the cigarette he could see Dana's profile in the glow. Morley withdrew quietly and returned home. He was puzzled. He'd have made book that she'd contact the blond guy, Conners, and that she'd do it via the pay phone. No dice. Of course she could have called from the room, but not likely, as that left a record; or she could have sent Lisha in the car; or most likely of all, the blond guy could have called her.

Morley pulled in under the porte cochere. Dana was waiting, very chic and striking in a light-colored pants suit of a kind of linen-like material. He reached over and unlatched the door and she climbed in. She looked friendly but serious. "Hi. You're on the dot."

"Yeah, but you can call me 'dot' for short."

This oldie brought a smile, so he knew she was in a positive mood. "Oh man, you really dug deep for that one."

"So solly. What kind of dinner sounds good to you?"

"Soup."

"Oh lady, now who's digging? That takes the prize. I give up. What would you like to eat?"

"Chinese?"

"Great idea."

She stayed on her side, and the conversation was light as they drove to a nearby Chinese restaurant. When they got inside he suggested that they have a drink in the bar before thinking about dinner. She accepted readily. They sat down and ordered. After they'd touched glasses and taken a first sip, Dana turned to face Morley. "You knew I'd call?"

"I *hoped* you'd call."

"I waited for you."

"I didn't think you'd want to hear from me again." He took her free hand and held it.

She smiled, widely. "You enormous fraud. You knew I couldn't just walk away."

"I knew. I didn't want you to but I was afraid it was too late."

"Do you still like me?"

"That's a bit bland."

"Really?"

"Dana Kelly, I love you, as if you didn't know."

"You didn't sound like it yesterday."

"This is today."

"What's different?"

"Time. I've had time to think. I don't want to lose you."

"Maybe you have," she said with a smile and an added bit of pressure from her warm hand that signaled otherwise.

"Maybe so. It was a chance I had to take."

"Why?"

"Because I saw you with that hood and figured what I had to figure. I had to find out. I couldn't go on unless I did."

"Suppose you're wrong?"

"I hope I am, but I don't think so."

"We're back where we left off yesterday." She stopped smiling.

"Not quite, honey, we're talking about it for a second time."

"What is it you want from me? A confession?"

"Just the truth."

"But I told you the truth yesterday."

"Not all of it."

"All you need if you love me."

"I love you, that's why I need *all* of it, if anything's to come of us."

"What could come of us?"

"Anything you want."

"You're serious, aren't you?" Her dark eyes were huge and

luminous. She looked like a vulnerable little girl. He wished they were in a more private place.

"I've never been more serious."

"I'm not really hungry, let's go somewhere private." My God, he thought, she's a mind reader. He laid some change on the bar and they left, waving off the young Chinese with an armful of menus with a "Be back later."

Morley drove the few blocks, parked, and then they were in his living room: low lights, fresh drinks, Dana propped lengthwise on the couch, and Morley seated alongside the curve of her middle. "Did you mean it—we still have a future?"

"Yes, ma'am, I sure did."

"What if I told you everything you suspected, everything you said, is true? What then? Washed up?"

"Not necessarily. Not if you don't want it to be."

"You mean if I've betrayed you from the start you'd still want me?"

"Sweetheart, I don't care about the past, just the future. If you feel the same, then there's no problem we can't solve."

"You mean it?"

"I mean it, honest."

"I love you. I really do. I know the time's been short, but I'm sure, really sure. Pat, honey, I don't want to lose you either."

"Then there's a future. All we have to do is be square with each other."

She put a palm on each side of his face and pulled him to her lips, then gently pushed him away so that she could focus her eyes on his. She spoke softly but clearly. "Okay. You're right." She didn't even blink as she went on. "I came to Florida for Conners. I was on that beach for Conners. And I dated you for Conners. But that's it, Pat. Honest to God, that's it. All of it. I don't know about any syndicate, or anyone wanting to hurt you; I wouldn't have come if I did. And I fell in love for *me*, not for anybody else."

"You're not Conners's girl?"

"No. He dated my roommate, Angela Mornay. But she really wasn't his 'girl' either."

"Conners just asked you to go to Florida?"

"He *offered* me an expense-paid vacation to Florida in the dead of winter."

"So you didn't care what you had to do?"

She pulled away, hurt in her eyes. "Of course I cared. I was bored, yes, and cold, yes, and jumped at the chance, but I cared."

"What *did* he want? What was the deal?"

"Simply to meet you, date you, find out if you were the Pat Morley he was looking for."

"And what Pat Morley was he looking for?"

"Well, he said the man's real name was Paul Morrison and he was an embezzler. Conners said Morrison skipped with a bag of money some years ago, from their Gary affiliate. They finally got a lead that Morrison was living down here in South Florida, but they couldn't identify him positively because nobody who knew him is still available, and—oh, yeah—the statute of limitations had run out, so they couldn't even get the law to help. Anyway, Conners said they hoped to shame or talk Morrison into paying or giving the money back. Somehow they figured he hadn't spent too much of it yet—but first they had to make sure he was who they thought he was." She stopped, looking very serious. "Does that make any sense?"

"Yeah. I guess so. Sounds pretty good."

"It really sounded good with that icy wind howling around my shell pinks up in Chicago."

"Yeah. I see. And so that's where you came in?"

"Right. For a couple free weeks of sun and sand I had to pump you about your background and help them find out if you're really Morrison. Are you?"

He shrugged exaggeratedly. "No man is an island, love. I s'pose there's a bit of Paul Morrison in every man. But no, I'm not ole Paul the embezzler, just plain Morley, nonembezzler. Honest injun."

"That's what I told Conners. In fact that's why I went to see him yesterday, to tell him I wanted out of the deal."

"Honest?"

"Honest injun yourself. That's why I felt so good when I came back here yesterday." She stopped and focused those eyes on his again. "And why I felt so bad when you pulled the rug out. I thought no harm'd been done and you'd never need to know that our meeting had been phony. Guess things never do work out that way."

"I honestly didn't—don't—care if the *meeting* was phony, long as the rest was real, but I did have to find out. I had to clear the air. I'm sorry."

"I know. I know. But you did shock the devil out of me."

"Like my old man used to say when he put the paddle down, it hurt me more'n it did you."

"I don't know, love, it hurt pretty bad."

"Where?"

"Right here." She pointed in the area of her heart, which happened to be slightly below and to the right of her left nipple.

"Let me kiss it and make it well." He did. "Better?"

She nodded.

"Honey, why did Conners send *you*?"

"What do you mean? He knew I hated Chicago winters, I guess."

"No, I mean why didn't he send Angela? He must have known her better."

She laughed. "I guess that's why. You don't know Angela!"

"She can't be a spook."

"Oh, God, no. She's very attractive. But she does have a mind of her own. Wow!"

"And you don't?"

"You know what I mean. She's a headstrong gal—capital H. I suppose Conners figured she'd have you up the wall inside a few hours. She's sweet, but she's a tease, a baiter, argumentative."

"Why not Lisha?"

"C'mon love, you're pulling my leg." He suited his action to her words and got a smiling "ouch." His hand lingered, softly caressing.

"Who is she?"

"She's a friend of a friend of Conners's. I suspect the 'friend' is here somewhere, but I didn't ask."

"Why not?"

"I really don't know her, and she made it clear she wasn't interested in talking about herself."

"Why's she here?"

"Conners said it'd look better if there were two of us. You know, two Chicago secretaries on a sun-binge vacation. I guess it made it look more like a long-planned trip."

"Is Felicia Martin her real name?"

"Hmmm. I guess so. I never thought about it. I didn't know her before this trip, and I didn't see any reason to question her name or whatever. Conners talked like she was just along for the ride, to make me look more real."

"I see. And as far as you know she's gone back to Chicago?"

"Far as I know. Though I'm starting to doubt everything now."

"And you were reporting back to Conners?"

She lowered her eyes for the first time, then raised them again and looked right at him. "Yes, I was. 'Til yesterday."

"What did you tell him?"

She looked hurt again. "What you told me about yourself. You know, the background stuff. I was sure you weren't Morrison and I wanted to prove it to him. None of the private stuff—our things—just background: where you came from, where you had worked and lived, that kind of stuff—just all that."

"And what did he say to 'all that'?"

"He said he thought I was probably right—you weren't

Morrison—but he wanted me to hang on for a while longer and make sure."

"So what did you say?"

"I said no. And he asked me if my reasons were 'personal,' and I told him yes."

"And?"

"He said, 'Oh, I see,' or something like that, and asked me if I were going back to Chicago. When I said not for a while he asked me again to help him make sure you weren't Morrison so he could wash this lead out once and for all, but I said I didn't feel I could do it."

"You didn't tell him about us?"

"No. It was none of his business, but I felt somehow he knew everything."

"So what then?"

"I told him we were even—he didn't owe me any money or expenses, and I didn't owe him any more reporting."

"And?"

"And he said okay, see you in Chicago, or something like that. I don't remember exactly."

"Just like that?"

"Just like that."

"That was all?"

"Yup. That was all."

"I love you." He kissed that "hurt" again. This time it was more effective as a healant, as he had succeeded in nuzzling open the top two buttons of her blouse.

"Yeah, I know. And I love you, too, and I feel better—lots better—now. But, honey, there're two sides to this business; I think I should get some answers too. Fair's fair, as my new friend Morley is wont to say."

"I agree, fair is indeed fair. No longer can I hold out. My real name is Paul Morrison, and I used to be a poor stock-broker, but temptation, in the form of a large redhead with the most—"

"Hold it! Hold it! I think your real name is Harry Smart-ass. What's all this about syndicates and killers and them wanting to take you for a ride, or rub out, or whatever. Is this serious?"

"Maybe, maybe not, but it's a great story, isn't it?"

"You heartless bastard."

"Sticks and stones."

"You made all that up to needle me."

"No, not really. I knew our meeting had to be phony. Everything was too pat, if you'll pardon my pun. Then when I fell for you and (I hoped) you felt the same way, I just had to find out. I figured that shock treatment might be the most effective."

"You were right, cad. But why the syndicate and killer bit?"

"The worse I made it the better it was." Then he got serious. "Besides, maybe it's true. It could be, even if you didn't know it."

"Yeah, I guess so. But you know Conners is just a broker, don't you? He is, isn't he?"

"If you say so, love. I don't know the man personally. But my instincts tell me otherwise."

"You are harder to pin down than a Philadelphia lawyer, Mr. Morley. You sounded so sure about it last night. Were you just bluffing?"

"I lied to you. I was born and raised on a riverboat."

"I'm beginning to believe that. But—wait a minute. What about Matthewson, Conners's boss, did he really get killed? And Sandy Porter."

"For real, honey, really real."

She frowned thoughtfully. "Then *he* wasn't a broker?"

"No way. Matthewson was syndicate. That I know for sure."

"The brokerage is phony. Yeah, I see. And Dennis Conners? He's phony too. And his story to me? My God, who can I believe? It's all phony?"

"Matthewson had a brokerage business, but as I said, it

was phony. You couldn't have known that. Conners is probably a phony broker too. Now as for the story they told you, it may be mostly true. They may be looking for an embezzler of sorts, and they may think he's here. They may even think he's me. In fact they must suspect that or they'd never have gone to all the trouble they did. Who knows."

"But you knew who Conners was."

"No, honey, I suspected who he had to be. *You* told me who he was."

"But you knew he worked for Matthewson?"

"No, I guessed he might. You told me he did."

"And you knew he was at our apartment that night— whenever you said it was?"

"No, that was a 'shock bluff' too."

"You're not always a nice guy, Mr. Morley."

"I had to find out, sweetheart. It seemed like the best way. I was lucky in my guesses, but I did have some facts to go on."

"You're something else, love, you really are." She just sat back and looked at him, half smiling, shaking her head slowly back and forth. "You had me swinging by my toes. You see, I really didn't believe Conners's story about this Paul Morrison, at least all the way. But the deal was attractive so why rock the boat? And while I did think Conners was a broker, I knew somehow he was different and he probably *was* at our apartment 'til dawn some night. Angela wouldn't give a damn who saw him or who didn't. Yeah. I believed all your big bluff 'cause it was so believable."

"As I said, I was lucky."

"Yeah, I guess you were. I'm glad it's over."

"Satisfied?"

"Yeah, I guess so. 'Cept for one thing—how'd you know— or I guess I should say, why'd you suspect—that Conners was not a broker? How'd you even know who he was or what he looked like?"

"Well, let's just say I happened to see him in a place and at a time that made me sure he was a hood. As I said, you just confirmed my suspicions."

"And why were you in this 'place' at that 'time'? Wait a minute. I get it. Sure. You were there and that's why they're after you. Yeah, but why?"

"Right, except for one thing. Just like the Paul Morrison story, I think *they* think I'm somebody else."

"Now you've got me thoroughly confused." She smiled. "But, knowing you I suppose that was your intent all along. No?"

"Perish the thought, my dear. It's just that the situation is indeed a confusing one, and so I can't describe it in anything but confusing terms."

"Now, that is really confusing!"

"I know, but what's to do?"

"Nothing, I guess. I'm satisfied if you are."

"Me satisfied?" He put on his best stage leer. "Never, my love, my libido cup's hardly half full."

He reached for her. She came warmly and willingly. It was soon as it had been before.

14

Thursday, the last day of February. There was a slight chill in the air from the fuzzy southernmost edge of the latest cold front that was freezing the southeast U.S., but nothing that wouldn't be burned off before noon. Lisha had returned to Chicago, her vacation, or whatever it was, over; Dana had moved out of the Inn and into Morley's apartment. Morley rationalized that this arrangement was the only sensible solution to a difficult logistical and security problem. It was economical, no question of that. And energy saving, a very patriotic objective. And above all, it was efficient. Then too, it appeared consistent with her attitude toward Conners and the "job" for which she'd come here. Last but not least, it enabled Morley to monitor her activity, phone calls, and all that, with ease. So he suggested it to her. Surprisingly to him, she balked at first; even after he made a persuasive argument, she was not convinced. She felt there was a pretty distinct line between their routine of her spending the better part of most nights there and her moving in bag and baggage. And so Morley had to eat his logic and admit to himself as well as to her that his real motivation was entirely personal: he loved her and wanted her near all the time. At that point she admitted similar motivation and moved in.

It was easy to talk now, and talk they did—about everything but the future. By some unarticulated but mutually recognized pact, this subject wasn't mentioned, but Morley knew it bothered her. It had to. She'd blown her job and her life and friends in Chicago, and he'd offered her nothing substantial in return. It bothered him too. It was becoming clearer day by day to him that a future that didn't include her wasn't much. In bed, before he got up in the morning, his uncluttered mind warned him that the woman was far from "proven," but once she was awake, and he started to live for the day, this signal became inaudible, and his mind concentrated only on how to keep her.

This morning was about the same, except that during his daily reverie he decided he had to make a move, and then when she woke up and he collected his first kiss of the day, he decided the move *had* to include her. Luckily, he'd foreseen this possibility and included her, tentatively, in some of the technical arrangements he'd made. But first he had to touch base with Terry. Dana's proximity, with all its advantages, did preclude his making or receiving his more sensitive phone calls in the apartment. At first he made these calls from the travel agency, but then as his trips to the office became fewer and farther between, he'd begun to rely on the drugstore phone. It was okay for outgoing calls, but the incoming ones were a problem. He did not try to convince himself that Dana was unaware of these procedures, anymore than she was unaware that he'd effectively stopped working; both were subjects that, along with the future, just weren't discussed.

Dana gave him an opening by ordering him out of the kitchen so she could fix her "he-man number one" breakfast. Morley was indeed out of cigarettes (by prearrangement), so he announced that he'd run to the drugstore and get some while she chefed it up.

He got Terry on the second ring. He answered his own phone because it was only eight-fifteen. He was in a jocular mood and began with a needle. "Hey, passion flower, now that I'm forbidden to call you at home and interrupt your privacy or whatever—I still think you've got Widder Kelly in your den—I gotta wait for your call, and you're not one of the world's great communicators, y'know."

"Yeah, yeah. I didn't mean you shouldn't call, ever; I just meant not too often, you know, minor emergencies and above. It's just that I have lots of visitors and I can't always talk freely, but don't hesitate to call if you've got something you think I should have right away."

"Gotcha, pal. But you're not fooling ole Terrello M. Rourke. You're getting him excited, all right, but not fooling him."

"Nothing could be farther from my mind, ole Terrello M. Nothing."

"Happy to hear it. I've got some goodies for you from California and points east. I'm not sure you'll like 'em all, though."

"Try me."

"Okay. First of all, you are psychic. Chew on this one: Miss Angela Mornay was born and raised in Ventura, California. That has to be our Kelly connection. Right?"

"Uh-huh. Unless the third roomie's from Ventura too."

"No, she's not. Has to be Mornay—too much coincidence. Now, Mornay also went to high school in Ventura, a year ahead of Dana Hayes, then went on to USC, graduating with honors in business administration. Evidently she was a top student, and she got a job with the L.A. office of a large national brokerage outfit. She's gone up the ladder fast—two major promotions—first one moving her to St. Louis, the second to Chicago, their home office. She was as clean in L.A. and St. Louis as she is in Chicago, although I didn't go very deep either place. In Chicago she has a first-class reputation at the brokerage house, her landlady thinks she's a 'lovely person,' and the doorman rates her at 'four whistles'—high for Chicago. She's lived peacefully at that Delaware Ave. address since shortly after her arrival in Chicago three years ago. She has dated various men about town, the latest of whom is one Dennis Conners, employee of a quote investment firm end quote, owned and operated by the late and not too lamented James Matthewson. How you lika dat, boy?"

"Not bad. Confirms what the girl said. How'd you get all this stuff, by the way?"

"Relax. There weren't any *real* live interviews and all the questions were oblique. My boy just ran into some gushy citizens."

"Good. I shouldn't have asked."

"True."

"Any more California stuff, Ter?"

"Nothing significant. She's described as a brunette, Mornay I mean, very good looking and with a luscious figure, that's l-u-s-c-!"

"Awright! Awright!"

"Well, anyway, she's very well stacked—won a 'Miss California' contest when she was still in high school. And smart as a whip. Or is it a whippet that's so smart?"

Morley groaned. "How can anybody be so smart-assed so early in the morning?"

"Easy, pal. It's not so early for us working types who've been out on the bread quest since seven A.M."

"Apologies in profusion, to you and all working types. Now tell me, where is Mornay now? Chicago?"

"Funny you should ask. We don't *know* where she is. Best we can determine is that she's somewhere 'on vacation,' supposedly with roommate Kelly. The doorman confided that Ferris, the third roomie, told him that. He figured it had to be someplace nice because Ferris said she wished she were with them. Oh, yeah. One other thing. The doorman also said that they hadn't gone away together. Mornay left a couple days before Kelly. I don't know what that means, but I thought it might be interesting."

"Hm. It is, interesting, I mean. Ferris *is* still there, isn't she?"

"Was as of six P.M. last night."

"And how about Felicia Martin. Anything?"

"That's another interesting item. There just ain't no appropriately aged Felicia Martin in Chicago. That has to be a phony. Your Felicia Martin is a nonperson. Say, Pat, you don't suppose she's—"

Morley cut in. "Angela Mornay? I don't know, Terry. You can't ever account for tastes in ladies or race horses, but I wouldn't have called Felicia Martin 'luscious,' though come to think of it, she did have a pair of jugs that would make a revolving door nervous. No. I don't think so. You got pictures of Mornay and Kelly?"

"Yeah, you should have 'em both today at your P.O. box. I have to warn you, though, they are a bit dated. Best I could do on Kelly was a college yearbook, nineteen-seventy. Mornay's 'seventy-four."

"Was Mornay ever married?"

"That was odd. Her last two years in USC she was listed as Angela M. Talley, but then when she went to work she was Angela Mornay again. Only information I could get was that it was Charles J. Talley, and there was no police or any other kind of record for him in the L.A. area. No marriage record, either."

"And Mornay's college was four years, no interruptions?"

"Right."

"What about Ferris?"

"Roomie number three: Marjorie Banks Ferris. Like Gibraltar she is solid, my friend. Comes from downstate Illinois, secretarial school in Chicago, been with same firm, that large produce-marketing outfit, for seven years, rising from apprentice steno to girl Friday for the boss. She's engaged to a young attorney, wedding planned next fall. She's been at the Delaware Street address almost six years, so possibly it was she who took Mornay in. There was another—unknown—roomie at that time. I don't know how they met, she and Mornay, or if it *was* her for sure. Anyway Ferris is an all-American girl—church work, charities, hospitals, and all that stuff. Reputation is spotless, all records A-plus. She goes to work every day, sees her fiance every night—properly, that is—church every Sunday, pays her bills every month, and bows toward Washington every night before beddie-bye."

"Anything else on the ladies?"

"Not that I can think of—or read from my notes."

"Okay. How about the ubiquitous Mr. Conners? How'd you do on him? I know the time's been short."

"We had some fun and some luck. Interesting case."

"So give."

"Well, Conners is an anomaly. He just doesn't fit the mold any way you turn it. Guess I'll begin at the beginning."

"That *would* be nice."

"Born 1954 in Cincinnati, only son of Leon and Magda Kanarsky. Baptized David Carl Konarsky. Father was a butcher—is still—with a local food chain. Salt of the earth, middle-class type; church goer, faithful voter, volunteered for naval duty in World War Two, that kind of good citizen, you know. Police, credit, everything clean. There was one other child, Ilona Jean, born 1958, now divorced and living in Chicago, under the name Ivy Retsinger."

"Don't tell me Delaware Ave."

"Okay, I won't, but it's not too far away. North side. Near Loyola. I'm trying to get a picture of her. Should have it shortly. Maybe she's Felicia Martin."

"I was thinking the same thing: Conners brings younger sister to keep tabs on the lovely Kelly. Hmm. Could be. Keep trying on the picture. Now tell me about young David."

"David was the epitome of the all-American boy. Went to a tough private high school in Cincinnati, graduated number one in his class, 1961, starring in basketball and track. Had some collegiate offers for his athletic ability, but passed them up to take a merit scholarship at the state university. David rolled right along, straight A's and a list of student honors and clubs as long as your arm, graduated and was accepted at the number-one law school in the country." (Terry didn't elaborate; he didn't need to. He'd gone to that law school himself and was always quick to award it that "number one" status.)

"David ate 'em up in the big leagues just like he'd done at home, and was leading his class when he suddenly quit law school in November 1976. I was intrigued, so I overstepped your restrictions just a bit by calling an old friend of mine and asking her to give my man the details on Kanarsky's legal demise. My friend happens to be the dean's secretary, and she's the soul of old New England discretion. My man gave her an appropriately cloudy cover story, fed her a ridiculously expensive lunch, and got the whole story.

"The lady remembered the incident well even though it was more than a decade ago, because she knew and liked Kanarsky and because it was 'that kind' of an incident. It seems David had a good friend, very rich, very well-placed, a 'Brahmin' so to speak, and they played together on those rare occasions when David took his nose out of the law library long enough to play. Oh yes, this 'Brahmin's' family was not only dough, prestige, background, and all that, but they were one of the principal factors in the university's perennially successful endowment drives.

"One autumn night, after a football game, there happened to be a party, kind of unplanned and casual, but with lots of drinking and pairing off. David and his friend happened to happen upon this soiree and proceeded to join in the fun. They met a couple of college girls and offered to take them home, and since David didn't drink often or much, his friend asked him to drive *and* to take his own date home first, so the Brahmin would have more time to assault the defenses of his young lady. They dropped off David's date, then proceeded to the other girl's house. The Brahmin had brought a flask with him and by this time both he and the girl were pretty well oiled.

"David waited while his friend took the girl in. Fifteen or twenty minutes went by, then all at once there was a lot of commotion inside the house—lights went on, doors slammed, and neighbors started peering out. Then the girl came to the door and staggered out, her dress in tatters about her waist, a cut and swollen place on the side of her face, and blood smears across her cheek, chin, and naked chest. She was screaming hysterically. David got out of the car and went to help her, but she screamed and beat on him, getting him mussed and bloody, just as the cops arrived.

"Now, Pat, I've gone into detail on this 'cause I think this incident and its aftermath give you a good idea of the kind of man this Conners is. I got a feeling he's important in whatever it is you're involved in. This is no run-of-the-mill-type.

"The cops came, saw the scene, and ran David off to jail on a rape charge. You see, the hysterical girl didn't know, or at least couldn't tell, what had happened. David's 'friend' left him in the lurch. David got out on bail, but on Monday he was expelled from law school despite his protestations of innocence. The 'friend' was hustled out of town by his family, and the young girl, who was not yet eighteen, stuck to her identification of David as the culprit. Finally David got a smart young lawyer who stirred up enough newspaper trouble to get the muzzles off the police force, and of course, the young victim reversed her story under pressure and cleared David. The law school offered to reinstate him, but not until the next semester when the scandal would have blown over. The dean's lady told my man that David suggested to the dean that he perform a physically impossible but vulgarly correct feat with his law school, and that was it.

"David went back to Cincinnati, sold cars for a while, and then went into the army. He got a commission and was assigned to the Criminal Investigations Division in the Far East. He had a superb army record, made captain, and was recommended for a regular commission, but he finished his tour and left. We next picked him up in Las Vegas—routine finger printing for employment in one of the casinos. Vegas police records say no arrests, no problems while he was there, almost two years. Then, he graduates to the big time. The Corporation makes him an offer he could refuse, but doesn't. Young David Kanarsky, now known as Dennis Conners, arrives in Chicago a couple years ago, sorta the new boy in the Corporation town, and inside two years he's moved along to the point where rumor has him in the running as Matthewson's replacement. How's that for a success story?"

"Then you figure if he's around anyplace, say here for instance, he'd be in charge of the show?"

"Oh yeah. And I'm sure he's working out of the hip pocket of that old fart, Mr. Henry, who runs it all, ultimately, from that castle in Jersey."

"Hmmm, I see. Wonder what they're up to?"

"Yeah. I'll bet you do."

"Anything else?"

"Where does Conners live in Chicago?"

"North side. Yeah, yeah, not too far from Delaware."

"That figures. And Terry, you did take care of those materials with our mutual friend, like I asked?"

"Yeah, reluctantly, but yeah."

"Thanks, pal."

"That's it?"

"That's it."

"Gimme a call tomorrow or the next day if you have any problems."

"Yeah, Ter, but maybe it'll be long distance, real long distance."

"Oh, I see. Yeah. Well lemme know when you can. Good luck."

"Thanks. I'll be seeing you."

When Morley opened the apartment door, the aromas were mouth-watering. She didn't say anything about his having had to go to Carolina to get those cigarettes, but just hurried him to the table. The breakfast truly deserved the appellation of "he-man number one." Afterwards they sat with their last cups of coffee, talking and laughing. She thought to herself that she could get to like this lazy life. She had quit commenting about

Morley's soft job—after all, she didn't even have one any more, and at least he did go over to the office once in a while, even if it was just for show.

She hit the table lightly with a spoon. "What's on the docket today, your honor?"

Morley looked out the window. "Oh, I think it looks like a Miami day. Let's drive down there for lunch."

"Sounds fun."

"Why not? Then after lunch we'll get you a passport."

"A passport!" She was all attention. "A passport. What for? Where are we going? What should we bring? You cad. Just like that! Where? You have a tour to guide or something? When do we leave? What's the weather like there?"

"Whoa! Whoa! Whoa! One at a time. I just thought it'd be fun to take a trip, a surprise trip, and maybe you'll need a passport."

"You love. What a nice surprise. But I've got to know what to bring."

"Okay. It'll be warm. Like a South Sea island."

She looked at him, unbelieving. "You mean it?"

"Yes."

"Oh. Oh. Oh. I can't believe it. When?"

"About a week, maybe a little sooner. Okay?"

"Okay? You bet it's okay! Anytime!"

"How about your job in Chi?"

"You joke, mister. I resigned by phone, collect yet, when I left the Inn. Didn't I tell you?"

"You mentioned something about it at one of those strategic moments women use to float certain things, when men's attention is centered elsewhere; I didn't know you'd cut the cord. Oh, well, the man is always the last to know."

"Poor baby. How long will we be gone?"

"I dunno. It's up to us. However long we want to."

"C'mon. Really?"

"I mean it. Whatever we—really, you—decide."

"And where?"

"Same deal."

"You're not kidding, are you?"

"No, sweetheart, I'm not."

"You really know how to get a girl's attention."

"Well there is that other way—y'know—start by whacking them on the head a couple of times."

"Okay, okay. You've got mine. Now let's get with it. What next?"

"Let's leave about eleven. I'll run over to the office for a few minutes. You know, scare 'em by pretending I'm coming to work today."

"Yeah, everybody fears the unusual."

"Funneee."

He drove to the office for a heart-to-heart with Roger, telling him he'd be taking some time off and not to count on him for a month or so. Roger was disappointed but not surprised, and said he'd be welcome whenever he returned. Roger did ask him point-blank if he was "serious" with Dana. Morley responded affirmatively and Roger looked pleased. Morley had brought Dana over a few days before and the three of them had lunched at Roger's "place." Roger had been totally captivated by Dana, and being a true friend, his commercial disappointment was outweighed by his delight with Morley's good luck. He had seen enough of Morley during those dark months after Monica's death, when he had to argue against Morley's conviction that somehow he'd been responsible for the tragedy, and he had actually feared for the man's mind. Now, at last, he seemed recovered, so Roger was not about to question the prescription. Morley needed a woman and this was some woman; lucky for him!

Before he left, Morley asked for a favor. "Hey, Rog, you know that rental car outfit you do business with at West Palm Airport."

"Sure."

"Would you give them a call for me?"

"Sure."

"Thanks. Now this is what I'd like them to do. . . ."

On the way back home Morley stopped at the post office and signed for a registered letter from a Mr. A. Parsons in Los Angeles, obviously Terry's "good man." He went out to his car and opened it. There was a short note clipped to two pictures, identifying them by numbers placed on the back of the respective prints, and initialed "A.P." Then Morley looked at the pictures and the numbers and thought to himself that even "good" men made occasional mistakes. He turned the pictures to the light and looked closer, studied a while, and decided A.P. *was* a good man after all. He drove home with a thoughtful expression on his face. It was real. He had a lot to think about.

Dana was ready when he got back. He asked if he'd had any calls and she said no. As he was changing his shirt in the bedroom he checked that phone. The tiny piece of thread was still exactly in place. He did the same to the living room phone. Also in place. It made him feel good.

Morley went down I-95 all the way to the end, beyond downtown Miami. He was erratic in his speeds, sliding from forty-five to seventy and sitting for various periods at most of the in-between numbers; he kept a close watch in the rearview mirrors without swiveling his head. He even left the interstate at Pompano, slowed for a nearby gas station, made a U-turn, and got back on the big road again, heading south. Dana noticed all this, of course, but stayed silent. At the end of the highway Morley made a fast exit and continued south for a couple of blocks, then he made two quick right turns, drove a block, made a left, another block, two more rights, and pulled into a drugstore parking lot, putting the car far back behind the building. They went inside the store and watched out the front window for a few minutes. Finally satisfied, he led the still silent but obviously amused Dana back to the car, and proceeded, again by a roundabout route, to a small photography shop in a block-long shopping area amidst an otherwise residential neighborhood. Again, Morley found a parking place where his car was shielded from the street.

Once inside the shop, Morley asked to see "Mr. Alvera" and was led through a door into the back of the store where there was a lot of drying and printing equipment and a small, nonprivate office area. There was a thin, dark man sitting on a stool in front of a table with stacks and rolls of prints and a film cutter on it. He came over and shook hands with Morley, then bowed low to Dana. "Señor Morley, it is good of you to come, and this lovely senorita—she is in need of a passport?"

"Yes, Mr. Alvera."

"And your time, Señor?"

"Soon as possible, please."

"May we get started then? This way, Señorita."

The whole thing only took about twenty minutes, posing, signing, and so forth. Mr. Alvera was fast and fluid. He knew his business well. They thanked him and were on their way.

They drove up to Ft. Lauderdale, and being starved by this time, stopped at a small restaurant on U.S. 1. They ate like vultures and then settled back over a leisurely second cup of coffee. Dana, an amused look in her eyes and a smile playing around the corners of her mouth, pushed the cup away, captured Morley's gaze, and said, "And now Mr. Pettybone, *if you please.*"

Morley smiled in spite of himself. He knew better than to pretend he didn't understand. "It's a long story."

"Time I got plenty of."

"Okay." He got serious. "I saw your friend Conners—"

"Ex-friend."

"Right. Sorry, love. Anyway I saw this soldier Conners in Palm Beach two days ago. He passed by the office in a car. I just *happened* to be at the window, and I just *happened* to look up and out at exactly the right time."

"Oh God, Pat, please!"

"Not that, honey, not that. I know it's nothing to do with you. But I am afraid Mr. Conners has not given up the idea that I'm his man. He's given up on you helping him, but he's sure not convinced I'm clean. That's why I did all that Mickey Mouse stuff on the way to see Mr. Alvera."

"I was afraid it was something like that. But there wasn't anybody, was there?"

"I don't think so. They'd have had to be awfully good—*or* have us bugged, and I know that's not so."

"I won't ask how."

"Good."

"And Conners, you still think he's a syndicate hit man."

"Honey, I'm sure of it." Her face started to cloud. "But I believe he works under cover of being a broker of sorts, and there's no way you could have known differently."

"Thank you. I mean that."

"You're welcome. I mean that."

"And Conners, he's doing all this chasing around? Maybe?"

"Him and his men."

"His men!"

"Oh sure, he's got at least two, maybe more, with him."

"All for a lousy embezzler?"

"You just answered that one with your own question."

"Yeah, I see. So what does he want? You, or that something he thinks you've got?"

"Exactly. Only, as I said, I haven't got it. I think I know why they think so, and what it is, but I still haven't got it."

"So why don't you go up to him and explain? Put an end to it."

"It doesn't work that way, sweetheart. That's just in the make-believe world. In real life it has a reverse effect: he becomes sure I *do* have it. You know, 'methinks he doth protest too much.'"

"I see. So what can we do?"

"You just made it all worthwhile."

"I did? How?"

"With that 'we.'"

"Well, it is 'us,' isn't it?"

"All the way."

"So we run? That's what Mr. Alvera was all about?"

"Uh-huh. But don't act so sad about it. I prefer to think of it as a hard-earned vacation for both sides, with us out of town and them cooling off."

"And, all this secrecy and phony name stuff I signed and those credit cards—all those papers and things Mr. Alvera had—that's so they can't follow us?"

"Right on, lover."

"And you just expected me to sign on the dotted lines, ask no questions, and tag along?"

He smiled and shrugged his shoulders. "So you just flunked your blind obedience test. But you passed the one on smarts. No, my dear, I'd've been worried if you hadn't asked."

"Aha. Me comprende. You're one smart travel agent, with some very odd connections and friends."

"I wasn't always a travel agent."

"I know. You were also a soldier and a pen-pusher. Sure, I imagine you pushed a pen about like you sell plane tickets."

"So I met some nice people who taught me some nice things."

"And some not so nice, I'll bet."

"Perhaps."

"Like your friendly neighborhood document maker, Mr. Alvera?"

"He's a gem, love. A real gem. Actually he's a friend of a friend, to be honest."

"Hey, that's good. Keep it up. Be honest." But she tempered her blast with a smile. "And so all this stuff is just in case—in case we want to leave quietly and stay lost?"

"You might say that. Maybe we won't need it, but if we do, it's nice to have it on hand. It would be better all around."

"Then when we come back they'll be gone and we can live peacefully ever after."

"Something like that."

"Patrick, my boy, as the old lady said when she kissed the cow, 'bullshit'! Talk about make-believe world!"

"All right. All right. I give up. My father told me never to marry a smart woman; they drive you crazy taking your excuses apart."

"Come on, lover."

"Okay. Yes, I think it's imperative that Conners people not learn of our plans to leave the country. Yes, I'm sure they'd stop us from leaving if they knew. No, I don't think it will blow over, but I think we will be better off if we disappear from their radar for a while. Although it might just convince them that I do have their goodies, it will also give them a chance to look at some other possibilities. Who knows, maybe they *will* find the culprit, and then we would be home free. Anyway, I think it's much healthier for us to leave and let things cool off while we bask in the sun somewhere."

"Hmmm. More like it, but it still sounds a little vague. But then you can be quite vague when you want to be, my boy."

"Vague is as vague does."

"Oh crap. So when do we leave?"

"We'll know tomorrow. Got a few items to take care of first."

"Can I help?"

"Just make everything look slow and easy and routine. No different or sudden moves."

"Then you *do* think they're watching us?"

"Honey, I am positive of it!"

"Oh."

"Sure you want to go? I don't think they'd ever harm you, but I can only guarantee it'd be over my dead body."

"Yes, I'm sure. She looked squarely at Morley, her dark eyes huge and probing. "You're going, aren't you?"

"I have to!"

"Then I have to, too!"

He reached over to kiss her; she raised her face and met him halfway. "I love you more today than yesterday."

Her eyes twinkled. The serious talk was over. It was settled, whatever it was. "I didn't know you felt that way about yesterday."

He grimaced with affected pain. "On second thought, you'd better stay here. Not sure I can stand those terrible puns all the way to Bali Hai or wherever."

"I promise—no more puns. Take me with you."

"No, no promises. You wouldn't be the same, and I want you just as you are. I'll take you, puns and all."

"Then it's settled."

"Yeah, honey, it's settled."

15

March came in like a lion—a modified, South Florida-style lion, but still a lion. It was windy, and an ominous bank of clouds moved in inexorably from the west northwest. A gloomy day, but Dennis Conners, Chicago businessman, was anything but gloomy. He had just had his perfunctory chat with Savilli and was waiting for his liege lord to come on the line. He did. "Good afternoon, Dennis. I hope you have some good news. It's a lousy day up here. I need to be cheered up."

"I think I do, sir. We have Santa identified for sure and we will pick him up tonight!"

"Wonderful, Dennis, wonderful! I am cheered up already. Which one is it? Or was it a new, dark horse you've kept from me?"

Conners chuckled. "No, sir, I'd never keep anything from you. It's Morley, sir."

"Hmmm. How did you decide? I must admit I would have bet on that other one, the one with the boatyard."

"He was my choice too, sir, at first. When he picked up all our bugs, I was sure, but then Morley picked 'em up too. The Bahama angle was another thing. We still haven't resolved that fully. Then we discovered that Morley went to work for that travel outfit right after the heist and left for Europe and Switzerland three days afterward. He made another trip not too many days later, same itinerary, then he just about quit working at the place. This got me thinking *he* might be number one, but we got the clincher about an hour ago from California. I think you'll enjoy this, sir, it's rather ironic. Morley's mother was a very religious woman and his full baptismal name was Saint Patrick Morley!"

The old man really erupted on that one. "Santa, Santa, Santa. Of course! Poor Dante, what a waste! He did have a wonderful sense of humor. Santa! Well, well. Yes, Dennis, that was certainly the clincher. So when will you pick him up?"

"Tonight, sir. As soon after dark as we can. He never stays in the whole evening, so whenever he comes out we'll take him."

"How about all those things you were worried about earlier: friends, insurance policies, all that?"

"I'm convinced he's a loner, sir. We've watched him loosely but steadily for almost three weeks now, and I'm sure of it. I believe he's alone, he's greedy, and he's vulnerable. I think he'll cave in."

"But I thought he was one of those supermen from, what did you call it, 'Squadron C'?"

"Yes sir, Squad C. But I'm sure he's severed all ties, and I don't think we have to worry about him scuttling himself with a cyanide pill or any of that. No, sir, I don't think he's a superman any more."

"So where will you sweat him?"

"We've got a boat. The captain is a Miami employee, and we'll go out far enough from land and go to work."

"And afterward?"

"Nothing 'til we have the money and the books in hand."

"Good. And then?"

"I recommend one last trip to sea for Saint Patrick."

"We think alike, my boy. Excellent! And the girl, Dennis, is she still with him?"

"Yes, sir, but he watches her like a hawk. She hasn't been able to risk communications with us since she moved in with him."

"You still trust her?"

"Yes, sir, completely."

"And so you'll just let her go?"

"Yes, sir. She'll go back to Chicago."

"And no trouble, Dennis? It seems to me she knows a great deal about our business."

"Well, sir, she's in as deep as any of us. But, no, I don't think she'll give us any trouble anyway. She really doesn't know *too* much, and we've got a good hold on her, sir—she'd like to work for us again."

"All right, Dennis, I rely on your judgment. Now let me go back a little. There's one item that bothers me. This Santa man, Morley, he was with the federal government how many years?"

"Almost ten—three in the army and about six and a half with Squad C."

"So, Dennis, why are you so sure he's a loner, an opportunist? Is it not possible that he could be a plant? How do you call it, a sleeper? Why do you feel so certain he has cut his ties with this Squad C? After all, you told me that his Pentagon file is still held secretly."

Conners hesitated, nodding at the old man's logic, then came on slowly and distinctly. "Anything is possible, sir, you are right. But I *am* convinced that it is not so in this case. First, Morley's background is now pretty open to us—I mean there are no real black spots. And this we know: he *was* overseas with Squad C; his wife *was* killed in a plane crash; he *did* take it hard, leave his job with Squad C and come down here; he *did* inherit enough money to be a beach bum for more than a few years. These are facts, sir. Then too, he's been living here doing nothing for more than two years—no mysterious deviations, contacts, trips—until recently of course—and nothing that looks out of line."

"I know, Dennis, and I agree, but still, would he not be careful to be just so clean and normal if he were a sleeper?"

"Yes, sir, of course he would, but two things convince me it

... 171

is not so. One is the fact that Squad C's jurisdiction is narrow and limited to overseas activity; the FBI handles all these anti-terrorist activities in the U.S. The other is the time element. It's going on three years since his wife died and he quit the government."

"I see. I see. You feel that Squad C would not be either able or willing to set him up as a sleeper?"

"Exactly, sir. It's completely out of their bailiwick. And if any other outfit, say the FBI, for example, wanted to use him—well, sir, they just don't operate that way. Three years! On the beach in Florida! No, sir! What were his targets, his objectives, which merited such an expensive cover setup. It just doesn't make sense."

"Hmmm. You make a convincing case, Dennis. One last question—his Pentagon file?"

"According to the insider—the Pentagon sergeant our contact man squeezed in Washington—this is just routine. Squad C puts 'secret holds' on the files of all its people for five years after their separation."

"So you are satisfied he is not a plant, this Santa man?"

"Yes, sir, I am satisfied."

"All right, Dennis, again I accept your judgment. But he is a very tricky fellow, and it is this that worries me. You know, tricky fellows are so often not what logic says they should be, and they don't behave as logic says they should."

"Yes, sir, you are of course right, anything could be possible but I do feel that we must proceed on our best judgment. To me that means assuming Morley is in general what he purports to be—an opportunist whose past experience makes him a tricky enemy. To me, sir, this whole thing only makes sense as a heist by Morley. You see, if he were a Pentagon sleeper, what is it that he and his bosses are after? Why wait? No sir, they'd have started the roll-up by now and we'd have alarms going off all over."

"Yes, I see. That is a good point. I like that. Why should

they wait. But Morley, he would wait for the right time and place, no?"

"I'm convinced of it, sir, and to me that would have been the proof—when Morley came to peddle the notebooks back to us."

"I agree, Dennis. Let's proceed as you suggest. Handle it as you have planned. Keep me informed as you move ahead."

"Yes, sir, I will."

At about the same time Conners and Mr. Henry were calmly planning his watery demise, Saint Patrick Morley was answering the insistent summons of his telephone.

"Hello."

"Patrick—sorry to be calling you at home, but this shouldn't wait."

"No problem, Terry. Not to worry. What gives?"

"You know that little piece of cheese you left out in Santa Barbara?"

"Yeah."

"A rat came for it yesterday."

"He got it?"

"Sure. You said no stops."

"Right. I did. Any idea who he was or from where?"

"Al said—my man Al Parsons—that the guy used the name James Smith on the sign-in book and gave an address in L.A. that's nonexistent. Al said he came during the lunch hour when the place was understaffed and seemed a little put out when he was told he couldn't examine the old books by himself."

"I don't suppose anybody recognized him; you know, he could be a local."

"No way. Big guy, fairly well dressed, not too friendly, and nobody in the place had ever seen him before. Al's principal contact happened to be the one who waited on him—there's only three there—so she was particularly careful. The guy asked for three names; the other two were not locatable. He paid his two bucks for a copy of your birth certificate and left."

"Aha. Very interesting."

"Yeah, I suppose it is. I wouldn't know. Can I call off Parsons now?"

"Oh, sure. And thank him for me; he played the whole thing exactly as I wanted him to."

"All right, lad. I won't push any farther, but some day fill me in on all this, will ya?"

"For sure, pal, for sure. Right now suffice it to know you've helped an old friend one hell of a lot."

"I'm glad, old friend. Anything else today?"

"Not a thing. In fact, I think you can close the file for a while. I'll be away for a month or so. When I come back we'll get together and I'll answer any questions over a huge steak— on me."

"You're on. I'll look forward to it. Meanwhile, be careful. I mean I've got a feeling you should be careful."

"Your feelings are valid. Take care yourself. My love to the family. See you soon."

"Yeah, Patrick, good-bye."

He'd hardly hung up the phone when it rang again. This time it was the telephone-keyed front door. He buzzed the lock open and then waited until the visitor arrived. It was Alvera's assistant with a small package. Morley thanked him and told him that if he met anyone who asked him where he'd been he should give them Morley's neighbor's name and apartment number. The man understood, saying that he also had covered the call board with his body when he punched Morley's door-key code number. Morley relaxed. He should have known that Alvera's man would be cautious. He opened the package and was looking at the documents when Dana came out of the bedroom. She was enough to take any man's mind off his work. Fresh from the shower, attired only with a towel around her waist, she was using another to dry and fluff her hair. He turned back to the papers and she came and stood behind his

174 . . .

chair, looking over his shoulder. She leaned down to get a closer look and he felt the weight and warmth of a bare breast on his shoulder. This ruined his concentration completely, so he turned his head to brush its softness with his lips. He liked the taste, and started to turn further to improve his angle of osculation, but a gentle hand guided his head and eyes back to the pile of documents. "What're those? Mine?"

"All yours."

"Mr. Alvera's contribution to our trip?"

"Exactly."

"How'd they get here?"

"His boy brought 'em."

"Just now? While I was in the shower?"

"Uh-huh."

"Why the rush?"

"We're leaving. I mean we, if you still want to."

"Try leaving without me."

"I won't. Can you be ready in half an hour?"

The mischievous twinkle started in her eyes and spread. "Darling, do I not look 'ready'?"

"Yes. Yes. That's why I hated to ask. How soon can you be dressed and ready to go?"

She stopped and looked at him full on. "You're not kidding? Today? Now?"

"No, I'm not kidding. Now. Right now."

"Give me half an hour."

He looked at his watch. "Your time has begun." Then he looked serious. "No bags! The little one you packed yesterday will have to do. And, honey, slacks, no skirt. Okay?"

She nodded assent as she moved toward the bedroom. Twenty minutes later she was back—hair dry, face perfect, carrying her largest shoulder bag and dressed in a casual, light pants suit. Morley shook his head. "Amazing. I wouldn't have believed it possible."

"All is possible, master, if the spirit, she is willing."

"Okay, okay." He laid the three passports out on the coffee

table and had her sign them with the appropriate names. Then he matched the three stacks of credit cards and pocket litter with the passports, gave one stack to her for her purse, and put the others, in separate and numbered envelopes, into his small briefcase. He placed an envelope on the dining table, picked up a grocery sack that was sitting by the door, and they left— without even a backward glance.

Conners was pleased. Things had gone well. First, the old man putting him in charge, then Matthewson's exit—funny, he hadn't had any problem with the men, even Paul, over that— and now the operation was falling in place. He'd really been sure when Morley had picked off the second bug, except that Roamer had found his too. Something all along had told him it had to be Morley. That's why he'd risked the girl on him. She was damn good, for an amateur. She'd picked up a hell of a lot of corroborating items, and of course she'd given them the Santa Barbara lead that broke the whole thing open. She'd get a good bonus when she got back to Chicago. He smiled to himself. Of course, she'd go back, and then he'd be the boss and could give her a *real* job. That was another thing. That bastard Morley kept the girl so tightly leashed. Hell, she hadn't been able to call him for a long time, and he had to admit to himself that it made him squirm to think of the two of them up there alone in Morley's apartment.

Well, Morley was smart all right. The more he learned about him, the more respectful he got. The decision to move tonight was born of this same respect. He didn't want the slippery bastard to get out from under. Might never see him again! Trouble was, he was a real pro. They'd taught him well in that "Squad C." It was a lucky break having their Pentagon man run into that enlisted man in a Washington bar. Of course he'd spotted the guy earlier as possible entrée into "Squad C"; nevertheless, he got a lot of interesting poop out of the man. It made Morley's skills much more understandable when you realized he'd spent almost six years with this supersecret outfit.

Supposedly they were the worldwide frontline defense against terrorists and nihilist activity aimed at the U.S. and its friends. The Squad C operators were legendary already, and from what the man said, this Morley was one of the best. Good thing Morley wasn't aware of *who* they were (Conners hoped) even if he did know *what* they were and *why* they were there. Still, the other guy Roamer was a Squad C graduate too. He'd quit for money, Morley for despondency, but they both had the skills and the training. It was the name thing in California that did it. Without that, he'd've had to toss a coin. Think of it! The damn answer was there all the time in a simple public record.

And yesterday. Shit! They'd had two cars on him and he got loose. They knew he'd been lost somewhere in a mile-square section of South Miami for almost an hour before they picked him up again heading back north on I-95.

Whatever it was he went there for, it was probably too late now to do anything about it. The Miami boys had taken a look at the area, but nothing there was immediately suspicious. Damn! He wished he'd hear from the girl, but that sure as hell was no cinch either. The only lesson learned in that Miami fiasco was that they had to be better from now on. And so today he'd used everybody sewing up that damn apartment building like a drum. There had been no use trying a third bug inside; he probably had the place booby-trapped. And anyway, the bastard would find it in no time at all. They did get a bug on his car, one of those new ones that are not good for much distance and are hard as hell to spot without the exact calibrated receiver. It was working fine as of Krupa's last call. Still, it was amazing what Morley had done in a few weeks, right under their noses. As Mr. Henry had said—jokingly, Conners hoped—maybe they should let the guy keep the money and hire him just to get him on their side. Conners had laughed, but he didn't think it was too funny. Okay, so the guy had shit all over them, getting the dough and then getting it out of the country. The big trick was to get to use it.

Tonight was it. Then his worries would be over. Conners

was glad he'd got the two extra hands from Mr. Henry. They were good men, and with the way Morley operated, he sure as hell needed them. Again he wondered about the girl. She'd be no factor tonight. She'd play his way, or she'd take the big swim with Morley but he really wasn't worried. She was too smart and too hung up on excitement to throw this chance away. He suspected that Morley's plans to leave—he had to be planning a split—included the girl, although he'd fuzzed this with Mr. Henry. Why Morley'd go to this kind of trouble, he couldn't figure. She was a doll baby, but the kind of money Morley had would buy lots of those. Oh well, he thought, smarter guys than him had had their heads ruled by their cocks. So what else is new?

He mused. It would be nice to be back in Chicago again, with spring coming on.

The phone rang. He pounced on it before he realized how keyed up he was, and then hesitated a moment to compose himself. "Yes?"

It was Krupa. "Dennis. They've been in that apartment all day. Car's still sitting in the parking area and the bug's working fine." He stopped, obviously wanting to say more.

"So?"

"So I got one of those feelings. Somethin's wrong. It feels too quiet, you know? Dennis, I think somethin' spooky's happened."

"Like what?"

"Like maybe they sneaked past us!" There, it was out of the bag now. Krupa obviously felt better.

Conners' voice was icy. "And how could they do that, Sal? How could they sneak past you four professionals? How?"

"I don't know, Dennis. I swear we've got this place locked up. But I'm just afraid."

"You try the phone?"

"Fifteen minutes ago. No answer."

"Any activity there at the building? People in and out? I

mean unusual things—too many people, too many cars, that kinda thing?"

"No. It's been strictly routine."

"So you wanta go in and look? That right, Sal?"

"Yeah. I think we should. Figured I could get a pair of overalls and a plumbing outfit—you know, tell 'em I'm working next door but need to get at a pipe fitting from their side. Somethin' like that."

"Okay, Sal, I agree we should go in, but I don't want you to do it. Use one of those new guys from up East. Use Rocco. and tell him *not* to go into the place. He's to go to the door—no farther—and if they answer, he tells 'em he's working next door and asks 'em to made sure their taps are closed while he cuts a pipe, just five minutes or so. He's not to go inside, no matter what. And, oh yeah, if the guy *is* there, then Rocco should go back in five or six minutes and tell him it's all okay again. Got it?"

"Gotcha. Will do, Dennis. I'll be back to ya shortly."

Conners sat by the phone nervously. Now he was worried too. It wasn't even dark yet. Could the bastard have slipped by them? And with the girl? Conners hadn't told anybody that he figured Santa might have "made" him at the airport that first day; if he had, he'd probably made Krupa too. So if the guy saw Krupa at his front door in a plumber's outfit or any other kind of outfit, no telling what his reaction would be, only that it'd be bad for them. It was almost twenty minutes later that Krupa called. "Sorry it took so long. We had to get into the maintenance room to get some overalls and stuff. No luck, Dennis; either they're gone or they aren't answering the door. Quiet as a church in there. Nobody moving. Rocco waited and listened for three or four minutes and not a sound. I'd like to go in. How 'bout it?"

"Damn it, Sal, I'm worried that may be just what the sonofabitch wants—to get his hands on one of us."

"And I'm worried he's skipped out."

"Okay. Okay. I guess you're right. Let's go in and see. Okay, it's now six twenty-one. At exactly six-thirty—that give you enough time?"

"Yeah, I'm next door, but make it six thirty-five to be safe."

"Okay. At six thirty-five you and Rocco be at the door to that place. I'll phone the number and let it ring seven times, no more, no less. I'll hang up after seven rings, then you guys move in. No problem with the locks?"

"Dennis! Rocco is an expert. The best."

"Yeah, I forgot. All right, now, don't go in if the phone doesn't ring at six thirty-five or if it rings more or less than seven times, 'cause then it won't be me and something will be out of whack. Got it?"

"Right. I understand."

"And Sal—"

"Yeah?"

"Splash a little booze on your shirt so you can give it the 'drunk-wrong apartment' bit in case the bastard's in there playing possum. And Sal, whatever you do, don't hurt 'em and don't bust up the place. No rough stuff. Got it?"

"Gotcha. What if they *are* in there?"

"*Persuade* them to come with you and we'll just move our timetable up a few hours. But watch that bastard closely. He's slippery as hell."

"Okay. Got it."

"Good luck. Remember, seven rings."

"Right."

At thirty-four minutes and fifty seconds after six o'clock Conners dialed Morley's number. It clicked in and then rang. Once. Twice. Seven times. He hung up and sat back in the dark to wait. At six forty-four his phone rang. He had a sinking premonition as he reached for the instrument, but there was no alternative to answering. "Yes."

"There's nobody there. I think they've split."

"They couldn't have gone out the back, to the beach?"

"No. Arnold's been on that exit all afternoon."

"And the front? You're sure?"

"I'm sure, Dennis. They got past us some way."

"Lotsa people in and out of there, you said?"

"Yeah, last hour or so especially. But that's normal for this time a' day."

"Couples?"

"Yeah."

"Walking?"

"None at all. Everybody that came out the front got into a car. None of them looked like Morley and the girl."

"But you think one of them was?"

"'Fraid so, Dennis. It has to be that way."

"Clothes in the apartment?"

"Yeah, lots of them. Both kinds. But who knows how much or little they mighta taken with 'em."

"You're right."

"Oh, and Dennis, there was an envelope on the dining table. It's addressed to you."

"What!" He fumed. "To me! Why didn't you say so?"

"I just did."

"Yeah. Sorry, Sal. Took me by surprise. What's in it?"

"I dunno, it's sealed, so I didn't open it. Want me to?"

"No, thanks. Just bring it to me. How's the apartment look?"

"Normal, like they'd gone out to dinner or something. No sign of panic or rush, if that's what you mean."

"That's what I meant. Okay, Sal, you and Arnold c'mon back here. Leave Paul and Rocco, one on each exit, just in case. We gotta start a lotta things in motion."

Krupa was back to the motel in twenty minutes. Conners opened the envelope with steady fingers and a half smile on his face. Inside he was churning like mad. There was a one-page typed letter in it, and he read it, his heart sinking deeper with each line. He sent Krupa to call off the surveillance and bring the boys back, then he got on the phone to Miami and got some help covering the airport and steamer sailings. When the boys got back he gave them pictures of Morley and the girl and sent them to Ft. Lauderdale Airport, Port Everglades, and the West Palm Airport. He knew damn well these were all futile exercises, but he had to go through the motions. That smart bastard Morley! But how did he know? The girl didn't know. Could Morley have been that lucky? Sonofabitch! Well, no use delaying any longer. It wouldn't get any easier. He dialed the New Jersey area code and that number, went through that polite charade with Savilli (didn't that spook ever sleep?), and then the old man was on the line. Conners began to sweat. "Sorry to disturb you, sir, but there's been an important development."

"Good news, I hope." The temperature of the old man's voice belied his optimistic words.

"No sir, not really. Santa has disappeared."

Mr. Henry's voice was like an icy wind. "I'd say that was definitely bad news, Dennis. Tell me why you don't think so."

"Because it's triggered the action we wanted, sir, even if it's not in the way we expected. He left a note, and now we know many things we didn't before. We know he's Santa, that the deal was a heist, that he has all our materials, and what he wants for them. But best of all, sir, we know he'll meet with us for an exchange."

"Because he says so, Dennis?" The icy wind cut again.

"No sir, because he has to. I think you'll agree when you read the note."

"Where'd you find the note?"

"In his place, sir. We decided to go in. It was too quiet, and they didn't answer the phone, and we were worried."

"And the note was there. Addressed to whom?"

"Me, sir."

"How'd he know your name, Dennis? The girl?"

"Could be, sir. I don't know. Maybe he was at the airport that day when I covered the aborted delivery. I don't know. Maybe the girl had to give him the cover story I gave her in case he ever pinned her down. She wasn't supposed to give the true names, but sometimes these things happen."

"And how'd he get past your coverage and get away?"

"I think he used disguises and borrowed or stole another car."

"And the timing, Dennis. How'd he manage that? Just under the wire? You think he knew your plans? Did the girl know?" The icy voice was still like a whip.

"I don't see how he could know, sir. Only six people knew the timing: you and I and the four men here with me. The boat captain's on standby, and I haven't talked to the girl in over a week. I don't know if anything spooked Santa. Maybe he was just lucky. What I do know, sir, is that he is playing for time and position. He wants our money, and he wants to talk about it, but he wants better control of the situation than he had here. I *know* we'll get another crack at him."

The icy voice warmed about ten degrees. It was still damn cold. "Well, Dennis, maybe you're right. These things do happen. I suppose you're taking all reasonable action to try to track them—the girl is with him, I assume—down at airports, et cetera?"

"Yes sir. I've set all that in motion. And yes, sir, the girl has to be with him."

"You're still sure of her?"

"Yes sir. I am. I think the problem is that Santa has suspected her from the start and has watched her like a hawk, especially the last week or so. She's following my orders, as I told her *never* to risk her cover by trying to communicate with me when conditions were not favorable."

"So you feel we've got somebody in the other team's huddle, after all?"

"Yes sir. I sure do. I guess all this was why I did *not* consider his escape a disaster."

"I see, Dennis. I see." The voice warmed another ten degrees or so. "Well, I want to see that note from this Santa man.

You'd better come up first thing tomorrow and bring it with you. And, Dennis . . ."

"Yes sir."

"Maybe you're right. Maybe this isn't a disaster. We'll see. Sleep well."

"Yes sir. Good-bye."

Everything was the same: the airport, Savilli, the ride, the castle, the old man's eyes, everything. Even the wine and the table on the patio. Mr. Henry dismissed the butler as soon as the wine was served and reached out for the note. He read it slowly and carefully, maddeningly slowly. Conners sat there silent and outwardly composed; inside he was a scared and worried little boy. He remembered almost every letter of that typed page. He could almost see the words coming off Mr. Henry's slightly moving lips as his hooded eyes moved slowly across the page. It read:

Mr. Conners:

We have not met, yet I feel we know each other quite well. My congratulations on the speed and efficiency with which you zeroed in on me.

I will be brief. I have the materials you seek, and I am willing to surrender them to you—if you are willing to meet my conditions.

I have four items: 1) the original and only series of six notebooks, "Amalfi one through six," which detail D.C.'s entire system and its personnel; 2) D.C.'s proposal to the Corse (carbon copy of the original he delivered in person to M. Marcella in Sept. '84; 3) the original and only copy of D.C.'s personal plan for the piecemeal implementation of the Corse takeover of "Amalfi" (I do not know if M. Marcella was given an outline of this plan—it is possible); 4) D.C.'s personal and additional "insurance policy" against a Corse double cross.

That is the merchandise; these are the prices: For items

one, two, and three—two million two hundred twenty thou-
sand dollars. ($2,220,000). For item four—one million dol-
lars ($1,000,000).

If you wish to purchase items one through three you
simply renounce all claim to the funds I am now holding. If
there is any question about the value of items two and/or
three, please note that their sole possession by the Corse
would be <u>most</u> undesirable.

Item four. This document is of <u>personal</u> interest only to
M. Latellier of the Corse. It is deadly and damning for him,
but I have assumed that you may wish to let him purchase
it, because he would be most grateful to you if you did. The
operative words are "Quetta, Samir, Paris, and December
83." M. Latellier will recognize these, and I am sure will
agree that $1,000,000 is indeed a bargain. However, I do not
care who the purchaser is; I am only interested in receiving
my price.

I will contact you via your Chicago office regarding time
and place for an exchange. This contact will be made be-
tween March 26 and April 6. You may attempt to follow me
if you wish, but it is not necessary. As you see, I do not
intend to be "lost" for long.

> *Santa*

Conners began to lose his outward composure as the old
man started his third reading of the letter. Christ!! What's to
read over and over? And that damn signature. The final insult.
Now Conners was personally involved; before he'd just considered the whole deal as a steppingstone for himself, and if
one of those steps was Santa's dead body, then so be it. But
now he wanted the bastard. "Santa" my ass! Old Cappacino
was probably still rattling his coffin over that one. Conners was
jolted out of his musings. The old man had finally looked up
from the paper and was starting to speak. Conners was happy
to note that the tone was almost lukewarm. "Well, Dennis, it
seems we made the mistake of underestimating our opposition.

I mean both you and I. Dante was much smarter than I had imagined, and this Santa man, he's much better than you expected. Right?"

"Yes sir. I mean, yes, I underestimated Santa's ability."

"I do not like this man, Dennis. He is a smart-ass and I've never liked smart-asses. But I must admit, this is a very clever man. Very clever. And very well prepared. And organized. Yes, organized. Hmmm." The old man nodded thoughtfully, apparently mulling over his own words, then went on. "I realize you do not have all the facts concerning the items in here—" he tapped the papers in his hand—"but I'd be interested in your thoughts about it."

Although Conners had expected such a question and had given it a lot of thought, his ideas on the subject were still a jumble; nevertheless, when Mr. Henry says speak, you jump up, wag your tail, and bark. "Yes sir, I agree Santa is smart, but I think the problem is that we underestimated other things more than that."

"Like what, Dennis?"

"Like his professional knowledge and his contacts."

"Hmmm. Interesting. Explain."

"Well, we felt from the beginning that he wouldn't have tried to get away with our materials unless he were confident—very confident—that he could swing it, but we thought he was relying on his own intelligence. Now I don't think that's true. I believe he not only planned this operation for a long time but he had some help in pulling it off."

"But you've said all along, he's a 'greedy loner.'" A touch of that ice came back in the old man's voice.

"Oh yes, sir, and I still believe it. In fact, I think that note in your hand proves it. He's willing to risk all in a face-to-face meeting just to get more money."

"What do you mean by 'help'?"

"I mean that Santa not only learned a lot while he was with that superspy outfit in Washington, but he made a lot of contacts in and out of the U.S. I'll tell you why."

"Please do." This was sincere. Most of the ice had gone.

"Well, sir, starting with planning, everything he did was smart, smooth, professional. This was his training and experience. He found our bugs, he beat our surveillance, he anticipated our moves. But the big thing—the important thing—was that he wouldn't have planned the whole operation unless he was sure he could get away with the dough *and* his life whenever he wanted to. I think logic proves this was no spur-of-the-moment caper that Santa thought up when Cappacino died, but a cold, calculated operation; therefore, he had help lined up in advance."

"What kind of help did this 'loner' have?"

"Blind help, sir. People who helped him because they were old friends, not because they had a piece of the action. I'm thinking of things like false documentation, overseas contacts for help with hiding the money and with secret travel arrangements, and of course his travel agency friends. And also—I figure this *had* to be, sir—he had somebody out in California tip him off when we checked those records on his name out there."

"Could be. Yes, I like that. I like it a lot better than thinking there must be a leak in our organization. So then you think he *did* get our materials out of the country?"

"Yes sir. I think he did—probably to a Swiss bank. With contacts he could have handled it easily, and I think the guy's got lots of contacts in Europe. The girl told us that's where he lived most of the last ten years, and we have an idea about what he was doing during that time. Or, sir, he *could* have simply used Dante's systems and people."

"By God, that's so! He could. Now, Dennis, I assume you are no longer worried that he might have an 'insurance policy'?"

"No sir, not really. I don't think it's consistent. If he's a loner and greedy, he doesn't want any *knowledgeable* help, and he has to deal with us, and deal by himself. Any kind of an 'insurance policy' would require him to change this basic plan. At first I thought he might well have arranged something, but I think his skipping out—a play for time and position—proves otherwise."

"Yes, I see. Now, where do you think he will set up the exchange?"

Dennis smiled. "Just somewhere with conditions more favorable to him than South Florida, sir. But where, I could only guess. I'm sure it will not be in the U.S."

"Why not?"

"With all that illegal blackmail money, he wants to be as far from the feds as he can. He'd figure we might even arrange to turn him in."

"And so, Dennis, we come to the nub of the situation. How would you propose to handle it from here on in?"

"Depends on your opinion of Santa's proposal and what kind of, uh, punishment you want him to get."

The old man chuckled, quietly at first, then louder, and finally slapping his thigh in glee. "Very good. I like your way of getting to the point, my boy. Let's have some food and we can talk about it."

It was small talk, sports, politics, weather, until the dishes were cleared away. Then they both sat back, each with a large snifter of some incredibly old and smooth brandy. Conners had again been amazed at the width and depth of the old man's knowledge. He was well informed, articulate, and interesting, and in addition, he seemed very willing to listen. Finally, he set his snifter on a small table and swiveled his chair to face Conners. It was obviously business time again.

"Oh yes, Dennis, you asked two questions—simple, good questions—and I'll try to answer them in kind. First: yes, as a proposal, this Santa man's offer appears reasonable. You might say a reasonable business exchange, assuming that the notebooks are the property of the late Dante Cappacino. But this Santa man does not know that Dante planned to use these books to harm us, his friends, his people. This changes the whole thing. So, Dennis, my answer is no! I do not like the proposal. I do not want this man to tell us what we can and cannot have of those things we *must* have to survive. I do not like his conceit, I do not like his style, and I will not agree to let him live happily on *our* money in return for a silence I can get more surely in other ways." The old man's voice was icy, his eyes like hot coals. "Dennis, I will not have this amateur piss on me to the tune of two or three million dollars, and then ask to wipe his cock on my face towel. I *can* not have it. You understand?"

Conners nodded, then the old man sat back and seemed to relax a bit. "I suppose I have answered both your questions at once, have I not?"

"Yes sir, you have. Very clearly. And what of Mr. Latellier?"

"Oh, Frankie's problems are his own. You know his real name is Lavarelli and he's still under indictment in New York for murder one on those two feds—treasury men. With this and the aftermath of the Dante business, he's got more trouble than he can handle right now in the Corse. If this Santa man's date and place—that Paris business—refers to what I think it does, Frankie will consider one million to be a bargain, a very good—oh yes, and necessary—business investment. But in any event this is what *I want* and I can assure you that when I tell him so, Frankie will be happy to go along with us. Dennis, I want this fucking Santa man's head on one plate and the notebooks on another. The money if you can get it will be a sweetener, but it's secondary. I will *insist* that Frankie buy into the deal. I don't want his secret. We got enough problems without causing a Corse blowup along the way. We'll help Frankie save his ass and we'll give it to him as a present. Maybe that'll give us a couple more years of peace before some other asshole works out a plan to steal our operations. Okay?"

"Yes sir, I understand."

"So what would you propose to do, my boy?"

Conners swiveled his chair so that he looked out over the still, snow-covered grounds of the estate. Then he turned his head to meet the old man's gaze and started to talk.

16

Martine Vallin looked with critical satisfaction at the naked body in the floor-to-ceiling mirror of her bathroom. At age twenty-nine—and who was alive to question her arithmetic?—she still had the gamine face that had appealed to men since she was twelve, and her slender frame still bulged in only the proper places. She was pleased. Martine's body was her fortune. The face was attractive—an anomaly with the blond hair and blue eyes of her French father and the dark golden brown complexion of her Arab mother—but it was her perfect body that had propelled her from the alleyways of the Marseilles waterfront to this mansion high on a hill overlooking the bustling Riviera. She had learned about men the hard way at age thirteen when she was brutally raped and sodomized by two drunken sailors in a waterfront hotel, and that day she had resolved that henceforth she would "use" men. She had kept this resolution. At twenty-five she had been one of Marseilles' most successful madames. That was when she met François. He was old enough to be her father, but he had young ideas and seemingly inexhaustible supplies of money, so when he proposed that she come to live with him in Nice, she had accepted with alacrity.

The arrangement was most attractive for her. She had her own suite of rooms in the huge house, and François had his. She came to his only when he asked for her, and he honored her privacy in the same fashion. But best of all, at last she had an acceptable status in the community. François was sexually demanding but financially generous; in return he asked just two things, her body and her loyalty. She had given both, willingly and exclusively, until four weeks ago.

Martine shivered slightly at the recollection. The handsome dark-haired young man had approached her in the greengrocers—she always picked out the ingredients for François's meals herself—and two nights later they had become lovers. Mon Dieu! What she had been missing these many years. Of course, to make love for love, not for money, that was the answer. Khaled was young and strong and passionate, and he treated her with a gentleness and respect that was totally new, but most of all he was expressing his love for her person, not just using her body to satisfy the bestial needs of his manhood.

Before the first week was up, Khaled had told her why he had sought her out and approached her, but he swore that the love that had sprung up between them was as real as it was unexpected. She believed him. He said he was a Palestinian patriot, but not, he assured her, a terrorist. Finally, he told Martine a bizarre tale of cross and double cross and explained his real objective. She trusted him implicitly, so when he told her what she must do to assist him, she agreed readily.

Martine turned from the mirror as her intercom buzzed. It was François. Could she visit him in fifteen minutes? She agreed. She sat there frowning. François with his coarse impatient hands, his often-limp organ, and his strange demands had begun to sicken her once she'd made love for love with Khaled. But she had to keep up the pretense. Khaled was returning tonight, then in a couple of days it would be all over. She made her face with the wet red mouth and darkened eyes that François preferred, slipped on a high-necked flannel robe, and began the familiar journey to the master suite.

François Latellier had just hung up the phone. He had been talking to Giacomo Malfalcone, or as he was known today, Albert Henry. Always bad news. He could not remember ever getting good news on the long distance. Always bad. And this call had been no exception. Latellier remembered most of the conversation word for word.

"Frankie, it's Jake from Jersey." He had laughed, as expected, at this old private joke.

"Jake, my friend, how are you? It's always good to hear your voice."

"I'm fine, Frankie."

"And all the boys?"

"Great. Just great."

"And business?"

"Not bad, Frankie, not bad at all. But we do have a little problem, I guess you could call it a mutual problem, which is why I'm calling today."

Latellier strained hard to keep the coldness out of his voice. "A problem, Jake? What kind?"

"Well, Frankie, we had a heist some weeks ago. Some dirty fucking bagman hit us for a couple mil and some real hot records. The dough we could write off, of course, but the records, Frankie, they're another matter. The feds could kill us with 'em!"

"Yes, I see. Business records, huh?"

"Sort of, Frankie—but really more on the order of personnel records. You know, people secretly on our payroll."

Holy shit! François thought. That old bastard is talking about Dante's courier system. Fer Chrissakes, why is he being so cozy? That's the stuff Dante wanted to sell us. Old Jake must be senile. Didn't he think Marcella would have told his old pal Frankie? Then, he realized he was running ahead without the facts. Jake was still talking. ". . . and this little asshole wants two point two mil in clean green to give us back our own records."

"He sounds like a candidate for a long swim in a cement suit, Jake. Got a line on him yet?"

"Yeah, we're on his tail and got somebody inside, but still

the guy is tricky. Don't worry, though, Frankie, we'll squash him like a bug."

"I'm sure a' that, Jake, but what is the 'mutual problem'?"

"Well, Frankie, it seems that this guy has another document, which he *says* is of interest to you fellows. No, as a matter of fact, Frankie, he didn't put it quite that way. He said it was of particular interest to *you*."

"To me? What is it?" This time Latellier did not succeed in keeping the hardness out of his voice.

"We don't know, Frankie, but maybe you can figure it out. The blackmailer said to tell you that the key words were 'Quetta, Samir, Paris, and December '83.' We do know he was in touch with our late friend, Dante, and it is possible that he found this document in Dante's place, or even that Dante gave it to him; what it refers to, I cannot even hazard a guess."

François's blood pressure was soaring. He could feel the pulse pounding in his temples and it seemed impossible that he would be able to speak, but finally he forced the words out in a surprisingly steady tone. "That's interesting, Jake, but I don't see what it is to me."

"I don't know either, Frankie, but this asshole bagman seemed pretty sure it would be important to you. In fact, he wants one million green for it. He said you'd consider that a bargain. What a nervy little bastard, huh?"

"I'm glad you plan to squash him, Jake. He's too smart to live." Latellier seemed to have his composure back at last.

Jake went on. "As I said, the story doesn't mean a thing to us, so we're certainly not interested in buying it at any price. Our only concern was to make sure it would not be harmful to you, so I'll leave the decision up to you. Frankie. Oh yeah, I forgot—the little bastard said he really didn't care who bought the document as long as he got his price."

Latellier was thoughtful. "How much time do we have, Jake?"

"At least a few weeks. We still gotta hear from the little asshole as to time and place for an exchange."

"Well, off hand it doesn't ring a bell, Jake, but since we've got time let me check around a bit and get back to you. And, Jake . . ."

"Yeah."

"I really appreciate your coming directly to me on this. Don't know if it's important, but thanks for handling it this way."

"No other way among old friends, Frankie."

"You're right, Jake, but sometimes our friends forget this."

"Sad but true, Frankie. Take care of yourself."

"Will do, my friend. Let me know when you hear from the blackmailer, and anything I can do to help—just ask."

"Right. G'bye."

"Bye and thanks again."

He sat there a moment just shaking his head. Of course he hadn't fooled Jake anymore than Jake had fooled him. The old bastard had probably figured out the bare bones of the situation, but he couldn't know how critical things really were. Jake knew about the Corse relations with the Palestinians and why they were necessary; what he didn't know was that the Quetta story could really blow old Frankie *and* the Corse out of the water. If that document was what he suspected it was, a million green was a bargain; in fact it was such a bargain that it was obvious the blackmailer didn't realize what he had. But then neither did Jake. In fact nobody but ole Frankie had all the facts, because only he knew about the plans of the half-breed bitch and her long-cocked gook lover.

To think he'd almost taken that bug out of her bedroom. She'd been clean as a whistle for four years, played it his way, done everything he'd asked. He'd almost felt guilty about bugging her place and listening to the tapes every couple days or so. But something told him to leave it in; after all, it had brought him one bonus that had been terrific. A year or so ago, he'd listened to the methodical and artful seduction of a young housemaid by Martine. He'd almost got his rocks off just running the tape while the sounds and whispers went from shocked refusal to willing and compliant participation. Then it had become a steady thing, and he'd tired of this aural voyeurism; he'd almost decided to "discover" it and end it, although it hadn't seemed to affect in any way Martine's servicing of him. In fact it might just have enhanced it a bit, but he got a better idea. He did pretend to discover their affair, but instead of punitive action, he simply ordered them to provide personal performances for him when he so desired. The bitch hadn't liked this at all, but she had no choice. And the maid—hell, if the bitch said "shit," she'd squat and strain like one of those fucking Russian dogs. It had ended a couple months ago when the girl ran off to another town and got married. He'd let her go. He was getting tired of that too, although at first he'd considered having her and her new husband killed just to tie down the loose end. He figured it was better this way anyhow. The little peasant had a fascinating body and Martine had taught her tricks you wouldn't believe. Hell, all he had to do was hint that he'd mail a few glossy prints to her new husband and she'd be on her back or knees, whatever he wanted, up in his bedroom. He'd relished the idea of having a backup whore whenever he needed her.

And then a month ago—bingo! He had hit the jackpot with his little bug. Mother of shit! He was so fucking mad the first night when he heard her moan and gasp and whimper for the gook's cock that he almost went down there and shot 'em both, but his good sense told him the gook was after something besides the bitch's pussy, so he hung in there and listened.

Good thing he had. In between having to listen to the love-sick Arab bitch tell the gook how wonderful he was and how she'd do anything for him—and from some of the sounds that came over the mike, she really meant it—he heard at first hand the details of a very clever plot aimed at ridding the world of one François Latellier! This bothered him, of course, but he knew how to handle this kind of thing. Shit! Better people than this gook had been trying to kill him for years. What really shook him up was the reason. There was no doubt in Latellier's mind that the story the gook told the bitch was a reference to Quetta. That was really bad. It had to be that treacherous son of a bitch Samir. Goddamn those soldiers for letting him get away. Samir must be feeling the pangs of remorse and so he's told somebody about Quetta. If the Palestinian leaders ever got a whiff of that from anybody they believed, scratch one Frankie Latellier. That one, even he couldn't handle.

Latellier shrugged resignedly. He knew he had to go along with the blackmail. In fact he had to pick it up himself wherever the crazy guy wanted—unless, of course, he choose the U.S. Anyway, whatever happened, this was one that Frankie Latellier had to handle himself, and handle it he would.

He'd called the bitch and told her to come up. Might as well have one more ride before he killed the pony. It was all set for tonight when she and the gook crawled into the sack. Vicente would seal the windows and then pump the carbon monoxide in through the heat vent. They'd be found, probably still hooked up like a couple dogs, in the morning, and the flics would find the faulty heat unit. Vicente would have stripped the tape off the windows long before, and of course, the flics would understand why Monsieur wished a hushed-up affair and a quick burial: after all, cuckolded by a gook! They'd understand.

A knock at the door. Martine came in. She was so lovely. What a waste! What a body. Once inside the door, she automatically reached up and began to unbutton her robe. It had always been the rule that she wore nothing while she was in the master suite. Naked, she stood by the door, head bowed slightly, obeisantly awaiting an indication of his desires. There was such a variety, she thought, so many nights, so many pictures—she was disgusted remembering the albums and blowups in that horrid room off his bedroom—so many debasements, so many rituals. He had to have the mind of the devil to think up all these things, but she had done them and taken his money in return. She disgusted herself. But soon, just a couple more days, and it would be over forever. Then she and

Khaled would become real people—married, babies. Oh God, let it be. Please let it be!

The degenerate old man just sat there in his chair looking hungrily at her body, then finally he opened his robe and gestured expressively with his head. Martine Vallin walked slowly to him, knelt, and slowly began the ministrations he had commanded.

17

The harried stewardess envied the handsome honeymoon couple from Milan relaxing in their wide, tipped-back chairs in the front section of the huge jet. The plane was passing over the lush, river-veined jungles of the Ganges delta at 40,000 feet. It was a spectacular scene in the gray light of early dawn, but the couple seemed interested only in each other. The girl, curled in her seat so that her head could rest on the man's shoulder, was the picture of connubial contentment. No one had told the stewardess they were honeymooners. No one had to. It was obvious from the way they looked at each other, the way the woman openly admired and twisted those gorgeous rings, and then too by the way they always seemed to find reasons for touching. They'd been on the flight since Geneva, where the stewardess got on, and they, too, were going to Hong Kong. Oh, they were friendly enough if you asked them a question, but mostly they seemed to want to talk to, look at, and fondle each other. The man was very dark and handsome in a classical Mediterranean way, but the girl was something else. With that long straight hair, black and shining, and that perfect complexion, and those fabulous chiseled features. She was much too beautiful.

The "honeymooners" stayed three days and nights in Hong Kong. It was endlessly bustling and fascinating, a fairyland of sea, sky, islands, and mountains, each vista more compelling and spectacular than the one before it, and they crammed action into each moment. It was a reluctant couple who dragged themselves back out to Kai Tak Airport the last morning to board the flight to Sydney.

Four days, two jet flights, and two feeder hops later, the couple arrived at the island. Their first view of it was eye-boggling. They came in from the southeast just before sunset, and it seemed to pop up suddenly on the horizon like a dark green emerald, gleaming and sparkling as the sun's flattened rays lit, shadowed, and bounced off the mountains and trees and sand. As they came closer they could see the town as it spread back into the jungle and along the lagoon from the harbor, picturesque but busy with people and various types of vehicles. They made their final approach over the lagoon and the bride was speechless as she looked down from several hundred feet and saw the multicolored coral sea bottom through the crystal clear water. She clutched the groom's arm in delight, and he smiled broadly at her. The airport looked adequate, but they could see why this last hop was handled by that two-engine piston plane of World War Two vintage. The packed crushed-coral strip looked tiny compared to the major airports they'd visited lately. They swished in over the trees, fast turning dark in the first moments of the short tropical dusk, and then bounded and rolled to a stop in front of the small wood and metal terminal. A small plaque over the main door said "Vera Ti."

There were only three other passengers on this final hop: a dour, fat Dutchman and his fat and ever-smiling wife, who said their name was Voors, and a young—twentyish, thirtyish, but how can you tell?—Chinese man. Voors said he sold heavy equipment, not further defined, to the plantations; the young Chinese—friendly, loquacious, personable—said he was returning from his studies in Hawaii to assist his uncle in the operation of the town's "best" hotel. His name was Sam Kee, and his English was excellent—he explained he'd lived ten years in Hawaii—and he insisted that his new Italian friends receive the best suite in the hotel at a reduced rate. The Italian couple also spoke excellent English, having lived in the States for several years with their respective parents and later for university schooling. Nobody seemed to think it was unusual that an obviously rich, newly married Italian couple were coming to Vera Ti for part of their honeymoon.

Dana Kelly, alias Signora Maria Vitali, alias several other names and nationalities, was lounging on a comfortably padded bamboo setee on the lanai of their "deluxe bungalow." Sam Kee had been as good as his word. The bungalows, set out along the white sand beach on either side of the hotel's main building, were positively luxurious, and theirs was undoubtedly the best, being larger and at the end of the row so that their lanai, bounded by the ocean and the shrubbery wall of the hotel, was like a private backyard patio. In fact, it was even better, since they stepped down from it to the soft white sand of their own private beach. Dana was luxuriating in the satin warmth of the tropical night, having showered and slipped on a light beach cover-up. The night was truly out of the travel folders—balmy, star-filled, with an almost full moon sending sparkling lasers thousands and thousands of miles down and across the water until they seemed to be aimed directly at her. The surf slapped gently at the sand a short stone's throw away, and the sound of soft music and the tinkle of glasses and dishes drifted over from the hotel dining room and lounge. There were even occasional giggles, musical and foreign, from the dark area back of the hotel where some of its servants were quartered. It was all fairy-tale stuff; but then, the whole trip had been so. She'd loved it. Every minute. And Pat really had been like a bridegroom: attentive, flattering, always there, always looking for ways to make the trip more pleasurable for her. He'd hardly left her side day or night. Well, of course, never at night! She smiled pensively, remembering.

They had left Morley's apartment casually, dressed as if they were going out for a very informal evening, but once in the elevator, everything had changed. He'd cut the power and let it sit between floors while he dumped a grocery sack's contents at their feet.

"Here, put these on."

"Good God, overalls. I see why you insisted on slacks. Oh well, I assume this change is necessary?"

"You'll see, love, the worst is yet to come. Now the cap."

"I look like a fugitive from a labor crew."

"That's the idea."

"I get it. You think somebody's watching for us to leave?"

"I *know* they are."

"And we're gonna walk past 'em like this?"

"Wrong. We're gonna drive past 'em like this."

"In a truck?"

"Right."

"Stolen?"

"Borrowed—or I guess rented's a better word. I greased a palm and there it was. I mean, there it better be."

Morley had taken a gray-black wig and mustache out of that seemingly bottomless bag, put them on, and restarted the elevator. Out a side door they went, into the building's maintenance garage and into a small truck. He handed her a pipe. "Here, keep this in your mouth—oh God, wipe the lipstick off—and pretend you're smoking it as we leave." He pulled out a fat cigar for himself and mouthed it.

"Trade ya."

"Just work on looking good with the pipe, love. The cigar'd make you sick."

"Wanta bet?"

"No. Now seriously, the next few minutes will be the most critical part of our trip, honey. Let's make it good."

Out through the drive and right on the highway. Nobody seemed to be following them as they moved north up the island, Morley watching closely in the rearview mirror. After a mile he pulled into the driveway leading to a nonsecurity high rise, made a turn through the porte cochere, then, shielded from the road, pulled into a parking area. He started to get out. "Short trip. Why'd we need the passport?" she said.

"Funny. C'mon move, lady, time for jokes later."

"Okay, okay."

Morley was already moving away, looking at parked cars. He called. "Here, this is it.

"That's what?"

"Our next steed, my dear." He was standing by a small light-colored car. He opened the hood, reached in, and came out with a set of keys. "Here, open her up, get in the back, take off that crazy outfit, and sit on the floor."

Dana did as she'd been directed while Morley got two small suitcases out of the truck bed where they'd been covered by a tarp. Then they were off again. She hadn't been able to follow their route for the next half hour but she knew without seeing that it had involved lots of stops and starts and turns and reverses. When he'd finally told her to crawl over and join him in the front seat, they were pulling into a turnpike toll-booth. "Okay Patrick, what the hell gives? Enough is enough. Backseat driver, maybe I *could* be; but back floor rider? Never. C'mon, give!"

He laughed. "You're cute when you're angry."

"Yeah? I'm not even angry yet, but I will be if one uncute bastard doesn't start leveling."

"Awright, awright. I told you somebody was watching. I didn't want them to follow us."

"That I figured out, pal. What I'm looking for is reason. Why so sudden? Why so secret? Who's watching? What horrible thing would happen if they did catch us? Those kinds of questions! How about some answers? Whether I like it or not"—her eyes softened—"and I do like it, I'm in this too, for keeps."

He reached for her hand, got it, squeezed it, and answered. "Okay, you're right. You are in it for keeps and you are entitled to the facts—those I have, anyway."

"Yeah?"

"Well, I learned from a friend in my hometown that a snooper was around looking at city hall records about me and it didn't take much of a genius to figure out who and why, or to figure I might be about ready to be grabbed."

"Grabbed? You're kidding."

"Wish I were, honey, but I mean it. I don't know, of course, but I sure wouldn't have bet against it."

"Hmm. I thought you were just doing some of that, you know, contingency planning, when you got all this passport stuff."

"Well, I was, really. Then I decided that this was a contingency."

"When you say 'grabbed', you mean 'grabbed'?"

"Exactly."

"And then what? What would they do?"

"Who knows? Maybe nothing, but then again, maybe something, in fact maybe something drastic."

"And your angry, cute associate—what about her?"

"I hope she'll always be my cute associate, angry or not."

"C'mon, c'mon."

"Well, I have never thought you were in danger, or I'd have played it very differently."

"Like leaving me back there?"

"Yeah. Like safe back there somewhere."

"So?"

"So this is the last chance to get off the Morley express to oblivion. You stay on, and you go all the way."

She had giggled in spite of herself, never one to miss a potential double entendre. "My dear, whatever made you think I'd 'go all the way.'"

He patted a tender part and said, "Oh I dunno, just a feeling I had."

"Watch the road, buster."

"Yes, ma'am."

"Go on."

"Yes, ma'am. I suppose you want the 'who'?"

"You suppose right."

"Well I suppose it's gotta be Conners and company."

"I figured that, too, but the 'why' still doesn't make much sense to me. I mean why do they insist you're their boy, while you tell me they're wrong? I still don't get it."

"I can't answer that, love. I mean I would if I knew, but I just don't know. But this I do know—I once helped a guy out and it got a bit more complicated than I'd bargained for. Then Conners's guys came into the act. I think they assumed I was more involved than I was, but as I said before, I really don't blame them for making that assumption."

"And as I said before, your story is confusing, and, I suspect, intentionally so."

"I just don't want to overly worry you, love."

"Sure. Sure. I understand." Her raised eyebrows belied the statement, but Morley was minding his driving and didn't appear to notice. She went on, this time in a lighter vein. "And what now?"

"Well, we'll turn in this car at Orlando, and—"

"Yeah, this car. Where'd it come from?"

"I arranged to have it waiting there—at that condo."

"You arranged?"

"Yeah, thought we might need it."

"Okay, go on." She was shaking her head in amused bewilderment.

"We'll take a plane from Orlando to Atlanta, then to L.A., over the pole to London, and points east."

"Now you're starting to sound like fun. That's all?"

"Not quite. I still want to confuse anybody who follows us, asking questions at airline counters and so forth."

"So?"

"So I want you to wear a little disguise, and we'll take separate flights from Orlando to Atlanta. Then we'll meet in Atlanta and change disguises and identities for the rest of our trip."

"Disguises? To go with those funny passports you got from Mr. Alvera."

"Bingo!"

"And when does this start?"

"Before we split up at Orlando."

"Sure we'll unsplit at Atlanta?"

"Never been surer, my love."

And it had worked just that way. She went to Atlanta as Helen Benson of Winter Haven, an attractive but mousy-looking woman with her hair in a severe dark bun. In a ladies' room at the Atlanta airport she became Senorita Delores Madillo, a very Latin and attractive young lady from Bogota, Columbia. She met her "father", Senor Madillo, at the Delta information desk as arranged, and the two boarded a flight for Los Angeles. The Senor spent the early part of that hop briefing the Senorita on her cover story. She was an apt pupil. Overnight in a motel near the L.A. airport, and then on to London. The Madillos had two fun-filled days and nights covering all or most of the sights, smells, and sensations of London town, then on to Geneva.

Switzerland had fascinated her from the air, with its white-tipped Alps and its valleys and picturesque chalets and it was even better close up. They breezed through the customs and immigration formalities, and then as she'd been instructed by Pat, she'd gone into the women's room and changed identity. A new wig, this one a modern, long, straight fall of black, her own eyebrows again, heavy eye shadow, and a small foam rubber pad high inside each cheek, and she'd become Maria Vitali, the distaff side of a young Italian honeymoon couple. She joined her "bridegroom," handsome Pasquale Vitali, in the waiting area. Pasquale was about the same height and weight as Senor Madillo, though he *appeared* a bit taller and more slender but it was the face that was so different. His hair was coal black and cut full like the sideburns. The pencil-thin mustache also made a difference, but Dana couldn't put her finger on what it was that really swung the change. She guessed maybe it was his whole personality. He acted, as well as looked, like a rich, young Italian honeymooner.

Again they had all the necessary documentation, complete with "evidence" of a honeymoon ski week at a Swiss resort. Dana was finally impressed as well as amused by the "Mickey Mouse" routine of documents, disguises, and such. Had she been more knowledgeable, she'd have been amazed as well. The passports with all the visas were truly works of art. The ID was just as good.

Shortly after they'd settled into their suite in a Geneva hotel Pat took all the Madillo disguise and documentation materials and went out to dispose of them. He was gone about an hour, returning with his small briefcase and a large smile. She'd spent the intervening time profitably by washing her real hair and then perfecting her Vitali disguise in front of the mirror, but mostly by looking, awestruck, at the view from the windows of their sitting room: the Rhone bubbling and rushing far below as it spilled from the magnificent lake and rushed enroute to its destiny in France against the background of medieval roofs and chimneys of the old town. She was disappointed when he said they'd have to leave the next day, but he explained that Switzerland was the most critical stop on their journey, because if he'd had the materials Conners's people thought he had, it would be logical that he'd have used a Swiss bank for a hiding place, so they'd have their best troops watching here. She wasn't sure she understood, but she agreed anyway. They went on another shopping spree, and when they got back she ripped out a number of the new clothes' labels and replaced them with labels from Milan and Rome that had appeared miraculously, along with a small sewing kit, out of Pat's cornucopian briefcase. Next morning the airport formalities went without a hitch and they were off for the Orient.

And so here she was in paradise, the lady from Ventura, luxuriating on a beachfront lanai on her own South Pacific island. She stretched langorously, smiling to herself. Yeah, a gal could sure get used to this life. At least from the little she'd seen of it, she assumed she could.

Inside the cottage, Morley was standing under the needles of a cool shower. Strangely enough, he too was recalling the excitement and the pleasures of their long journey to Vera Ti. He guessed maybe he'd been the happiest in Geneva—for two reasons. He and Dana had both passed their tests!

He'd left her that first morning at the hotel and gone to see Lt. Jean Benet at a nearby unmarked government office. He told the receptionist who he was and was immediately led into the Lieutenant's office. He was a severe but good-looking blond man in his late thirties, and he stood to greet Morley. "Signor Vitali, it is indeed a pleasure." His Italian was very good, although heavily French accented.

"It is my pleasure, Signor. Very kind of you to assist me."

Benet's severe look slipped slightly as his eyes showed a trace of humor. "But of course, Signor, a good friend of Colonel Stehrli is, how you say, a good friend of mine."

"Both you and the Colonel are too kind."

"It is nothing, Signor." Then, the French amenities dispensed with, he had become all business. "The hotel switchboard and the floor concierge are in the charge of two of my trusted men, and I have arranged for the coverage you requested at the airport tomorrow."

"Excellent! And most appreciated."

"My pleasure, Signor. When you return to your hotel please contact M. Delon at the service desk on your floor. He will be expecting you, and he will give a report in full." He picked up the phone, speaking quickly in French, and shortly there was a knock on the door and two nicely dressed young men entered.

Benet stood for the introductions, which he conducted in French, not even raising his eyebrows as Morley responded in his near-perfect Parisian accent. The young men left and Benet switched back politely to Italian. "They will be available as you wish, Signor, from two hours before your departure time, at the airport. And now, if there is anything else, anything at all, Signor, that I can do to make your stay in our city more pleasant, I am at your service. And, oh yes, here is the package Colonel Stehrli asked me to give you."

"You have been most kind, sir. There is nothing else. I am most grateful for your generous assistance."

They had shaken hands and Morley left. He walked down the street still marveling at the ease and efficiency with which Willi had arranged things and chuckling at the savoir faire with which Lieutenant Benet had discussed with the Signor the arrangements for surveillance of the latter's bride. Those French! Even the Swiss version! And so he had returned to his "bride" an hour later, euphoric in the knowledge that she had made no attempt to contact anyone in person, by phone, or by mail, and that no one had contacted her either. He had silently begged her forgiveness, but had known it was a precaution he'd had to take. Switzerland was indeed the critical point in the journey.

If he'd had any doubt of this, it would have been dispelled the next day at the airport. Some half hour before they left he'd spotted the well-dressed but tough-looking dark man who was so intently inspecting each of the passengers in the departure lounge. He had a magazine in one hand, and every so often he'd open it and look inside for a moment before resuming his scrutiny. He'd looked long and hard at the Vitalis, especially the woman, twice sneaking additional looks at whatever was in that magazine.

Eventually, he seemed satisfied and resumed his inspection of the other passengers. Morley had signaled with his head and eyes to the two young men he'd met the day before at Benet's office. It had been unnecessary; they'd already zeroed in on the dark man and were moving closer as he left, apparently to visit another departure area. From then on, it had been a breeze.

Morley came out onto the lanai, hair still wet, clad in a pair of white duck shorts. He walked to the edge of the porch, took a long look at the gorgeous tropical scene, then turned. He murmured, almost as if he were thinking aloud. "Beautiful. Spectacular."

"You called?"

"Hmmm. Yes, you too, Signora. Not too modest, but definitely beautiful. And focusing exaggeratedly on the sparsely covered area of her bust, he continued "Yes, and the view, definitely spectacular." He took a cushion from the end of the lounge, put it on the floor next to her, and sat on it, his arm resting lightly on the curve of lounge next to her thighs. "You are superb, my love. The magnificence of the night is only backdrop for your loveliness."

"Shakespeare?"

"I just made it up, honest."

"Boolsheeta, Pasquale. You may have made it up but you're not honest. Not to worry, I love it anyway."

She moved around to touch his bare shoulders with her fingers and began a slow, rythmic kneading that was at once soothing, relaxing, and exciting. He purred with contentment as the kneading deepened down his chest and back and then became a series of light caresses. She interrupted his silent enjoyment but maintained the action. "Now we can have fun, on our island?"

"For sure! But you mean it hasn't been fun?"

She bent to kiss his warm shoulder. "I didn't mean that. You know I've had more fun, and been happier, than ever before in my life, since I've been with you. You know that."

"I know. Me too. Yes, we can have some island fun now, anything we want to do. It's our island."

"You Robinson, me Friday."

"You don't look like Friday."

"What does Friday look like?"

"Oh like mostly sunny, with a thirty percent chance of afternoon showers. You know, the usual thing."

"I asked for that."

"Indeed you did, sweetheart." He moved his face to the

opening of the cover-up and nuzzled the soft tan satin of her hip. She held his head tightly to her body for a moment, then relaxed her hand. "Can we talk?" Then smiling, "First?" She started that slow caress down his back again.

He pulled back, returning her smile. "Sure. Long as it's just first."

"How long can we stay on our island?"

"How long do you want to? A week? A month? Who knows? Maybe you won't like it. Maybe you'll love it and go native and want to stay forever."

"You mean it'll be up to me?"

"Basically, yes, honey."

"Basically?"

"Well you know—mice and men's plans and all that. But I don't really see why not."

"How about you? What do you want?"

Morley took her hand from his shoulder, kissed it, and held it. "Honest to God, sweetheart, I want you to be happy."

"Oh, Pat, I am. I really am. But I'm concerned about our future, too."

"Why, honey?"

"Woman reasons I guess. You know. Are we always gonna be just two lovers on vacation? Hold it, I'm not knocking it, it's wonderful, but as you said, we do have to have some kind of plans. Don't we?"

"Of course we do. I agree. I just thought we could defer them while we enjoyed the vacation."

"Yes, I know things are still unsettled, and I'd be much too stupid for you if I wasn't able to figure out why, but what about long range? Are we gonna live here? Are we gonna work, or just play all the time? Are we gonna be Pasquale and Maria for the rest of our lives? That kinda stuff. That's what I mean. Guess I just want to be clued in on what's in store for us. Guess I mean for *me*, to be honest."

"Fair enough. God knows I owe you that, for openers. I owe you any answer you want to anything, really, but some of 'em I just can't figure yet. But, okay, to start. We have enough dough—I know that has to concern you too—to last us a couple years full blast, and maybe twice that, skimping a bit."

"Your inheritance?"

"Yeah, and some investments that may or may not pan out. But I don't think we should play until all that runs out. No. It's a question of what we want to do and where we want to do it."

"Okay, I agree, but money was a minor concern. We can always *earn* that when we need it. I guess I'm more interested in the personal side."

"Marriage, love, kids, home, business, all that?"

"Something like that."

"That's easy. I love you. I don't ever want to leave you. I *will* marry you tomorrow, next week, whenever or wherever you say yes and want to. I want the kids and home, long as they're our kids and our home, and most of all I want you to be happy—with me. What we decide to do with our lives and where we decide to do it? To me these are secondary. First, is that we do it together."

She didn't say anything. She was looking out towards the sea and her face was in profile. A tear made a rivulet down her cheek and dropped noiselessly. Morley leaned over and kissed the wet spot at the corner of her eye. She clutched him and held on tightly for a moment. When she relaxed he pulled away to look at her. Both cheeks were wet now, but she was smiling widely and it was like a rainbow shining through the last vestige of a spring shower. "Thanks. I needed that."

"That's all?"

"No, darling, that's not all by any means." She poked him gently with her balled fist, then loosed it to caress his cheek. "That was the sweetest speech I've ever heard. I'm not a speech maker, so I'll steal your words. I love you so much it hurts. I love these rings." She held up her left hand. "And I love what they mean. I want them to be real. I mean, to be mine for keeps. I want to be your wife, and have our kids, and live with you and be with you, so I guess I don't really care where it is or what we do to get along. I know we have to wait a while, to get our 'Italian divorce.' I don't even care what our names are—as long as they mean Mr. and Mrs."

Morley leaned back, smiling widely. "Wow! For a non-speech maker, lady, you make one hell of a speech."

She returned his smile, then got serious. She cupped her hand under his chin and moved his face so she could look directly into his eyes. "One more thing, Pat. Is there some reason why we can't go back to the States or can't ever use our real names?"

He was thoughtful. "No, not if you mean 'ever.' We have to stay here a while, Italian style, until I get this business with Conners's people taken care of, but then, after that, no problem.

"This 'Conners business,' when will it be over?"

"By the end of this month, I hope."

"And there *is* a lot of money involved?"

"You know there is."

"Oh God, Pat, not that again! Please! Please!"

"Okay, I didn't mean it that way, honey. You're my life and I'd trust you with it."

"Enough to level?"

"Yes, as far as I can. I mean, whatever I know."

"Okay, what's the money?"

"Ever hear of the Corporation?"

"Not really. Like the Mafia?"

"Sort of, but not. An outgrowth, but basically the modern-day version of organized crime. A meld of legit and illegit business."

"Yeah. I see. And they think you have something of theirs?"

"Yes, honey, and I do." There, it was out, finally. He was relieved.

She just looked, unsmiling, as if she'd always known. "And Conners? He really is their man?"

"One of their best."

"And Matthewson? He was too? Like you said?"

"Exactly, honey, like I said."

"And they want their stuff, whatever it is, back?"

"Of course."

"Can you give it to them?"

"Yes, I intend to. For a price, and soon."

"What then?"

"I hope, peace and quiet."

"How and why'd you get this, this stuff, in the first place?"

"That's a long complicated story, darling. I guess I could sum it up by saying I was in the right place at the wrong time and got greedy, but now I've learned my lesson."

"Conners's story to me was completely phony?"

"Of course, as you suspected from the start."

"I guess I did really know it all along. Guess I was able to stifle my conscience pretty easily with the prospect of an all-expense trip to Florida."

"Don't blame you."

"Honest?"

"Honest."

"How about you, Patrick Morley? You're no travel agent, are you? Never have been. Right?"

He looked at her squarely and said with a half smile, "No more than you're Dana Kelly, my love!"

She was magnificent. No shock was evident, but she hardly moved, maybe even a bit of humor showed around the eyes, mixed with relief. "You know! You always knew, didn't you?"

"Not always, honey. Not 'til I got a picture of Miss California."

"You cad, I was just a child then. Why'd you suspect?"

"I didn't really, but I knew something was out of kilter. Then when I saw the picture I knew what it was. Hell, everything I'd learned about the lovely Miss Mornay fit *you;* everything I'd learned about the Kelly girl didn't."

"You didn't care? And you knew before we left Florida?"

"Oh, I cared all right, but I thought I understood. After all, I'd held out a few things on you too, but it didn't mean I was playing you along. What's in a name? I was in love and I believed you'd been honest with me in all the important things. Right?"

"Oh God yes, Pat! Yes! Yes!"

"So why fret, huh?"

"You're quite a guy, Patrick Morley."

"Well, you're quite a girl, Angela Mornay!"

"My friends call me Ann."

"I'm included?"

"Numero uno, paison."

"Tell me, honey, was the name change your idea?"

"Oh, no. Conners said it would be best to do it that way since Morrison might get somebody to check back on me in Chicago."

"Yeah. And so?"

"And so they'd find no connection between Dana and the brokerage business. With me they would have."

"And the same about a connection with Conners?"

She lowered her eyes, but almost immediately snapped them back up proudly. "Yes, that's true. I did date him and I did like him. He's a *very* nice gentleman. But, I wasn't his 'girl,' and I didn't love him."

"I'm sorry, honey, I didn't mean that."

"It's okay. It's time to clear the air, let's clear it."

"And Dana, the real one?"

"Conners's company gave her plane fare to L.A. and two weeks pay to keep her out of Chicago."

"What did she think *that* was all about?"

"She really didn't care. I told her it was in connection with an investigation job that Conners's and my firm were cooperating on. She did it happily, for me and for the free trip home."

"What's your connection with Dana?"

"We're first cousins. Our mothers are sisters. I'm sure you noticed the family resemblance."

"Yeah, I sure did, and it almost threw me for a minute. Might have even fooled a casual friend."

"Yes, we've done that on occasion."

"So she came to Chicago because of you?"

"Sure. She was like a younger sister. We grew up three blocks apart in Ventura. I had a younger brother but no sisters—she filled the gap."

"And the aunt in Racine? She's yours too?"

"Right, she's the third Magnelli sister. All of them married Northern European types, ending a long line of thoroughbred spaghetti benders."

"I like the half-breeds best."

"A man of good taste."

"Do you know where Dana is now?"

"Of course not. How would I? I suppose she's back in Chicago. What do you mean, is she okay?" She was really alarmed.

"No, honey, there's nothing wrong. Last I heard she had not yet returned to Chicago."

"Oh, she probably stayed on in Ventura past the two or three weeks they paid her for. Don't you think?"

"I'm sure that's it. Say, sweetheart, since you're not Dana Kelly, what about all that 'Dana Kelly background' you gave me, marriage and all that."

"Would it matter?" She was dead serious.

"Not a bit. Forget it." So was he.

She smiled in relief and reached again for his shoulders.

"No. You deserve it. The background was me—true—I just changed the names to protect the innocent."

"The whole thing?"

"Yeah. The whole thing. It was my father who died and my mother who married again and me who got widowed in Vietnam and all that."

"And Dana?"

"She did get married and quit UCLA, but her husband, he was the Ventura high school athlete, was killed in a car accident, drag racing, and that's when she came to Racine and then Chicago."

"And you? Mornay?"

"Mornay's my maiden name. I married Chuck Talley, a man from San Francisco, in my sophomore year at USC, and he did go to Vietnam and he was killed. I was devastated. I loved him very deeply, but I knew I had to go on, and I knew I had to do it on my own. So I got the dancing job and continued and finished at USC. I took my maiden name back since it was more acceptable to be Angela Mornay than Mrs. Chuck Talley in the business world those days."

"And your family?"

"They're still in Ventura, except my brother Joey. He's a successful young attorney in San Diego. A great kid. You'll love him."

"He like you?"

"People say we'd be twins if I were his age."

"Then I'd love him for sure. Your parents?"

"Friendly but cool. My stepfather is about thirty degrees to the right of Attila the Hun. He thinks John Birch was a radical. We never did see eye to eye, but I guess it was that 'Miss California' thing that really blew it."

"Why?"

"Oh, I was only seventeen at the time, lied about my age, and did it as sort of a lark. It grew out of a thing we had at high school, a mock beauty pageant. Anyway I won, and the story of my age came out and it was in the papers, and Albert F. Mornay, Esquire, president of the First National Bank, the Rotary, and I don't know what all, was fit to be tied. He told me I'd disgraced the family, but he never explained just how, so I resented that and moved out when I started college. Stayed in the dorm and didn't even visit home 'til my sophomore year. Then when I got married, Albert, Esquire, was sure I was pregnant and about to disgrace the family again, so he practically disowned me, without a trial."

"You weren't?"

"What?"

"Pregnant."

"Yeah, I had triplets—girls—who grew up and became the Andrews sisters. Surely you've heard of them? No, damn it, I wasn't. Chuck wasn't the type. He was old-fashioned too, but a sweet, sweet man. You've had loved him too."

"That I doubt, but go on."

"That's about it. I got a job with an L.A. firm, got transferred to St. Louis, which I loved, and then Chicago, which I didn't. I met Dennis Conners at several business functions before I ever dated him, but I never ran a Dun and Bradstreet on his company. Guess I should have."

"But how'd he select you for the Florida job?"

"Oh, I guess I led into that. We'd discussed jobs and places, and he knew I was getting bored with my job and with the prospects for advancement. Let's face it, account executives who make their vests stick out and fill the round places in their slacks have a tough time advancing. And he knew I hated cold, cold Chicago. So he'd told me before that his company did a bit of business that required travel, sometimes foreign travel, and he'd investigate the possibility of getting me a shot at it. This Florida thing was kind of a trial, and of course I jumped at the chance, as he knew I would, and didn't ask too many questions, as he knew I wouldn't."

"So what's a nice young girl from Ventura doing on a South Sea island?"

"Loving it." She looked serious again. "Then I'm forgiven?"

"What's to forgive?"

"I mean the lies. I got in so deep, then when I decided I loved you for real and didn't want to lose you, I was afraid to tell you the truth. Afraid you'd boot me out."

"I know how you felt."

"Your secret?"

"Yeah. You've always known too?"

"Not always. In fact I still don't really know 'what.' I guess I only know 'why.'"

"Uh-huh. Y'mean I couldn't be as dumb as I sounded."

"Remember—you said that! But it's close. Yeah. You weren't going to all that trouble for peanuts or because some brokerage outfit was sizing you up for a pitch. Then I got to thinking about Conners and Matthewson, and Matthewson getting blown up, and it all started to make sense—except for you. You didn't make sense, and neither did your story. I could easily cast them as heavies, but I loved you by then, and I couldn't fit you in that mold, emotionally or any other way."

"You sure you're not just prejudiced?"

"Of course I'm prejudiced, but I know you—God, how I know you, Pat Morley—and it just isn't your bag. But you don't have to tell me anything now. Some day, when you're ready. But you decide."

"There's not really much to tell. You've figured it out, most of it, already. It's really much simpler than it appears at first glance. Imagine a lazy, peace lovin' beach bum, sliding along trying to decide where to go with his life. He meets a pleasant and interesting old man, and then the old man asks him to do a favor for him. That favor leads to another and he's in deeper, into something he knows isn't kosher but he's hooked. He was bored and now he's got some kicks and it isn't hurting anybody. So the old guy gets himself killed and the beach bum figures the hoods who did it want some things that belonged to the old man as well as to them. Now the beach bum—"

She interrupted. "I resent that, let's call him 'B.B.' for short."

"Okay. So B.B. takes a chance. He collects all these materials and he sits tight waiting to see what will happen while he makes some tentative plans to blow if things get too warm. Then the plot thickens. Comes the love interest. She's a lot like B.B.; we'll call her, say, L.L. Now L.L.—"

"Wait a minute, What's L.L.? 'Lithsome Lulu?'"

"No. she's 'Lust for Life.' She's like B.B., as I said. She's bored and doesn't look too closely at a proposed adventure that appears anything but boring."

"Okay. Go on."

"Well, B.B. gets a brilliant idea. Why not give the hoods the materials they want, the ones that really belong to the old man they killed, who doesn't have any family, and charge them for his services, say, about the same amount as the money of theirs he already has?"

"And why not? Did he do this?"

"Yes, but first he decided things were getting a little too hot and he'd better skip town, with L.L. of course, and give everybody a cooling off period."

"Did L.L. cool off?"

"Thank God, no."

"Okay. And then?"

"B.B. proposed the exchange and they agreed to go along."

"When?"

"Not set yet. I'd guess about a month."

"And then?"

"Then B.B. and L.L. go in peace, never to fight again with the heavies."

"You really believe B.B. can swing it?"

"Yes. B.B. has a couple aces up his ying yang that provide a kind of life insurance these guys understand. Still, it's a little dicey."

"What about little L.L? Do they know she's with B.B.?"

"Oh sure, they figure she has to be. They may even figure she's waiting for her big moment to help."

"They're wrong! B.B. knows that, doesn't he?"

"Of course he does."

"So meanwhile?"

"Meanwhile B.B. and L.L. live it up and make love and things like that."

"Does the story have a happy ending?"

"Of course. All stories do."

"Can L.L. help B.B. in any way?"

"She is, already, just being with him. But on the deal with the heavies? No. No way. B.B. wants her to stay out of sight. Hopefully the heavies won't know exactly where to look or have time to hunt. If she stays low profile they won't see her. He hopes."

"So no more secrets."

"Not really."

"What's that mean?"

"There are a few details, but better you don't know them. On my honor they in no way affect you and me, our relationship."

"Okay. And what is our relationship?"

"Why Signora, look at your finger."

"Oh yes, Signor, my rings. I sometimes forget." Then she stopped to look more closely. She got serious. "They are beautiful, Pat. I just love 'em. I wish they were for real. I mean for me, and that they meant what they should. Oh, crap, you know what I mean. I'm repeating myself."

"Honey, those are yours, honest. You earned them putting up with me. And if you're good, I'll get you another set, bigger and better, that says Ann and Pat instead of those crazy names."

"I'll be good. Try me." Her eyes were large, unblinking dark pools as she sat up and the flimsy cover-up fell back on both sides. Morley got that old tingly feeling and felt his heart begin to race as his eyes traveled down the smooth, unrestrained satin of the beautiful body he knew so well. She reached for his head, pulling his face toward hers, and said in her soft throaty voice, "And now, my love, where were we before I so rudely interrupted?" Soft sighs of pleasure blended with the muted rustle and slap of the night surf and the gentle whirring of palm fronds outside the lanai. Soon there were no other sounds in the world. Just those.

18

The island was everything they'd dreamed it would be—and more. Days slipped by in a montage of sea, sky, sand, surf, jungle, and mountains. They stayed at the hotel for almost two weeks, letting Sam Kee's very fat and very talented chef try to shape them in his physical image, fighting back with calorie-burning romps on the hotel's superb beach and its king-sized bed. Morley made a number of moves during this period. He bought a thirty-nine-foot Australian-made ketch with luxurious fittings and an oversized, overpowerful inboard engine. He arranged the rental, for sixty days, of a small copra and vanilla plantation about ten miles from town, with a lovely, reasonably modern main villa and its own stretch of beach. *And* he sent that letter to Conners. Dana, Angela, Maria—he had compromised by calling her "honey"—was ecstatic about the boat, excited about the plantation, and excluded from any specific knowledge of the letter.

The boat was an integral part of the plan Morley had formulated over the past weeks; in addition, it was the most fabulous toy he'd ever had. Dana/Angela loved it more than he did. He introduced her to deep-sea fishing, skin diving along the reefs, "sailmanship," and she ate it up, every minute. The plantation, too, was part of his plan. It had been arranged by his ubiquitous friend, Sam Kee, who had learned that the French planter-owner was returning to France for three or four months and wanted someone to live there while he was gone. The rent was less than nominal.

The letter was delivered to Conners nine days after it was mailed, on the fourth of April. Unknown to the addressee, it had been mailed originally to an address in Zurich, where Willi had removed the outer envelope and posted the inner one, unopened, to the States. Conners noted the Swiss posting, but his preoccupation with the contents soon overwhelmed that as a matter of interest. He called Mr. Henry, and as expected, Mr. Henry suggested he fly in from Chicago "tomorrow."

This time Conners arrived in mid morning. He'd spent the previous afternoon at a Chicago library, and the evening thinking, and he felt he was as ready as he'd ever be for his big chance. This time they had coffee in the old man's study. It was a miserably wet, gloomy day, and the "terrace" looked uninviting. Again the old man read with agonizing slowness, and again Conners sat nervously and watched. Again he remembered the letter's every line. It was dated March 26 and it read:

Mr. Conners:

I trust that you and your principals have had sufficient time for reflection and have found my proposal reasonable. I am sure that M. Latellier shares your view. Regarding the redemption of your materials, I must insist that you accept the procedures below.

On the 25th of April at four P.M. you and M. Latellier will be in the main cocktail lounge of the Maeva Hotel, Papeete, Tahiti, French Polynesia. You will be allowed to bring to Tahiti and to have present at this meeting one other person of your choosing—a total of three. My representative will meet you there shortly after four P.M. I have decided that M. Latellier must be there in person. It is not that I do not trust you to act as his agent, but for my own protection I must be assured that he is personally convinced of the authenticity of the material he receives and that there is no misunderstanding between us as to what has taken place. The third party on your "team" will serve exactly the same function vis-à-vis Mr. Henry.

You will understand, I am sure, the need for me to have prepared an insurance policy. It is very simple: the last existing copies of all these documents—both yours and M. Latellier's—are at the moment sealed and safe in the hands of a friend. If I make a coded phone call on the 25th of May these copies will be destroyed unopened by incineration; if I do not make this call they will be mailed on the 26th of May to interested and very powerful parties. I am as anxious as you are to avoid the latter contingency. The existence of these copies should neither surprise nor alarm you. I like life, and I realize its continuation will be dependent upon my keeping my part of our bargain. After all, I do have the money already, and am asking nothing additional for the return of the books—the ownership of which is a moot question—simply to assure that we can go our separate ways in peace.

One last requirement. I must insist that you and your party arrive in Tahiti no earlier than the 24th of April and leave as soon as possible after the exchange on the 25th. I will consider any breach of this requirement a breach of our agreement and act accordingly. The same is true for the three-person limit of your party.

I will look forward to seeing you on the 25th.

Ciao. Santa

Mr. Henry finally put the letter down. He just sat there for a while, apparently deep in thought, tapping his fingers on the leather arm of his chair. After a time, he turned to face Conners. His eyes were hard, as hard as Conners had ever seen them. "Our friend, this Santa man, is worse than a smart-ass. I don't think I like him even a little bit." Then he relaxed his face into a near smile. "But you have a final proposal to take care of that for me, do you not, Dennis?"

"Yes, sir, I do. I have a basic plan but I need some more details, local things, to fill it in. Things I can't get until I arrive in Tahiti—assuming, sir, that you agree I should go."

"Oh, yes, Dennis, you must go. We have no choice. We must have those books and I see no way of getting them other than playing this Santa man's game. You *must* go!"

"Exactly my idea, sir. We must *appear* to be playing Santa's game until the final moment."

"Now after this final moment, Dennis. What about this 'insurance policy' business?"

"Frankly sir, I don't believe him. I mean the 'insurance policy' business I believe is a bluff."

"That's a rather significant point. Why do you think so?"

"I think there's no logical place for Santa to send those documents. Not us, not the Corse, not the U.S. government, not the French government, surely not the Palestinians. So where?"

"Hmmm. Interesting. But why not Washington?"

"Sir, Santa is a fugitive in every sense of the word. Why should he make things worse and just get more people looking for him, with no extra monetary gain? And why banish himself from the States forever, at least *with* all that money. Remember, sir, we have concluded his motivation has to be greed. There isn't any other motive or plan of action for him that makes sense."

"You should have finished the law school, Dennis, you have a persuasive tongue. I am convinced. So what can we do?"

"I need two men. I have them selected, subject to your approval."

"Who are they?"

"The Professor and a young fellow from Los Angeles named Lee Alakaua."

"The Samoan kid."

"Yes sir."

"And the Professor?"

"Yes, I have definite reasons for wanting both of them."

"I'm beginning to get the drift. I think I like it. So you'll be going into Tahiti early, too." The old man nodded knowingly. "Of course, if this Santa man is bluffing on the big matter he's also bluffing on the small ones."

"Exactly, sir."

"And why did he choose this place, this Tahiti? So far away."

"Several reasons I can think of. It's out of our bailiwick, unfamiliar territory to us but not to him. He's part of the scene there by now. I assume he's living around there somewhere, though probably not right on Tahiti—somewhere he can control better."

The old man interrupted. "What about the girl? Nothing? She could tell us."

"That's another reason for thinking he's off on some smaller island. You see, she hasn't been able to get word out to us. I'm sure that too was part of his scheme: he's neutralized our operator by cutting off her communications."

"Have you heard from her at all?"

"No sir." Conners hesitated a fraction of a moment, then went on. "But that was the arrangement. She was not to risk anything enroute. Now she can't do anything about it."

"You think she's still with us?"

Conners spoke quickly and convincingly. "I'm sure of it, sir, but I'm not sure it'll do us any good. I think Santa is on to her."

"What will you do with her?"

"Bring her back."

"Okay. That'll be interesting. So you and the Professor and the Samoan will arrive early."

"Yes sir, and we'll make our final plans. Then I'll slip out to 'arrive' with Latellier and the third man."

"I've decided to send Savilli."

"Fine. We'll arrive together—that is, the same day, different planes, and make the meeting."

"Frankie hasn't said he'd come yet."

"He will, sir. He has to, to get his papers. And now Santa has removed the last stumbling block. You see, Tahiti is French territory, and you can get there from France without ever touching U.S. territory, so Latellier should have no problem. Even if they knew he was coming, which I can't imagine, the U.S. officials couldn't do anything about it on foreign territory. The British or Australians, or Mexicans, whatever, are not going to antagonize the French by arresting or detaining a French citizen in transit because the U.S. may or may not want to extradite him. Latellier has to come, and now he can do it safely. I suppose, sir, that that is one of the principal reasons Santa selected Tahiti."

"You've done your homework, Dennis. Yes, I see. And now, about that plan to relieve me of all this trouble?"

Conners smiled quickly, then began a surprisingly detailed recital of his proposal for the final hours in the life of St. Patrick Morley.

19

The rainy season with its sudden torrential downpours, its steamy respites, and its drippingly humid days, had all but passed. The flora on their little island was an eye-bombarding gamut of bright colors, complemented and softened but never overpowered by the ever-present shadings of green. At the moment, the white sand and the aquamarine water contrasted with the naked brown woman standing at the edge of the surf.

Morley watched as he always did, tirelessly, while she poked at something in the water with a thin driftwood stick. She looked like a native. Her black hair had grown longer and all these days of the beach had given her a deep golden tan all over, unmarred any longer by the lighter shadings of the bikini she had eschewed after the first couple of days. She'd even developed a walk a bit like that of the native girls, with that uniquely Polynesian stride—erect, proud, fluid, and yet very saucily feminine.

The plantation was comfortable and always interesting, even if there was no work to do at this time of year, when the place practically ran itself. And there were so many fascinating, exotic, and exciting nonwork things to do that there never seemed to be enough time as the days melted one into the next. They had boated, in the big one, in canoes, in outriggers, and in an ancient motorboat belonging to the plantation. They had fished, day, night, with lines, with spears, with traps, and with nets. They had explored—jungles, rivers, mountains, shores, lagoons, and reefs. They had swum in pools fed by waterfalls; climbed partway up green, then jagged, volcanic peaks; and visited native villages so remote and untouched that *they* became the curiosity. But most of all, they had talked and laughed and enjoyed being together.

He looked at her standing there, surf lapping at her knees, queen of a South Sea island in every sense of the word. He watched as she walked slowly toward him, scuffing the sand with her heels as she moved. She'd stayed so slender, and he thought to himself, "she'll always be that way," and then the word "always" caught in his throat. This was their last swim together before he left for Papeete and his rendezvous with the Corporation. Whether he'd return to her or not depended on whether or not he'd guessed right on one hell of a lot of important points and on how badly they wanted to kill him. In any event he was worried about her. He didn't think they'd really bother with her, and he'd made a number of arrangements to provide for her if he *had* guessed wrong; nevertheless, he was worried for her. "For" was a much better word; he'd long ago quit worrying "about" her.

She sat down next to him on the grass beach mat, droplets of water still sparkling on her skin. She turned to face him. The face was sad, and he knew what was coming.

"Don't go! We don't need that damn money," she said. "Just send it to them. I don't trust those people at all. Just stay here with me—we'll never let strangers on our island. Never!" Her cheeks were wet with more than seawater now, belying the smile she was trying to manage.

Morley put his arm around the brown shoulders, drawing her closer, then kissed the line of her brow. "I know, sweetheart, but it's too late. I passed that corner a long time ago and there's no reverse in the wagon. I only wish I hadn't got you into it."

"Don't say that. I'm here because I want to be here. I got

myself into it, and I've got no regrets. I met you, I love you, I want to be with you—always. It's that simple."

"I know. I know. But like you say, I don't trust these people either. I'd be happier if you were sitting in Sydney under a phony name."

"Instead of Vera Ti under a phony name?"

"Yeah. I guess." He laughed, and this time she was able to squeeze out a real smile. Then he spoiled it all. "It's been the most wonderful time of my life, and I really don't wish you or I'd been anywhere else for even a minute."

"Don't say 'it's *been* wonderful,' dammit! That sounds like good-bye, or it's all over, or something like that, and it isn't. It isn't over. I won't let it be. I know, dammit, I *know* you'll be back here tomorrow night and it'll be the same again."

"That's right, honey. Believe it."

"You don't sound very convincing."

"I don't?" He still looked serious. "Maybe it's because I worry too much."

"About what? Tomorrow? Not beyond that, I hope."

"Yeah—tomorrow. If tomorrow works out, then the rest of the days should be fine."

"Not *the* days, *our* days."

"Right. Our days. Yours and mine."

"So why worry?"

"Oh, the usual. You know, 'best laid plans,' and all that. These people are not like your neighborhood grocer, and trust—in either direction—isn't one of their stocks in trade. They like to play with long odds in their favor, and I don't know what they've been doing to promote that situation."

"But you told me it makes sense for them to take your deal. You said they should jump at it."

"Yes, it does. Of course it does. But who's to say these hoods are sensible people?"

"Well, Conners always seemed sensible."

"Believe me, honey, I hope to God he is sensible. But sometimes even sensible people see things differently if their objectives are different."

"I'm not sure I like that. You mean they might have objectives other than getting their dough and those papers back?"

"Something like that, but I've been preparing for just that kind of situation. I just hope I've covered all the loopholes."

"And what if you haven't?"

"Then I gotta be quick, believe me."

"And I can't help you be quick, or sneaky, or anything?"

"No, hon. I know you *could*, but I don't want to expose you."

This did get a smile as she raised her eyebrows and gestured at her totally exposed body. She returned to seriousness quickly. "Where are the papers and everything? Do you have them ready?"

"They're in Papeete. All ready."

"Sammy Kee?"

"Uh-huh."

"Just you and Sammy against the world?"

"Not exactly. We've each got a friend, too."

"Four of you. That's a little better. You said there'd be only three of them."

"Three officially, yeah. But I'm sure they've got a few more hanging around."

"And your friends, do I know 'em?"

"No, but one of them will be around here tomorrow."

"To protect me?"

"No, not really. Let's say he'll be here in case you should need him."

"That's different?"

"Of course. You won't see him, but he'll be here. I mean you'd only see him if something very unusual happened, but I can't see that. You know what I mean."

"Yeah, I'm afraid I do, but it looks like there's nothing I can do about it."

"Let's say there's nothing you *need* to do about it."

"Okay, let's. So you're all ready?"

"I hope so, sweetheart."

"My money's on you, Patrick." Another forced smile.

"I was hoping it would be."

"Did you have any doubts, love?"

"Not a one, Signora."

"'Signora,' huh? Oh well, I guess I should know that signal. You want me to perform some kind of 'signoral duties.' Right? You mean here, on the beach? You animal."

"No, Signora, let's go home. I hate to see your beautiful signoral kulo all sand-scratched."

"You're all heart, Signor. Your concern touches me—right here." She raised a hip slightly and pointed. "Oh well. A signora's work is never done." She reached for the towel and her flowered pareu. "You're right, love, let's go home."

And then it was morning. She'd been awake long before she heard the first jungle noises, long before she saw Morley stir from his fitful sleep and start to get up. She waited until he padded toward the bathroom, then she slid out of bed, and covering her nakedness with a cotton shirt and shorts, felt her way through the semidarkness to the kitchen. By the time the coffee was perking it was quite light out, and Morley had arrived, shaved, showered, and dressed. She'd started eggs and toast and wouldn't accept no for an answer, insisting that he could at least begin the day with a decent breakfast. She didn't eat, just sipped her coffee and watched him. He finished quickly. "Guess I'd better get moving. Sam's waiting at the harbor."

"Can't talk you out of it?"

"Wish you could. I feel like the guy in *High Noon*." He reached over to cup her chin and followed up with a kiss. She didn't mean to, but she clung, and it became a long kiss. He pulled back finally. "Love it, sweetheart, but Sammy calls. Be back later this evening."

She didn't say anything, just nodded. Then they stood and

walked to the door, arms around each other. He opened it and stepped out, pulling her to him. "I love you, Signora, keep warm 'til tonight."

She tried a smile. It almost came through, but didn't quite make it. "*Si, si,* or whatever, *Signor.* Be careful."

"I will. You too. See ya." He held her tightly then brushed his lips across her cheek and left. He could taste the tears on his lips as he started the jeep and pulled away from the house. Her lips mouthed "See ya, yourself" as she watched until the vehicle turned out of sight.

Morley watched the bubbles surfacing on the placid water alongside his boat. A head broke water and he saw the smiling face of Sammy Kee, followed by his arm, raised triumphantly to show a grayish white box about the size of a book. Morley helped Sammy up the small boarding ladder and watched as he very carefully laid the box on the desk. Morley nodded approvingly. "Just as we thought. Where was it, Sammy?"

"Nicely done, right near the exhaust openings, blending beautifully with the color and contour of the hull." He smiled. "Right about where I'd've put it if I were so inclined."

"Uh-huh, that's interesting, but I suppose natural too."

"Yeah, I guess so."

Morley knelt beside the box and began prying gingerly with a small, thin screwdriver. The top came loose. He lifted it off very slowly and examined the contents. "Looks pretty simple: limpet, plastique, battery, wire, and timer. Very interesting, Sammy—the timer's set for four-fifteen P.M.!

"How d'ya figure that?"

"Guess I'd have to assume it was intended to remove our escape capability, not kill us."

"Hey, Patrick, I'd like to see their faces when they find out where the exchange is set to take place." Sammy almost doubled up with laughter.

Morley chuckled shortly, then turned serious. "But dammit, they'd've had to figure the boat as a possibility, wouldn't they?"

"Maybe not, Pat, maybe not. Maybe they'd figure we'd want to do the whole thing in a more public place—somewhere around the hotel probably."

"Yeah, I suppose you're right." This time he laughed harder, imagining. "Yeah, Sammy, it should be about four-twenty or so when we all arrive here. That oughta shake the bastards up a little. It should be fun watching 'em sneak looks at their watches."

This time Sammy turned serious first. "Pat, if we have to figure they just want to knock the boat out then it's gotta follow that they want us alive. Right?"

"Absolutely, my oriental Watson. I doubt those greedy bastards ever considered any option that let us walk off with the dough."

"I see. I was afraid that had to be the answer."

"Yeah, it looks like it, Sammy. Now let's get at it, we've got a lot to do."

Sammy smiled inscrutably, gesturing at the little box in front of Morley. "Okay, if you're sure you got that bastard turned off."

Morley raised his eyebrows and shoulders, palms turned up. They both laughed again. It was ten-seventeen by the boat clock.

20

At 3:53 P.M. on Thursday the twenty-fifth of April, a cab pulled
up to the functionally modern and beautifully landscaped front
entrance of the Maeva Beach Hotel near Papeete. Three men
got out and entered the hotel. High above them, on an angled
section of the tiered building, two men watched. They seemed
particularly interested in what happened after the men had
gone inside, their binoculars swinging in all directions around
and away from the entrance.

The tall blond man spoke. "Looks clean to me, Sammy,
but then they wouldn't be obvious, would they?"

"No way! I know they've got soldiers around somewhere.
Question is more when they'll show than where they're hiding.
Anyway, I'll feel better when we hear from Jackie."

The phone rang inside. The tall man went to answer while
Sammy continued sweeping the area with his glasses.

"Hello."

"Pat?"

"Yeah."

"Looks clean to me."

"Good, Jackie. Where'd you pick them up?"

"They took a cab from their hotel. Renny and I were waiting since about noon. Don't think they've been anywhere else
since they got in, but of course we can't be too sure."

"Yeah, they could've got out last night?"

"Right. No way we could cover the whole place after dark."

"No problem. It's now we're really interested in. You talked to Renny?"

"Yeah. No round eyes left the place after them—nobody suspicious or coming this way, I mean."

"Sounds like you're right. They must be clean."

"At the moment anyway." Jackie laughed and after a moment Pat joined him.

"Okay, Jackie, everything's set and you two know your routines."

"Like a trouper, boss."

"Good. I'll be seeing you shortly with our friends."

"With friends like those—"

"I know. I know. See ya in a few minutes."

Pat returned to the balcony. "All clear, Sammy."

"Good, good. I figured it would be. Those apes ain't gonna get mean 'til you make your deal."

"Sam, Sam—you have such a low opinion of your fellow man."

"Who's talkin' about men?"

They both laughed, and then Sammy went inside, put his glasses into a small flight bag, and came back to the sliding door. "Well, Patrick, guess I'd better get home and clean up the place before the company arrives."

"By all means, my boy, we would not want to offend their 'couth' in any way."

"Okay, see ya shortly."

Pat was serious. "I sincerely hope so."

They shook hands and Sammy left. Pat waited a few minutes, still using the glasses. After checking his watch, he too went inside, put his glasses into a small flight bag, and left.

Earlier that afternoon, long before Morley had made his way toward the lobby of the Maeva, Paani, who was sweeping the verandah in a typically slow but untypically efficient manner, watched as a small jeep pulled into the packed sand driveway in front of the main entrance of the villa on Vera Ti. A man got out, looked around, then walked toward the door. She stopped sweeping to stand quietly and watch. The man was obviously a Westerner, light hair and light complexion, about forty to forty-five years old, pleasant-looking, and dressed casually in plain tan slacks and a quietly flowered shirt.

He knocked on the door and Kaulu answered. The man said something in French and Kaulu went away, leaving the man standing outside. Madame came, dressed as usual in her native *pareu*. The man began talking to her in a language Paani did not know at all, using his arms and appearing very excited. Madame looked worried, then the man said something else and she seemed to smile. She opened the door to let him in, and they disappeared into the house. Paani went back to sweeping.

About ten minutes later Madame and the stranger came out. Madame looked around but didn't see Paani, who was now dusting behind some furniture. Madame and the man walked quickly down the drive and got into the jeep. She was now dressed in Western clothes and carrying a small valise, which she threw in the back seat. They seemed to be in a hurry, for as soon as Madame was in and seated the man started the jeep and roared away.

Paani found the entire incident puzzling, but then all Westerners were puzzling. She was glad that Madame had smiled. She didn't like it when anything made Madame sad. Paani shrugged. It was none of her business. She resumed her methodical sweeping and dusting.

At 4:06 P.M., Morley, dressed in a pair of duck slacks and a dark polo shirt, entered the sparsely populated bar lounge of the Maeva Beach Hotel. He saw the three men who he'd watched arrive by cab sitting quietly at a far window table commanding a magnificent view of the sea and the misty island in the distance. Morley walked directly to their table, stopped about two paces short, and nodded his head in greeting. "Good afternoon. I'm Patrick Morley."

They all looked up at him, casually, with no apparent show of interest, as if he'd interrupted their conversation. Finally, the blond man, whom Morley knew to be Conners, nodded back and motioned Morley to sit down. He sat and looked around. Conners close up was a handsome, clean-cut man, well dressed in an obviously expensive poplin jacket with the collar of his silk shirt outside. On his left was a man of indeterminate age, coal-black hair combed straight back from a widow's peak low on his forehead, dark eyes, thick black eyebrows, and incredibly white skin. His mouth was a crimson slash cut straight across his expressionless white face. All Morley could think of was Dracula. It made his throat itch. The third man, who he recognized from his pictures as Latellier, had not moved a muscle, but continued to stare unblinkingly at Morley. He had never before seen such intense and undisguised hate emanating from a human being. The man was a study in anthropology. He was fat but not pudgy, like one of those Japanese wrestlers—hard fat. His jowls were heavy and hung down like a bloodhound's, their bluish black sheen extending across his cheeks in a whisker line that plunged on down into the collar of his stiff white shirt. His hair was grayish black and sparse, and he combed it, from a point low over one ear, across the mottled, olive-skinned dome of his incongruously small head in a pathetic attempt to disguise his well-developed baldness. But it was the eyes that sent a chill through Morley. They were malevolent. They seemed to burn with the evil of the ages, and it was uncomfortable to be the object of their hateful scrutiny. Morley felt as if he were in the presence of the devil himself. This was a man without scruples, without mercy, probably without any human emotions. He was sure of it.

Conners broke the silence. "Mr. Morley, we are here as you requested. Can we get down to business?"

"If you are prepared for the exchange, I am."

"We are prepared."

"If you will accompany me I will take you to the merchandise."

They went outside. There was a cab waiting with an engaged sign in the windshield. Morley led them to it, saw them inside, then gave the driver some whispered instructions. A small car, driven by a young Polynesian, was idling in the parking area ahead of the cab. Morley got in the passenger side and it took off, the cab following closely.

The journey was short. In a few miles they came to a wide area in the road, where a narrow sandy path led to the left down to the shore. There was a small dilapidated dock extending out into the water of a sheltered cove, and tied to it was Morley's boat. Morley watched from the corner of his eye but could detect no signs of alarm or apprehension on the part of the three men as they alighted from the cab and took in the sight. Nor did they seem to notice the revolver that had appeared in his hand. He gestured with it toward the boat, and they obeyed, walking onto the craft and down the steps into the "salon." It was crowded but adequate. Sam Kee was awaiting them, standing at the far end of a table that formed the central furniture grouping of the room. Sam too had a pistol at the ready. The young driver took his place on the top step of the entrance stairway, now armed with Morley's revolver. Morley stood as the three visitors seated themselves around the table, then sat down in the end seat where Sam had been standing. As he did so, Sam moved smoothly off to a point that allowed both him and the driver an unrestricted field of fire. The three visitors still gave no indication that they had noticed the guns.

Without further ado, Morley reached down, picked up a briefcase from the side of his chair, laid it flat on the table, and opened it. He took out six black leather spiral notebooks and shoved them across the table to Conners. The third man, the vampire, reached out and intercepted the books and started to leaf through one of them. Conners just sat, unmoving. The fat, evil man continued to glare at Morley through those dark and unblinking eyes. When the vampire finished with a book he passed it to Conners, who repeated the page-by-page examination and then placed the "accepted" book in a small briefcase. They followed this procedure for all six books, although they didn't spend nearly as much time on the last couple. Conners put the sixth book in the case and looked up expectantly. Morley reached into the briefcase and produced two unsealed envelopes and passed them to the vampire. After the same procedure of dual examination, Conners put them in his case and snapped the combination lock.

Latellier had not taken his eyes off Morley or moved a muscle. He appeared to be totally disinterested in what was going on around him. He had yet to say one word. Slowly he shrugged, his head leaning to one side, and raised his hands, palms up in the traditional Italian expression of "what now?" Morley brought a sealed envelope out of the case and passed it to the outstretched talons of the devil-man, who tore the end of the envelope and pulled out a thin sheaf of folded papers. Reading them carefully but quickly, he put them back in the envelope and put it in his inside jacket pocket. Resuming his glaring at Morley, he reached down, brought up his briefcase, opened it on the table, and then shoved it toward Morley. It was tightly stacked with money. Morley pulled out a pocket calculator and began riffling through each stack and toting it up on the buttons of his little machine. He took his time, but finally he was finished. He nodded to Sam, who motioned for the young Polynesian to clear the stairs, then turned to Conners. "I see no need to repeat the terms of our agreement unless you wish to."

Conners shook his head. Morley continued. "Your taxi is waiting. He will take you to the airport. I will be aware of any deviation from this procedure and will consider such, or any attempt to harm or suborn the driver, to be a breach of our contract. I'm sure you understand. Likewise, I will consider similarly any attempt by you to leave the airport or to prolong your stay in Tahiti." Sam motioned with the barrel of his revolver as Morley continued. "Now please proceed to the cab. My assistant will escort you."

The three men left as instructed. As soon as the cab pulled away toward the airport road, the small car following closely behind, Morley moved up to the cockpit and started the engines. Sam was still below, working with some items he'd taken out of a box in one of the storage bins. After a few minutes he joined Morley topside and watched as they moved out through the lagoon and past the reef channel into the open sea. They turned onto a course that took them along the promontory and headed north toward Vera Ti. They were both smiling as they passed the port area and turned northerly into a following breeze, heading for the wide passage between the two islands.

A young Polynesian man sat calmly far out on a rocky shelf overlooking the beach north of town. There was a large, craggy promontory on his left, its sides inaccessible to anyone but an experienced and well-equipped climber, which sheltered him from the wind and other elements and from sight of the town. On his right the lush green hillside sloped gradually back to sea level on the seaward side of the narrow white coral road. His small French compact car sat by the side of this road, but the young man couldn't see it through the jungle growth behind him. Casual observers, of which, luckily for themselves, there were none, might have thought the young man was having a solo picnic. This couldn't have been further from the truth. His "picnic basket" held a large pair of binoculars, a deadly looking automatic handgun, and a small black box the size of a transistor radio. There was no food in it at all.

The man seemed to be straining his eyes looking out to sea along the length of the promontory. Every couple of minutes he'd stop looking long enough to glance at his watch. Suddenly, far in the distance, out in the interisland channel, a boat appeared. The young man snapped the binoculars into place quickly. It was the boat! He could even see those two smart bastards sitting in the cockpit. No need to wait any longer. He took the little transistorlike box, held it in front of him, flipped back a small but heavy plastic shield, and pressed strongly on the button underneath. Almost instantaneously there was a flash of fire on the horizon, and even before the dull boom reached his ears he could see that there was only fire and smoke where the boat had been seconds before. He watched with the glasses until there was no more fire, no more smoke, and definitely no more boat. No other boats were visible. There was not a sign that one had ever been there. Nobody had seemed to notice. As the young man repacked his "picnic basket" and headed toward his car, he could not help but marvel at the chemical and electrical genius that had made the whole thing so neat, so clean, so—possible.

21

The main entrance of the terminal at Papeete's Faaa Airport was crowded. The taxi dropped off the three men, who seemed to be in surprisingly good spirits as they entered the building's reception area. Conners checked his watch and started toward the side of the building that faced southwest. He motioned for the vampire and the devil-man to follow him as he went through a doorway and out onto a porch. A waiter seated them and took an order for drinks. He was back quickly with his full tray, and when he'd dispensed them and departed, the three men raised their glasses in what appeared to be a happy and friendly toast.

After a few minutes Conners again checked his watch. This time he nodded to the others. "Any time now, gentlemen."

They all seemed to be waiting happily for something, but as a couple of minutes went by, their faces began to reflect concern. Then, suddenly, there was a distant *boom*, flat and dull, but distinct and powerful sounding. Conners smiled widely, raised two fingers toward his right eyebrow in a mock salute, and said in a psuedo-grave tone, "Merry Christmas to you, Santa man!"

The devil-man actually smiled, raised his glass to Conners, and sipped from it. The corners of the vampire's horizontal mouth twitched, and then turned up, just a bit. The three men finished their drinks and ordered another round. Again they seemed to be waiting for something. After about twenty minutes an athletic-looking young Polynesian dressed in white slacks and a brightly flowered shirt appeared in the doorway to the reception area. He spotted the three men at the table and walked toward them, his face breaking into a wide, white-toothed smile. Then the young Polynesian looked directly at Conners and raised his right hand with the thumb and forefinger forming a circle. When the young man joined them, there was handshaking all around, more drinks and toasts, until the loudspeaker called them for check-in on their departing flight.

Ms. Leslie Cantrelle finished mixing a round of drinks for the passengers in the last row of first-class seats on Quantas's nonstop flight from Papeete to Acapulco. Those three blokes must either be scared or celebrating: they were quaffing the free whiskey as fast as she could mix 'em. On second thought, it had to be a celebration; they were laughing too much, as if they were sharing some huge joke. Except for the creepy old man with the weird hairdo! What a mean-lookin' bahstud he was. Always staring at her crotch like he could see right through the uniform. He made her feel crawly and dirty, and unfortunately the creep was going all the way to London. Oh well, as long as he didn't start groping when the lights went down she could stand the staring.

Her intercom station buzzed. It was the flight deck. "Les, would you come up here please. Captain would like to chat with you."

"Be right there." She delivered the drinks on the way, and the "creepy bahstud" stared at her crotch the whole time. She knocked at the flight deck door. It opened.

"Come in, Les."

She went to the space immediately behind the left seat and stood. The captain turned in his seat to address her. "Leslie, we've got a problem. It's minor in terms of safety but major in terms of passenger convenience, and I want you to brief the rest of the cabin crew so they'll be prepared to handle any questions or difficulties that may arise. We have an overheating engine, number three, and while there is no immediate danger, I and home base feel it would be foolish to continue to Acapulco. In a few minutes we will reach the point on our course where we are closest to Hawaii, and I've been instructed to proceed to Honolulu for necessary repairs. Now there's nothing to be worried about and I want you to make sure all attendants understand that. When you've briefed them, buzz me and I'll make the announcement."

"Yes sir. Will do."

"Thanks, Les, we're counting on you to carry this off."

Stewardess Cantrelle had performed her tasks as assigned and was delivering another drink to the creep and his friends when the skipper made his announcement. My God! She thought the old fart was gonna have apoplexy or worse right there in his seat. He turned green, then white, spilled and sputtered his drink all over, and generally looked like he'd been kicked in the bloody groin by a kangaroo. (Not a bad idea come to think of it.) Was he upset! And for what? He didn't seem that scared of the mechanical threat. The good-looking, polite, blond fellow finally got him calmed down by telling him that the stop was just an unforeseen emergency that had nothing to do with him personally; but creepy was still three sheets and looked like he'd founder any minute. About that time Ms. Cantrelle got a call for assistance from another station and happily left that grouping.

An hour and a half later they touched down at Honolulu International. The creepy old bloke tried to stay on the plane during the repairs but left quietly when the second officer told him rather forcefully that this was against airline and airport regulations and was strictly enforced. Leslie was the last of the cabin crew to leave, and she was following behind the creep and his friends when they entered the transient lounge. She didn't notice how it happened—there was no unusual commotion—but suddenly seven or eight men surrounded the three passengers. One of the newcomers said something to the creep and showed him a paper and what looked like a passport or card case. Then a nice-looking, well-dressed man took a pair of handcuffs out of his waistband and proceeded to put them on the creep's wrists and lead him away. The other two got the same treatment, but without the handcuffs. It was all over inside a minute, and they were gone, with those American blokes carrying the little briefcases those passengers had been so careful with. They didn't even go through customs.

22

Within days of the arrest of Frank Lavarelli—a.k.a. François Latellier—at Honolulu International Airport a number of interesting, and to the Corporation, ominous, events began to occur. As the drama unfolded they realized that it was disastrous, maybe even terminal. The scoreboard looked like this:

There were fifty-seven arrests of customs, immigration, and police officials—middle-to high-level—in eleven different countries and rumor had it that Interpol, supported and pushed strongly by the U.S. government, was in the process of getting cooperation from eight other nations for similar crackdowns on their exit and entry procedures. No matter, actually, because once the arrests started, even the braver culprits among the as yet unarrested were neutralized; they didn't want to play anymore.

In the States, eighteen middle- to high-level customs and immigration officers, divided almost equally among New York, Miami, New Orleans, and Los Angeles, quietly resigned rather than face charges. Thirteen of them were subsequently indicted by grand juries in their respective areas. The charges, while possibly not provable because of the absence of some critical witnesses, were sufficiently solid to cause these officials grave concern and to insure that they would not rule on official matters again in this life.

Two New Jersey men, employees of a construction company identified in the press as a Corporation front, were arrested by the FBI and indicted by a federal grand jury for the brutal, fake-accident slaying of John Rayboldt, Jr., M.D., on the George Washington Parkway, a federal reservation area near Washington, D.C., on the night of February 17.

Two other men, employees of a Chicago warehousing firm, similarly identified by the press as a Corporation front organization, and Bruno Bamowicz, a former professor of chemistry at an Illinois state college, were arrested and rapidly indicted in Chicago on the charge of first degree murder for the February 18 auto-bomb slaying of alleged Corporation official James Matthewson and his secretary, Cassandra Porter.

But in terms of arrests, the most significant incident of all was that which occurred in New Jersey on May 5. Federal officers arrested Albert Henry, alias Alberto Henrici, Giacomo Malfalcone, et al., on thirteen counts of income tax evasion.

Lavarelli, ex-syndicate official in the U.S., known in France, where he has resided since 1977, as François Latellier, had been under indictment since 1977 for the first degree murder of two special agents of the U.S. Treasury Department. He was scheduled for trial on these charges beginning May 31 but was found dead in his New York jail cell on May 2, an apparent suicide. Noteworthy in regard to this development were two separate but related events: one, the government of France had formally requested extradition of Lavarelli/Latellier on April 30 to stand trial for a double murder that occurred at his home near the city of Nice in early April. The victims were identified as his mistress, French citizen Martine Vallin, and Lebanese/Palestinian citizen Khaled Jamata. Two, the Palestinian terrorist group "Black September," announced via the Libyan press that *it* had been responsible for Latellier's death in the New York jail. No details were given, and no statement was made by federal authorities in New York.

The U.S. Drug Enforcement Agency, in coordination with a variety of local and state police forces, had in the first five days of May seized narcotics enroute into this country from abroad with a "street value" of more than eight hundred million dollars. One hundred twelve individuals had been arrested on charges emanating from these seizures.

The U.S. Coast Guard had seized and confiscated nine vessels of varying sizes and value, which had been used in the narcotics and other illicit trades between the Bahamas and several Florida ports and beaches.

U.S. Treasury agents had seized and confiscated over fourteen hundred firearms of all descriptions and more than one-and-a-half tons of traditional and sophisticated explosives in raids on two warehouses in the Jersey City area.

The French government announced the arrest of fourteen French citizens and the deportation of six aliens, reputed to be the top management of the new Corse crime organization throughout the Mediterranean area.

Eleven banking officials in three European countries resigned in the wake of rumors linking them with the widespread use of messenger services and credentials by organized crime in contravention of national laws and international banking agreements. Criminal prosecution was expected in most of these instances.

In Tripoli, Libya, one Samir al Faris, a Palestinian terrorist, sought by the governments of both France and West Germany for the hijacking-murder of seventy-seven Lufthansa Airline passengers in 1983, was killed when an explosive device on which he was reportedly working ignited prematurely. Friends of the victim said that he had been despondent recently over conditions within the Palestine Liberation movement but expressed doubt that he would have taken his own life. Libyan officials did not permit anyone to view the remains, which were cremated shortly after the tragedy.

The latest fallout took place in Bern, Switzerland, where a senior official of the Swiss government resigned in the wake of widespread European media allegations that he had for several years been circumventing various Swiss banking regulations on behalf of certain "foreign criminal organizations."

In Washington, D.C., Assistant Attorney General Byron Cawlfield, who had been put in charge of the Justice Department task force that was overseeing the nationwide prosecution of organized crime cases, told media interviewers that because of pending legal proceedings he could only comment generally at that time. Cawlfield went on to say that "current and projected arrests and indictments" should prove to be the "most serious setback" for organized crime in the last four decades. When questioned directly about the latest bombing in Chicago, Mr. Cawlfield stated that it was "relevant" to the overall Corporation case. The victims were reputed Corporation official Dennis Conners, alias David Kanarsky, and a woman identified only as Angela Mornay, Chicago resident.

23

The buildup of thunderheads over the island had raised the late afternoon humidity to its limit, but inside the hotel compressors and fans were winning their battle with the elements; it was cool and comfortable. In the lounge a young oriental man stood behind the bar stirring the ice in two glasses. He stopped, picked them up, and carried them toward a table where another man, a blond Occidental, sat watching and smiling. The Oriental delivered the drinks with an exaggerated bow. "Your Singapore Sling, *tuan*!"

"I ordered pink gin, you crazy Chinee!"

"I know, *tuan*, and I have bring same for you; but I prefer to call it 'Sling' so I can 'plactice' saying my ells! Besides, what's in a name? Just drink and enjoy, round eyes."

They both laughed as the young oriental sat down, then the blond man spoke. "Sammy, my boy, when the white *tuan's* labor unions arrive on Vera Ti to loosen your chains, you will no longer be able to wear four hats around here!"

"Four?"

"Yeah: bartender, room clerk, waiter, and comedian."

"Hey, thanks, old buddy, for that part about comedian. Most people don't appreciate that side of my many-talented personality."

"Don't put words in my mouth, Sam. One hat a comedian

doth not necessarily make. Now if I'd said scuba diver, then that'd be a different story."

Sam laughed unrestrainedly; the other man looked puzzled. "Oh, Patrick, it was so damn funny! I can't help laughing. You should have seen the look on the face of that fat Samoan bastard when the police boat picked him and his boatman up. Man, I thought he was gonna shit in his wet suit right there!"

"Maybe he did, Sam. How can you tell? Is he still in the town brig?"

"You bet your ass, friend. He's finally quit screaming for his lawyer, so now they'll let him cool down for a few days before they give him his hearing and sentencing."

"Sentencing? Really?"

"Hell yes, Patrick, I suspect he'll get six months or so on the road gang in the mountains. You can bet that's one hood who'll return to the land of habeas corpus a wiser, sadder, and thinner man. Maybe he'll even take up a legitimate business. Who knows?" Sam shook his head in wonderment. "Can you imagine that evil-eyed old turd, Lavarelli, giving you that dough in a waterproofed briefcase and thinking we wouldn't notice or figure out why? I'm amazed he stayed alive as long as he did! I thought that was a tougher league those guys played in."

"Don't kid yourself, friend, that league is tough all right. About the time you get to thinking it isn't, some soldier will stick a shiv in between your fourth and fifth ribs!"

"Uh-huh . . . Still, Pat, it was kind of a tip-off that they not only expected to get their dough back, but from a watery grave yet! Our grave, that is."

"I didn't say they were smart, Sam, just tough. Same with the bomb, right from the start."

"I know you were always convinced of it, but I never did figure out why you were so sure."

"Sam, it just had to be a boat bomb! Nothing else covered all the angles for them. You know, wiping us out with no mess or bodies or such. But there were two other factors that really convinced me. First, hoods love bombs! And remember we'd already identified their bomb expert, the Professor, in the area. Second, hoods hate strange and 'uncontrolled' territory. No way they were going to take us out with soldiers in our 'backyard,' not knowing the lay of the land or our plans and capabilities. They don't like short-odds operations even a little bit. Yeah, it had to be a bomb, Sammy."

"Not to mention that red herring of a limpet bomb on the hull."

"Which we were supposed to find."

"Of course. And then when we found the radio controlled device and learned at the same time that the stupid Samoan had been down to Harbor Control looking for depth charts . . . Not too smart, Patrick."

"Icing on the cake, indeed. At that point we could have written the scenario ourselves: no way but that blow-up point had to be past the populated areas of the harbor and the headlands but before we reached the deep of the channel."

"Like you said, Patrick, I'm glad *we* guessed right. You still think *they* think we're dead?"

"Yeah, I do. I don't think they'd've sent the Samoan out to dive if they didn't. . . . I don't think he'd have gone if *he* didn't. . . . Also, I don't think their man—I'm sure it was the Samoan—would have pushed the button that day if he hadn't thought those dummies with our clothes on were for real!"

"Uh-huh. I'll buy that."

Patrick smiled. "Unless the Samoan recognized you on that police boat! In which case we'll have to make sure he has an accident on that road gang."

"Not to worry. My own sweet mother wouldn't have recognized me on that boat. Besides, all Chinese coolies look alike— or so you told me!" They both laughed. "Anyway, I *had* to go. Those cops aren't very dependable, laddie, even under the best of circumstances, and with a fast-talking American-Samoan and an obscure old French 'treasure trove' law to work with, there was only one way to make sure they didn't cave in, take a bribe, or screw the whole thing up in one of a thousand different ways, and that was to be there myself!"

"I know, I know." Patrick smiled wryly. "I still can't figure how you talked the law commissioner into enforcing that old colonial statute."

"It wasn't easy, friend, but then, not too hard either: he plays poker with my uncle every Thursday. Well, anyway we're home free with this." He patted the briefcase. "Lavarelli's burning, Savilli's in the slammer, Conners is dead, destination unknown, and the Samoan will have his own little hell—for a while."

Patrick nodded, pointing to the briefcase. "That's yours, Sammy: as we agreed, twenty-five percent off the top."

"A very generous arrangement, my good friend."

"One gets what one pays for. You want first class you pay first-class prices. Seriously, Sam, no way I could've pulled it off without you, so spend and enjoy."

"And no income tax problems? I can put this in my bank in Honolulu?"

"Yup, you sure can. The deposit will be noted and passed on to the Treasury Department, but there's a file number you ask the bank to attach and the whole thing never gets on IRS records. There's a note inside explaining the thing. That was, and is, the deal I made with the U.S.G. and it's guaranteed by the General!"

"Yeah. That's the part I like best, Pat. His word I accept. Besides, he's got more clout in D.C. than anybody else except the First Lady. If he says it's done, I believe it."

"Well, Sam, he says so."

Sam looked serious as he moved his glass back and forth on the table. "Can I ask a question, old buddy?"

"Sure."

"You never told me what was in those notebooks and documents. From what's happened around the world in the last couple of weeks I can figure out most of it, but some things aren't quite clear. I can figure why you wanted to make a deal with the U.S.G. and why they would be anxious to accept it, but where and how does old Lavarelli come in? Can you tell me?"

"Sure. Why not? I'd've told you before, but you didn't ask." He laughed. "Your old training, I suppose. Remember I told you how I got involved, innocently of course"—Pat smiled and Sammy raised his eyes to the ceiling—"in a syndicate worldwide courier operation and just happened to get my hands on those notebooks, which contained the whole setup, chapter and verse? At the same time I got some interesting documents—all from the same source—indicating that the syndicate guy I was working for was actually like an independent contractor, and although he had a long background in the brotherhood, was truly on his own in this courier operation."

Sam interrupted. "Courier operation? Couriering what?"

"Money, plans, papers—all briefcase stuff, no drugs."

"You drew the line?"

"Would have, but didn't have to. Subject never arose."

"Okay. Go on."

"Anyway, some of these documents indicated that my boss was planning to sell his network to the Corse people, you know, the new French syndicate, which would have bugged old Albert Henry worse 'n a hot poker in the anus. Anyway, and this is guesswork, some syndicate enforcer had my boss knocked off *before* making sure he could get the documents! So I had the papers and they had zilch. This guy, my boss, had assured me some time before, and I believed him, that nobody but him knew who I was. I had a code name, and they knew that, but. . . ."

"Code name?" Sam smiled. "What was it?"

"Santa."

"Santa? Just plain Santa?"

"You got it, Sammy boy. Anyway, I figured I could take them for a good piece of dough, do the U.S.G. a good turn, and get immunity from the IRS, all at the same time."

"So you contacted the General and made a deal with him?"

"Yes, in essence. Actually I made a deal with Justice and Treasury, *through* him. But as I said, the best part was that *he* guaranteed that *they* would stand by the deal."

"Which was?"

"I gave them copies of the notebooks and the papers, and they gave me, and of course you—I'd already contacted you by that time—the IRS waiver, on the grounds of national security, on any monies I could bilk out of the syndicate on the operation. You know, they, the General and the whole USG, couldn't let the details of this case float around in government records that could be exposed some day! Or so I—and the General— told them."

"And Lavarelli?"

"He was a pot sweetener for them. You know, Lavarelli was one of Mr. Henry's captains at one time, 'til he murdered two Treasury agents, narc guys, in New York. He was indicted in absentia, having already skipped. He surfaces a couple of years later in Nice, France, as a second-level officer of the Corse. You see, he is—I should say, happily, he *was*—a pretty cagey old fart. He wangled the job as their contact man with all the Palestinian terrorists in Europe: advising, supplying, financing, whatever. And you see, as long as he was playing Daddy Warbucks to these finks, he was under their sponsors'— read Arab oil states—protection! France wasn't about to let him be extradited and annoy the oil people!"

"Uh-huh. I see. So you had to get him onto U.S. territory somehow. The plot thickens."

"Right. Now, one of the documents I nipped from that syndicate boss of mine was a letter he had received from one of his Arab contacts. The letter—it was really more of a confession— was from Samir al Faris, a Palestinian Black September officer."

"The guy who was blown up in Libya?"

"The same, and he *was* blown up. It was no accident, I'm

sure. Well, Samir stated in his confession that he was Lav-arelli's double agent penetration of the Black September and that he arranged, on Lavarelli's orders, for the blowing up of a hijacked Lufthansa plane a few years ago. He said their pur-pose—his and Lavarelli's—was the elimination of a young Corse officer who was on the plane. This Corse guy was under-studying Lavarelli, and since he was the brother of the Corse headman, Lavarelli saw the handwriting on the wall. Hell, old Lavarelli couldn't let anybody take away his Palestinian con-tacts and make him vulnerable to extradition! No way!

"This Corse man, the younger brother, was helping Samir set up the operation, and Samir was slated to go on the plane as an 'observer.' Samir feigned illness at the last minute and conned the Corse guy into taking his place. Samir had already put an acid-timed luggage bomb on the plane. It blew up and that was that."

"Yeah, I can see why Lavarelli had to have that piece of paper, but why was the syndicate helping *him*?"

"Oh, I guess they help their own. Also, I'm sure Lavarelli put in dough, maybe all of it. And the American syndicate guys who, I'm sure, know Faris's story, get themselves a free pen-etration of the Corse. Hell, after that letter they could say 'jump' and Lavarelli would make like one of those automobile ad guys, reaching for the sky!"

"So you set up the meeting in Tahiti to entice the old bas-tard, and they all had to come and they all had to pay!"

"Right. He felt safe, and they had no option. And of course, this was our territory, especially yours."

"So you got them on that Quantas flight to Mexico and France, had the Aussies fake engine trouble and land in Hono-lulu, where the Bureau guys were waiting with great big nets. Right?"

"Uh-huh, that's the way it happened."

"And all the good guys were happy. The U.S.G. gets to roll up a worldwide courier net, not to mention a lot of stateside plums to boot, including Lavarelli on toast; we get to keep the dough, tax free, while scoring lots of brownie points for the General and our old 'alma mater,' and last but not least, the enemy thinks we're dead!"

"Let's hope so, Sam."

Sam started moving that glass around again, lowering his eyes to watch the moisture tracks on the table. "Yeah, a real happy ending . . . for everybody but you, old buddy. I mean Angela. I really liked her, Pat. She was one fine lady."

Pat's eyes glazed visibly and he lowered them, but his jaw line tautened. "Yes, Sam, she was that, all right. A helluva lady, and lots more." He raised his eyes to meet Sam's. "I loved her, my friend, very much, and I came to trust her. But now, I just don't know any more."

"Pat, we really don't have any evidence that she betrayed us. Hell, if she had they wouldn't have made the meeting."

"She didn't know it was a trap. But you're right, we certainly don't *know* that she betrayed us. Still, I—"

"Patrick, we do *not* know for sure that she left Vera Ti that day willingly and wittingly."

"No, we don't. But the servants said she was smiling and stopped to say good-bye, and the charter pilot who took them from Vera Ti to Faaa said all was friendly and light. And of course the description of the guy she went with fits the Professor like a glove. And the Professor's from Chicago. You see, Sam, I want to believe, but these things keep piling up. It's hard as hell to think positive, believe me—much as I want to do it."

"There are lots of ways to get somebody to do something besides coercion, Patrick. She could have been conned into it, maybe even thinking she was being taken to you! Chicago's a big city, you can't assume she knew the Professor. . . . Hey! Did you tell her you'd left a guard on the island?"

"Not in so many words, but she could easily have inferred it. I did tell her not to leave the house and she'd be safe. But it's no use, Sam, it all then comes back to the most damning thing of all—she was back *with Conners* again the night they were bombed. That's the one thing I can't explain myself. That's truly the 'most unkindest cut' of all."

"I know. I know. But dammit, we still don't know the 'why' of it. The whole thing could have been part of the con job. We don't even know whether she thought you were dead or alive those days. Patrick, my trouble is that my gut tells me Angela was a straight lady. I believe there's an explanation for the whole deal even if we can't figure it out today, or ever."

"Thank you, my friend. I guess we'll just have to think the best of her and remember the good times—the way she was."

Sam nodded sadly. "So what happens now, Patrick. Back to the States, new name, new face, whatever, and spend your ill-gotten grubstake on birds, booze, and bets?"

Patrick laughed. "No, I don't think so, Sammy—at least not just yet. Think I'll stay around here for a while and let some more of the dust settle from that syndicate roll-up. You know, just see what happens. Maybe Mr. Henry'll get hit by a car or something. Who knows? You know they don't have a picture of me—to my knowledge—and their people who've seen me in person are either dead or in jail. Yeah, who knows? What about you? Back to hula land?"

"Yeah, eventually, I guess. Gotta go back to the business sooner or later, although little brother Tony is probably running it better than I could!"

"You'll hang on here a bit?"

"Uh-huh. You know, the old guy really is my uncle, and he sure as hell could use some help 'til he gets a bit more mobile. Guess I'll stay on for a couple months or so. Hey, let's go see what that crazy chef of ours is cooking for dinner tonight! Then we could grab a quick swim and another pink gin before he finishes stirring with his thumb and rings the bell!"

"You got it, pal. Let's go."

24

Assistant Attorney General Byron Cawlfield picked up his phone, listened a moment, and said, "Send him in."

The door opened and a tall young man of serious mien and somber apparel came in. He handed Cawlfield a small, tightly wrapped package. "Sir, this is the tape that Mr. Macalaster phoned you about yesterday—it's Mr. Rafferty's interview tape. Will there be any return message, sir?"

Cawlfield shook his head slowly, looking at the now unwrapped cassette. "No . . . no, I don't think so. Just tell him many thanks and that I'll take it from here, any problems I'll call him. And thanks very much."

The young man turned and went back through the door. Cawlfield got up and went over to a small, very compact tape system that sat on a section of library shelf, turned it on, and inserted the cassette. He pulled a chair over in front of the machine and sat, listening intently.

When the tape ended, he rewound it, ejected, and walked back to the desk looking thoughtfully at the cassette as he moved. He picked up the phone. "Marcia, please get me General Ashley at the Pentagon."

25

One of the servants came down to the dock to tell Morley he
was wanted on the radiotelephone. It was Sammy Kee. "Patrick, I've just received a cable from the General. It's for you,
and it's very interesting."

Morley laughed. "You've read it, you nosy Chinee?"

"But of course, *tuan*, it's my job. Seriously, why don't you
pay a call and we'll have dinner. I think old Wong is about to
make his special prawns with black bean sauce! Anyway, come
on over, read the cable, drink a pinkie, and we'll have some of
it. Okay?"

"You sure as hell know how to get a guy's attention, pal. A
secret message and prawns with black bean sauce! How can I
resist. Be there in an hour, give or take fifteen minutes depend-
ing on the water level at the ford. See ya."

Morley sat in his favorite chair in the lounge while Sam
Kee mixed him what looked like the granddaddy of all pink
gins. He brought it over, set it in front of him, waited while
Morley took a large, mouth-puckering swig, and then handed
Morley a white envelope. Morley took out several folded sheets
of onionskin paper, read the first few lines, and then stopped to
take another large sip of his drink. Sam waited quietly for a
moment until Morley picked up the papers again. "Patrick,
would you mind reading it aloud? I glanced at it as I was
breaking it, but didn't really get it all."

Morley raised his left eyebrow but said nothing. Finally he nodded his head and began reading. "Dateline yesterday, headquarters. Morley from Ashley. Received this date tape of conversation between Assistant District Attorney Rafferty, Chicago, and Dennis Conners, St. Joseph's Hospital, Chicago. Conners aware his medically hopeless condition and wanted get message to you prior death. Said quote: 'girl did not turn you in. Backed out in Florida before we identified you. Made no further contact. She was tricked into leaving island thinking she was going to meet you after exchange had aborted. She got wise in New Zealand, so they drugged her and brought her back as mental patient, later released her in Chicago. She thinks you are dead, but I know better. Figure you outsmarted us every other way, no way you would lose big one. Tried to tell girl but, she would not talk to me. Come get her, Santa, she is a "oner."' End quote.

"Rafferty told Conners that Mornay was killed with him in bombing. He became very agitated. Said it was not Mornay with him but his sister Ivy Retsinger, which was major cause his anger toward syndicate. When told Mornay ID found at bomb scene, insisted it was plant and that Mornay in great danger. Said Mornay probably hiding aunt's home Racine. At this point Conners became incoherent. Died twenty minutes later.

"U.S. Marshals, Milwaukee, took Mornay into protective custody same evening. Dana Kelly, cousin and roommate of Mornay, was shot by unknown assailant following morning at entrance their Chicago apartment. Kelly serious but will recover. No press release on Kelly who is similar in appearance to Mornay, since assume Mornay was target.

"Am forwarding package that will explain in more detail but felt you needed this info soonest. Best regards, Ashley."

Morley just sat there smiling and slowly shaking his head in wonder. He didn't move when Sam Kee got up and went out of the lounge, and he was still sitting and smiling when Sam came back. Sam said something he couldn't hear, then he seemed to come into focus audibly as well as visually. Pat turned to face him. "I said, Patrick, that the General's package has arrived. Would you like to see it?"

Morley came back to the world, fully. He nodded. Sam got up again, went to the door of the lounge, then stood aside to let a radiantly smiling Angela Mornay walk in.